"So are you going to frisk me again?"

Scarlet sank onto the chair and crossed her legs. "You've got good hands," she drawled. "If you know what I mean."

Adam felt something terrible rise inside him. He knew what it was. A crack in the surface of his calm. One that could untether his self-control and fling it to the four winds, allowing him to bounce around with no constraints, no rules, no goal. "You know damn well I never touched you inappropriately. To say any different—"

"Got you," Scarlet said, giving a wink. "You're so easy."

He'd process Scarlet and put her in the holding cell until she posted bond. Then he'd give himself another lecture on pretending the blazing-hot Scarlet was just another criminal who had handcuffed herself to a lamppost in a protest. Just another woman. No one who would interest the professional, responsible leader of a police force.

No one who made him fantasize about the various ways to use a pair of red-furred handcuffs.

Dear Reader,

I'm certain I learned drama from the best. The women of my family are many things: strong-willed, hard-working and very stubborn. But most of all we are queenly. Some are queen bees, some are beauty queens, and others are queen-sized, but we are all drama queens. So I got to thinking…are drama queens good heroines?

Whether you agree or not, drama queens are certainly interesting, as is my heroine Scarlet. Scarlet lives to enter the fray, boldly and dramatically wielding the sword to slay her dragons. And who should tame this flamboyant mudraker? A straight-laced lawman, of course. Scarlet was made to color Adam's world, no matter how much he resists the lure of the over-the-top actress.

I had such a great time writing a love story for these two characters, and I hope you will enjoy taking one last trip back to Oak Stand, Texas, with me. You'll see some familiar faces and say goodbye to some old friends.

I love hearing from my readers so feel free to email me at www.liztalley.com and let me know what you think about *A Touch of Scarlet.*

Happy reading!

Liz Talley

A Touch of Scarlet

Liz Talley

TORONTO NEW YORK LONDON
AMSTERDAM PARIS SYDNEY HAMBURG
STOCKHOLM ATHENS TOKYO MILAN MADRID
PRAGUE WARSAW BUDAPEST AUCKLAND

Recycling programs for this product may not exist in your area.

ISBN-13: 978-0-373-71738-5

A TOUCH OF SCARLET

This edition published by arrangement with Harlequin Books S.A.

For questions and comments about the quality of this book please contact us at Customer_eCare@Harlequin.ca.

www.Harlequin.com

Printed in U.S.A.

ABOUT THE AUTHOR

From devouring the Superromances on the shelf of her aunt's used bookstore to swiping her grandmother's medical romances, Liz Talley has always loved a good romance. So it was no surprise to anyone when she started writing a book one day while her infant napped. She soon found writing more exciting than scrubbing hardened cereal off the love seat. Underneath her baby-food-stained clothes a dream stirred. Liz followed that dream, and after a foray into historical romance and a Golden Heart final, she started her first contemporary romance on the same day she met her editor. Coincidence? She prefers to call it fate.

Currently Liz lives in North Louisiana with her high school sweetheart, two beautiful children and a passel of animals. Liz loves watching her boys play baseball, shopping for bargains and going out for lunch. When not writing contemporary romances for Harlequin Superromance, she can be found doing laundry, feeding kids or playing on Facebook.

Books by Liz Talley

HARLEQUIN SUPERROMANCE

1639—VEGAS TWO-STEP
1675—THE WAY TO TEXAS
1680—A LITTLE TEXAS
1705—A TASTE OF TEXAS

For my mom,
who is likely the biggest drama queen I know,
but I wouldn't want her any other way.

And also to the Ruby-Slippered Sisterhood.
Long live the drama queen!

CHAPTER ONE

SCARLET ROSE GLANCED in the rearview mirror at the lights flashing behind her. Damn. Who got pulled over for going 75 mph in a 65-mph zone? Wasn't there a ten-mile cushion or something?

Obviously not in Texas.

The cop was taking his time emerging from the depths of the silver cruiser, so Scarlet gave her lips another swipe of the Elizabeth Arden ruby-red lip gloss resting in the cup holder. After all, her lips were her greatest weapon. Overly large and plump, they had their own fan page on Facebook. She'd always thought the attention given to them a little absurd, but if she had to use them to get out of a ticket, then she would.

After all, who in his right mind would give the vampy Veronica Collins a speeding ticket? Her luxurious red locks, gleaming white teeth and kick-ass curves clad in the trademark catsuit inspired kinky fantasies for those who followed the new drama *Deep Shadows,* which had debuted six months ago to a rabid fan following. Currently, Scarlet was on hiatus, so she looked nothing like the naughty vampire Veronica. Just plain ol' Scarlet Rose in faded jeans and a ponytail.

But she did have those lips.

She slumped against the leather seat and watched in her side mirror as the cruiser's door opened and a police officer climbed out.

He was tall with a military haircut and wore mirrored sunglasses. Good body. Stiff demeanor. She had a fifty-fifty chance of getting out of this one.

Her director's voice popped into her head.

Veronica will smile at the officer, feigning innocence. Camera One, narrow to capture the gleam in Veronica's eyes as she knowingly plays with the unsuspecting cop.

Scarlet turned and delivered a smile. "Hello there, officer. Is there a problem?"

She pulled the end of her ponytail forward so it brushed her bared collarbone while curling her shoulders forward, smooshing her boobs so the cop had a nice vista of flesh to contemplate. She couldn't tell if it worked or not. His gaze could have been on her girls… or on the steering wheel. Damned mirrored sunglasses.

"Yes, we have a problem," he said, his voice nice and melodious, like an announcer on a game show. It was definitely cultured. No Podunk, Texas accent. He wasn't from Oak Stand. "You were doing seventy-eight in a sixty-five zone, and you have a brake light out."

She smiled again before giving him a flirtatious shrug. "Surely I wasn't going that fast?"

His jaw tightened. It was a nice jaw. Cleanly shaven and tanned. He had a good mouth, too. Straight lips with a slightly sensuous curve to the bottom lip. It was the kind of mouth a girl wanted to nibble into a smile. Total challenge.

But he didn't smile. "Surely you were."

"Sorry. Look, I'm trying to get to my sister's house before she runs off with some horrible, horrible guy. No one is answering the phone, and I'm worried, you know? I guess I should have had my mind on the road, but—"

"That doesn't explain the brake light," he said.

Scarlet tamped down the annoyance at being interrupted. Syrupy sweetness worked on hard-asses like this. At least it usually did. “I bought this car three weeks ago and had everything inspected. The light must have burned out without my knowledge. I’ll get it replaced tomorrow. Promise.”

He didn’t move a muscle. She could tell he stared hard at her, even though there was mirrored glass between his gaze and hers. Seconds ticked by. Had she worked it hard enough to get out of a ticket?

“Are you asking me to overlook a violation?”

Oops. Maybe not. “Of course not. No.”

“Because that’s what it sounds like.”

Scarlet tossed her flirting ploy aside and straightened. “I don’t always agree with the laws you enforce, but I would never ask you to compromise yourself.”

She gave him the schoolmarm stare she’d perfected in her off-off Broadway debut of *Mrs. Tingle’s Jingles.* He didn’t wiggle the way he was supposed to. He merely stood, straighter and taller.

“Just give me the ticket so I can get on with my day. I’ve got a wedding to stop.”

At this, the officer’s mouth drew into a line. No more semimocking curve. “What wedding?”

Scarlet gave him a New Yorker smile—kind of a smart-ass smirk. “Now, that, Officer—” she looked at his nameplate “—Hinton, is none of your business, is it?”

Officer Adam Hinton jabbed a finger toward the city-limit sign that sat behind her black BMW convertible. “This is my town. Everything in it is my business.”

Scarlet pulled on the viperous persona of Veronica as easily as she shrugged into a jacket. “Now, that’s where I’m thinking you’re wrong, Officer Hinton.”

Don't make me bite you, dude.

She loved Veronica, the alter ego she sometimes donned merely because the vampire queen could control everything about her world. So what if it were pretend? Playing the dangerous, sultry vampire allowed her to feel powerful. She showed him her teeth for good measure. It was a hard smile, sans fangs, designed to put him in his place.

"Can I have your license and registration please?"

Okay. So she had no effect on him. Fine. He probably squeaked when he walked. Even his damn badge was perfectly lined up adjacent to the button on his uniform shirt. He probably flossed three times a day and took a multivitamin. Jogged the same path, ate the same foods and cut his lawn with methodical precision.

She tugged her wallet from the oversize purse, flipped it open and pulled out the license she'd obtained last month. Her very first driver's license procured specially for the trip to Texas. As a New Yorker, she'd never learned to drive. Subways and cabs had worked fine.

She handed her license over without a smile. "Here you go."

"Registration?" he asked, taking the hard plastic license from her hand.

She leaned over, popped open the glove box and rooted around. Stefan had said he left everything she'd need in there. A string of condoms slithered to the floorboard along with a pack of cigarettes, a package of Zingers and a small airport bottle of rum. Nice. Her roommate had a weird-ass sense of humor. Finally she located a zippered owner's manual and found the registration inside, along with a proof of insurance. The insurance card had her name on it. Stefan must have placed it inside for her. Okay, she'd let him live.

"Here. Everything should be inside." She jabbed the manual at the police officer. Then she dismissed him, flipping down the visor mirror and checking her bangs, for no other reason than it pleased her to shut him out.

The sun pressed on her shoulders. The end of August was hotter than hell in East Texas, but it was her first road trip so she'd kept the top down most of the way along the East Coast and hadn't put it up on her trek across the South. She'd stopped to see an old friend in Atlanta, putting her behind schedule in getting to Oak Stand. She'd gotten even with the city-limit sign when Officer Tight Ass had pulled her over.

She was tired, too warm and not feeling friendly at all. Texas hadn't been on her list of vacation destinations, but saving her sister, Rayne, from the ridiculous fascination she had for Brent Hamilton topped lounging on the beach in France. Well, almost topped it.

Scarlet's bangs looked fine, so she snapped the mirror shut and tried to look bored as the lean cop scribbled stuff onto his little notepad.

"Have you been drinking this afternoon?" His voice seemed monotone. Automated.

Crap. The stupid minibottle of rum.

"Of course not."

"Would you mind stepping from your car, ma'am?"

"Actually, I would mind. Why do you need me to get out of the car if you're merely giving me a speeding ticket?" She studied the teal polish on her fingernails. It was very divalike behavior—something she never did. But at this point, she knew it aggravated Officer Hinton. So it felt good.

"Out of the car," he said, swinging the door open. "Step around to the back of the vehicle, place your hands on the trunk and wait. Please."

He'd nearly choked on the last word. She'd ticked the cop off. Might not have been the smartest move, but that was Scarlet's modus operandi—react, then regret. A car passed by on the highway, and she caught a glimpse of a curious driver. She waved.

"What an excellent way to make an entrance," she said, climbing from the car. She was glad she'd left her flip-flops at her friend's house, because the mile-high wedges she wore boosted her five-foot-eight frame by four inches and made her feel more powerful. It brought her eye level with the cop, who watched as she unfurled from the car.

Her tank top had tiny jewels embedded around the low neck and hugged her torso all the way down to the tight, ripped jeans. Aside from her plump lips, her body was her trademark. Scarlet had kicking curves that looked so good in a bodysuit they'd given her the part of Veronica before she even read for it. Not really. They'd made her read to make sure she could act. But still, she felt as if she'd been born for the role of Collinstown's audacious vampire.

Her director's voice came back.

Stroll to the rear of the car. Make sure it's a do-me walk. Then place your hands on the trunk, feet apart, and arch your back. Slowly smile at your prey.

Scarlet stretched like a cat, then moved into position. She purposely stood far away so the pose she struck looked seductive. She didn't know why she did it, other than she got perverse satisfaction in needling Officer Hinton. It was rapidly becoming her new favorite game to play.

Piss Off Hinton. Coming to stores near you. Oops, I dropped my license in the vodka. Is that a nightstick in your pocket or are you happy to see me? Make Officer Hinton crack, and you can win all the marbles!

He cleared his throat, snapping her out of the board-game commercial playing in her head. "Is this all the alcohol you have in the car?"

"Yes. And I have to say, your detective skills are lacking. That little bottle hasn't been opened yet."

Officer Hinton stared at her a good two minutes before approaching. "I'm doing my job, ma'am. Now, I'm going to briefly pat you down, Miss Rose."

"No dinner first?" she said as she stared at the back of her bucket seat and pretended she got pulled over and frisked all the time. No big deal that a cop was about to run his hands all over her on the side of the road. She braced herself for his touch.

His hands moved beneath her arms, over her ribs, down her waist and hips to her thighs. Quickly, his hand slid inside her knee and moved down to her calves. It was quick, methodical and professional. No reason for any match to be struck. Nevertheless, Scarlet felt strange. Little pulses erupted in her belly. It shocked her. She hadn't felt even a nudge of sexual interest since John. It made her want to get away from this small-town cop. Made her want to hide her emotions. Protect herself. Pretend she felt nothing.

The whole thing was crazy.

"Turn toward me, please."

He'd taken off his sunglasses and it was as if a mask had been removed. He was damn gorgeous in a Robert Redford/Clint Eastwood sort of way. His eyes searched hers, presumably for signs she'd been swigging cough syrup. But the perusal didn't feel accusatory. It felt raw. As though he was peering inside her soul. Inside to where her self-doubt hid along with her insecurities.

She pushed her sweaty bangs back and pretended she was on set.

Now Veronica portrays impatience. She needs to get rid of the cop. She can't allow the cop to see who she really is.

But it didn't work.

His green eyes were clear and searching. They unnerved, and she wanted to escape them.

"See? I haven't been drinking anything other than a Diet Coke." She looked down at the sunglasses she held. She should put them on. Protection from his all-knowing eyes.

"I'll be the judge of that," he said, sliding his hand under her chin and tipping her face so her gaze was forced to meet his. His touch sizzled. Like, seriously scorched her bare skin. He jerked his hand away and a frisson of unease crept into his eyes.

He wasn't supposed to touch her outside of the initial frisk. She knew that. Or she thought she knew it. But it had seriously felt…sexy. Almost like a caress.

Veronica will not react to the cop's touch. She must retain control. Even if she wishes to slide her hands up his shoulders, even if she wishes to taste the mouth of the man who could tame her, who could—

Please. Who got hot and bothered by a cop on the side of the road in some backwater town?

She had to be suffering from heatstroke. Or low blood sugar. Anything to explain her reaction to Mr. Tall Blond Jackass.

She needed him to give her the damn ticket so she could head toward Aunt Frances's bed-and-breakfast. Away from whatever strange thing pulsed between her and this cop. She'd driven too long without sleep and had to be partially delirious from road tripping.

"Okay, I've seen enough drunks to tell you're clean. Wait here." Officer Hinton spun on one motorcycle boot and stalked toward his cruiser. She was accustomed to following direction. Just not that of a pompous cop, so she sidled toward the open door of her car and sank onto the leather seat she'd abandoned moments before. She jabbed her sunglasses on her nose and tapped her fingernails against the steering wheel in an impatient manner.

She heard him approach. Heard the crunch of gravel beneath the boots. Heard the sound of a ticket being torn from the pad he'd carried.

"Here you go. Please note the ticket must be paid by the date on the bottom. There is also a court date listed if you wish to contest the citation."

He handed it to her. No flourish. Matter-of-fact.

"Slow down and be safe."

Bite me.

She took the ticket, slammed the door and cranked the engine of the secondhand-but-still-gorgeous convertible BMW. She also tugged the seat belt across her chest and clicked it. She didn't need another ticket, thank you very much. But the devil inside her wouldn't allow her to slink away like a meek mouse. No, the devil inside her bade her to crumple the ticket and toss it onto the floorboard.

The devil inside her usually won.

She flashed a blinding smile at Officer Adam Hinton as she pitched the wadded ticket toward the fast-food sack that held gum wrappers and gas receipts, along with the remains of her noon meal. "Thanks for the welcome home."

He blinked. He hadn't put on his mirrored glasses. "Home? Wait—" He looked at his notepad. "Summer Rose?"

She saw the dawning.

"You're Rayne's sister. But your stage name is Scarlet. The actress from the vampire show." His gaze swept her, taking her in. She wasn't wearing heavy makeup. No dramatic kohl-rimmed eyes or overly plumped red lips. No catsuit. No bra that pushed her boobs so high she could prop her chin on them. She looked very little like the vampire queen who ran the fictional Collinstown. And very much like a regular twenty-six-year-old.

"Wow. Your powers of deduction are better than I thought. You had my name right there and everything. A real brainiac." She gestured to the clipboard in his hand. She was being a smart-ass but didn't care. She was pissed at him for embarrassing her with the whole DUI test and for making her react to his touch. How damn weak was she? Getting turned-on by a random cop? Pathetic. And that made her mad.

Because he had no right to make her feel anything.

She wasn't ready to embrace any frisson of desire. Not ready to welcome that small pique of interest. Not ready to move past the ache she clung to deep, deep down in her heart. She was dead to love.

She fingered the charm on the gold chain about her neck and begrudgingly looked into the cop's eyes.

She'd crumpled his ticket, then insulted him. The veneer of control he wore like a shield had cracked. He looked not quite so in control. "I would have let you off with a warning. I'm a friend of Rayne's new husband. But since you seem as much of a bitch as the character you play, I'm glad I didn't."

Scarlet gasped. Yes. Gasped. "How dare you? I'm reporting you to the police chief. This is an outrage, a—"

"Good luck with that." He slapped a hand against the hood of the car and turned toward his cruiser. "Have a nice day."

Scarlet moved her hand to make the universal sign of disdain, barely an afterthought for most New Yorkers. But she stopped herself. He was an officer of the law and this was Texas. So she grabbed the steering wheel instead and pressed the accelerator.

It was totally immature, but as the gravel spun beneath her wheels, Scarlet felt a momentary flash of satisfaction. She hoped the bits of rock hit his polished boots and scuffed them. Damn him. Calling her a bitch. She wasn't a bitch. She played one, but wasn't one. Officer Tight Ass was wrong.

Okay, sure. She had it in her. All women did. But he'd been the one to play the power card and force her to be frisked and humiliated on the outskirts of town. So she'd been mouthy. What of it?

Bastard.

Scarlet's car ate up the two miles of dilapidated houses, appliance-repair shops and boarded-over junk stores that dotted the highway leading into downtown Oak Stand. As she rolled, she grew even more aggravated at the cop and his stupid speeding ticket. She didn't care how damn sexy he looked in his uniform. Or how his touch had heated her blood. A friend of Brent Hamilton? That figured. Brent was a creep extraordinaire with gorgeous baby-blue eyes and a body that would make a nun toss her habit. He'd romanced most of the women in town. In fact, the last time Scarlet had been in Oak Stand, he'd tried to hook up with her.

Ugh. She had to talk some sense into her flighty sister before Rayne got hitched to a player of epic proportion. Brent spelled heartache and she had already had enough of that in her life. Scarlet knew what was up. Brent had hoodwinked her sister with his greasy smile and hot bod in order to hitch his wagon to Rayne's rising star. As soon as she had mentioned the *M* word, Scarlet knew she would have to do more than protest from afar. She needed to go to Texas. Thank goodness she was on hiatus. Small favors.

But the cop had said *new husband.*

Scarlet's mind stutter-stepped. Surely, Rayne and Brent weren't already married. Her older sister had said maybe sometime in September. It was still August. Very hot, sticky, sweltering August.

Rayne wouldn't get married and not tell Scarlet. No matter how badly their last conversation had gone.

Would she?

The town square materialized in front of her windshield, withered green and stereotypically small. Large oak trees hunkered in the shady park that centered the town. Brick streets, tired businesses and faded signs wrapped round it, clinging to the park like a toddler. Last spring, a tornado had ripped through town, leaving many businesses damaged. The First United Methodist Church of Oak Stand still lacked a steeple and several businesses remained boarded up. But otherwise, Oak Stand looked the same.

She rounded the square, noticing it seemed busier than usual. Almost every parking spot was taken, including all the ones in front of the Dairy Barn, the hometown diner that masqueraded as haute cuisine here. Directly in front of the Oak Stand Baptist Church were several vans with Horizon Blue Production Company on the side panel. Horizon Blue was the company contracted to film Rayne Rose's *A Taste of Texas,* a cooking and travel show debuting on a food channel. But that was to be filmed at Serendipity Inn, her aunt's newly refurbished bed-and-breakfast. And production wasn't scheduled to begin until September.

Or so Scarlet thought.

She slowed her car as she approached the front of the church. Only one man stood outside the closed doors, camera held at his side. Hmm. Something was going on and she suspected it had to do with Rayne.

She searched for a parking spot, but there were none near the church. She circled the square again, looking for an empty slot, finally finding one on a side street next to the old green stamp store. She leaped out of the car, grabbed her new Marc Jacobs bag and pressed the lock on her remote key chain. She walked quickly through the shady park. Squirrels scampered out of her way and the fountain with the Rufus Tucker topper spewed tepid water. A trickle of sweat rolled between her shoulder blades and she prayed her deodorant worked as well as the ads claimed. 'Cause it was Texas hot. Beyond all degrees known.

She stepped onto the sidewalk on the other edge of the park as the double doors of the church swept open. Her sister, splendid in a soft ivory bridal gown, appeared like an angel on the elbow of the handsome Brent Hamilton. They were grinning from ear to ear at the cameras whirring around them. Brent caught his glowing bride in his arms and kissed her.

His timing couldn't have been better, though he was not an actor.

The happy couple clasp each other and stare into

each other's eyes, blissfully happy. Cue the family around them, basking in the love the couple shares.

Everyone behind them "oohed" and "aahed."

Exactly.

Camera Two, get a close-up of angry sister's face. She's bewildered, hurt and furious. She won't stand for what has occurred.

Scarlet narrowed her eyes and stalked across the street toward her sister and Brent. The hurt that thumped in her chest was soon overshadowed by the anger rushing into her, whooshing in her ears, shooting out of her fingertips. She couldn't believe her eyes. Couldn't believe the timing. The irony beat down on her. She'd driven across the country to stop this very event.

Brent and Rayne broke apart and everyone clapped. Arm in arm, they turned and started down the steps toward the limo that pulled in behind Scarlet. She planted herself in Rayne and Brent's path.

Rayne's smile faltered when she saw Scarlet standing in front of the car, arms crossed. Rayne looked beyond beautiful. Absolutely tasteful, refined and...a little scared. Scarlet couldn't believe her older sister had gotten married and not invited her.

The pain razored across her heart again, but Scarlet ignored it. "Guess I missed the 'speak now or forever hold your peace' part of the ceremony."

"Scarlet," Rayne stammered, glancing desperately at her handsome groom. "You came!"

Cameras edged closer, but Scarlet was accustomed to being in front of them. They were an afterthought. "Yeah. I came to stop this sham of a wedding."

Rayne's eyes grew as big as the diamond on her left hand. Which was pretty damned big. Her sister looked at Brent, who glared at Scarlet.

"See? I told you not to call her," he said.

"Call me?" Scarlet looked past the elegant lace on her sister's shoulder to where her mother and father stood with Aunt Frances. They looked fairly alarmed, too. "No one called me."

One cameraman came too close. Scarlet whirled. "Back off, buddy. This is between me and my sister."

He immediately stepped back.

Amateur.

"Scarlet, you're making a scene," Brent said, taking her elbow so he could move her out of the way.

"Really?" Scarlet asked, trying like hell not to cry. Rayne had *married* this too-good-looking waste of skin. Scarlet was too late. All that effort to stop Rayne from making a colossal lapse in judgment, and Scarlet had arrived an hour too late.

If only that cop hadn't stopped her. She might have made it. Might have burst in and objected…on the grounds that Brent Hamilton was a man-whore and not fit to lick the soles of her sister's shoes.

"I always make a scene," Scarlet said drily, wrenching her elbow from his grasp and ignoring him. She looked at her sister instead. "Rayne?"

"Sorry, Scarlet. I love you, but I love Brent, too. We're married and we're staying that way. I don't care if he screwed half of Texas, he's my husband now. So stop the drama." Rayne pushed past Scarlet, dragging Brent with her. The limousine driver opened the door with a flourish.

Rayne turned around. "You can come to Serendipity and celebrate with us if you'd like."

Then she disappeared into the depths of the car with Brent right behind her. Henry, Rayne's son, sped by Scarlet and leaped onto Brent's lap.

"Come on, Aunt Scarlet! We're gonna party!" he yelled out the window as the limo pulled away from the curb.

Scarlet didn't say a thing. She couldn't have if she wanted. She'd failed miserably. She felt like crying into a vodka tonic, but Oak Stand was a dry town. Hell. If there was any time she needed a drink, it was now.

Her mind tripped back to the little bottle of rum lying beside the crumpled speeding ticket. It was all she had to take away the sting of failure. The sting of hurt.

Man, this day sucked.

CHAPTER TWO

HE'D LOST HIS COMPOSURE.

Not cool. He shouldn't have baited her. Shouldn't have implied she was a bitch. And he damned sure shouldn't have touched her.

Adam Hinton dusted the dirt and gravel off his boots as he watched the taillights of the BMW fade into the distance. He'd polished the black motorcycle boots last night and now they looked dusty.

Damn it.

He reached inside the cruiser for the backpack holding an assortment of necessities. First-aid kit, flashlight, extra clothes and other things he might need when away from the small house he rented in the middle of Oak Stand. He pulled a package of wet wipes from the depths. Not the best thing to use on leather, but it would do. He'd apply another coat of polish later tonight.

He needed to stop by the Hamilton reception. He'd told Brent he would, even though technically he was on duty. It could count as his lunch hour. He liked both Rayne and Brent, though he didn't know them as well as others in the small town did. He'd only been in Oak Stand for nine months. But as the newly appointed police chief, it was in his best interest to drop by the much-anticipated event. Nearly everyone in the town had been invited to the wedding and reception, which was being filmed as the premiere of *A Taste of Texas,* a new show featuring Rayne Rose, a rising chef in the culinary world. Not only was it a joyous celebration of the love shared between the couple, but also of the opportunity Rayne Rose had given Oak Stand when she'd talked the network into using Serendipity Inn as the base for filming the show. Everyone was thrilled about the potential benefit to a town still trying to get on its feet after a tornado ripped through last spring.

Everyone except obviously one smoking-hot redhead.

The image of Scarlet arching against the rear of the BMW like a naughty advertisement for porn popped into his mind. She'd had him salivating at the blatant taunt. He'd done his best to remain impassive, but inside his libido had ratcheted up several notches and revved to near out of control.

She was everything he wanted and nothing he needed.

Adam felt his groin tighten. Oh, yeah. Scarlet Rose was the type of woman he lusted after. Lush, brash and absolutely naughty. He liked the girls who wore their clothes too tight, drank Bud from a bottle and had tattoos of *La Vida Loca* on their backside. Years ago, he'd gone through a parade of women who threw things at him when they got angry, wore cheap red lace bras and drove him totally over the edge.

Why he preferred trouble to perfectly acceptable in a sweater set escaped him. He supposed it had something to do with his father and his sexcapades. That's exactly what his shrink would say. Perhaps Adam could explore that line of reasoning the next time he went to Houston and saw Dr. Fitzgerald. Maybe he could find out why coiffed blondes with monogrammed stationary turned him off. Why cute soccer moms with juice packs and empty smiles left him cold. And why women who went to Bible study and drank hot tea with lemon made him want to run for the hills.

Because those kinds of women were what a police chief needed. An acceptable lady. Not a sex kitten.

He gave himself a mental shake and pulled his thoughts from women of his past, present and future.

He was on the clock with a job to do.

He tossed the soiled wipe into the trash bag he kept on the floor of the idling cruiser and climbed inside. One pass around the town, then he'd stop at the reception. Hopefully, the redhead hadn't caused any problems. By his watch, she would have been too late. But something told him she wouldn't let Rayne and Brent get in her way.

Desire unraveled in his belly. He tamped it down.

Scarlet Rose spelled trouble. With a capital *T*.

And if there was one thing Adam didn't need in his life, it was that kind of Trouble.

ADAM CLIMBED THE STEPS of the century-old house that served as Oak Stand's only bed-and-breakfast. It was a gingerbread of a house, freshly painted a cool blue with bright white trim. Lush ferns greeted visitors as they made their way onto the wide porch featuring rocking chairs and a porch swing. He could hear the hum of the crowd, most of which likely filled the interior and the pristine backyards of both the inn and the Hamiltons who lived next door. No one was on the front porch.

Except Scarlet.

She sat on the porch swing, looking as if someone had kicked her. Hard.

"Hey," he said, a little too loudly.

She started. "Oh, it's you."

"Yeah," he said, for want of anything clever to say.

As he stood there contemplating a feast for the eyes, his libido tapped him on the shoulder and whispered, "I want some of that." Libido was hard to ignore.

She sighed and leaned back, causing the swing to tilt and her breasts to thrust forward. A gold shoe charm hung from a chain around her neck, nestling right in the middle of her breasts. He wanted to be that little shoe. His mouth went dry at the thought. His libido resumed the incessant tapping.

"Wow. Not only are you competent in the art of detection, but you excel in the art of conversation, too. Bet the ladies in town are lining up." Sarcasm didn't drip from her mouth. It gushed enough for him to shove his libido under a rock.

"No luck in stopping the wedding?"

Her eyes narrowed. "You gave me that DUI test on purpose."

He shook his head. "No. I detained you because a bottle of liquor fell from your glove compartment. I'm entrusted with a job to protect this community."

She snorted. "Yeah. I'm a real danger. Hide your children."

"Just doing my job."

She shrugged. "I wasn't in time. Guess we bitches don't always get our way."

He winced. "I shouldn't have implied you are a bitch. It was unprofessional. I'm sorry."

She averted her eyes toward the large magnolia tree that squatted in the yard between the inn and the street. "No problem. I am a bitch. Everyone knows it."

Silence descended on the porch. He thought he heard crickets.

"I'm sure you're not, um, well, not to everyone."

Damn. What was he? A tongue-tied virgin standing in front of a wet-dream fantasy girl?

Amusement twitched at her mouth and her gaze caught his. Her eyes weren't brown like her sister's. More of a hazel with flecks of gold and green. They looked like the granite on his kitchen counter. Mesmerizingly gorgeous. Of course, he couldn't see them from where he stood, but he remembered from earlier.

"You're being nice to me."

He shrugged. "Not really, but I sense you need someone to give you a break today."

"Like you did earlier? You gave me a DUI test on the side of the highway a mere—" she glanced at the red leather watch on her arm "—forty minutes ago."

He glanced through the glass in the oval door. The parlor looked to be a crush of people, talking with their hands, sipping punch. It looked uncomfortable. He moved toward Scarlet. "Again, just doing—"

"Your job. Yeah, I get it," she muttered, not moving from her spot on the swing.

"So, are you in time-out or something?"

At that, she laughed. It sounded like tinkling bells and his groin tightened. "Yeah, something like that."

He gestured toward the rocker in front of the swing. "Mind if I sit?"

"It's a free country."

"Not really, if you think about it," he replied, sinking into the flowered cushion of the rocker. "We pay taxes."

She jerked her gaze to his. "You're strange."

"I think I'd rather you call me a bitch," he said. Did everyone think him strange? Hell, he'd heard nothing but the same from his own mother every day of his life.

Along with his father. And nanny. And tutors. The list could go on and on.

She lifted her eyebrows and laughed. His libido climbed out from under the rock where he'd stuffed it and punched him in the gut. A match struck, desire flamed. He needed to get his ass off the porch, shake a few hands and choke down some wedding cake. He didn't need to tempt himself with the woman in front of him.

Yet, he didn't move.

"So *are* you a bitch?" she asked, a twinkle in her eye.

"Is that code for asking if I'm gay?" he said.

"Are only gay guys bitches?"

"I really don't know," he said, finally cracking a smile. It felt creaky. Unused.

For a moment they sat, measuring each other. It was a far different vibe from the one they'd engaged in earlier.

"My roommate's gay. I'll ask him," she said, scuffing one heel against the painted boards. She set the swing going a bit and stared off into the distance at a stop sign at the end of the street. Or maybe it was the Weeks's old Chrysler parked in their driveway. He couldn't tell.

"Your roommate's gay? Interesting."

"Yeah. The best roommate a girl can have. He cooks things like reductions and flambé, cleans with pure vinegar and knows what sweater goes with my newest wedges. I should probably marry him. He'd love that kind of cover." She smiled again, shifting her attention to him. It felt good having her regard. He wanted to stay there, under her gaze, under her spell. "My roommate is Stefan Horton. And I suppose I should tell you he's not out. So…" She made a lock motion, tossing the imaginary key over her shoulder.

She said it as though he should know the name. He searched the recesses of his mind. No clue. "Stefan Horton?"

"He plays Karakas on *Deep Shadows.*"

"Oh." Adam had never watched the campy drama, though plenty of people around town had buzzed about it since the day it debuted. Everyone knew the demonically sexy queen of the vampires was played by Frances's niece, who happened to be Chef Rayne Rose's younger sister. The *Oak Stand Gazette* had done a feature piece on Scarlet and had even netted a telephone interview. He'd perused the interview one night while sitting on the outskirts of town, waiting for the roughnecks at Cooley's bar to get rowdy the way they did every ladies' night. He'd remembered her publicity shot. The alabaster breasts threatening to topple out of the black spandex. Those red, red lips and haunting eyes.

"You don't watch, I take it?"

He shook his head. "The existential angst that underpins the soap opera doesn't fit my ideal viewing parameters."

"Big words. And it's not a soap opera," she said, flipping her ponytail over her shoulder. Though her skin was remarkably fair, she was not freckled. Her shoulders were smooth and faintly golden from the sun, as if awaiting his kiss. "You're not from around here."

It was a question. "No. I'm originally from Houston."

"You don't sound like you're from Houston."

He leaned forward and clasped his hands. He was accustomed to questions. Everyone in Oak Stand wanted to know who your mama and daddy were. And where you attended church. But he hated answering questions about his past. "I went to prep school on the East Coast. They force Texas twang out, much like I'm sure you did when you trained as an actress. You don't sound Texan."

"I'm not a Texan. I'm from everywhere." The mood shifted. No more lightness. Something darker had awakened in her. For a moment she didn't speak, seemed caught in her thoughts. Then she looked up at him. "You know, I have some wicked fantasies about prep-school boys in stuffy oxford shirts and sweater cardigans. About getting them out of those khaki pants."

It was off-kilter. Almost sarcastic. She vamped him and his blood responded, heating like lava, making him forget who he was. Her gaze narrowed to smolder and her pink tongue appeared at the corner of her plump lips, throwing gunpowder onto the fire.

He couldn't stop himself. He dragged his gaze over her fantasy of a body. The tank top was tight and outlined what he wanted to see. Even her blue-green nail polish looked provocative. He knew it was wrong. He knew he'd poured his own fuel onto the fire that blazed between them. "I had some pretty wicked fantasies myself. The best one involved a smart-mouthed redhead with long legs and big—"

"Are you flirting with me?"

Her words were like ice water, dousing the flickering flames within him. What in the hell had he been thinking playing with her like that?

"Are you flirting with me?" he countered with a deadpan expression.

He found his cool. No need to let her know how much he wanted to handcuff her in a very unprofessional way. No need to let her see the weakness he held when it came to women like her.

She leaped to her feet. "No."

She walked toward the front door, not bothering to glance back at him.

His body bade him to follow her, to find out how it would feel to have her perfect white teeth nipping his earlobe, to have her abundant flesh filling his hands. To discover the way she'd feel beneath him, on top of him, around him.

But Adam didn't move. He was no slave to desire. Not anymore. So instead of watching Scarlet walk away—which he knew had to be a great view—he focused on a moth fluttering above some flowering bushes ringing the porch.

Brother, you've lost your mind. Don't forget who you are in this town. You are the law. And you are currently on duty. No indulging in witty repartee with a bold strawberry tart who broke the law less than an hour ago. Get a grip.

He rose and straightened, donning his resolve and doffing his uniform hat.

Then he traced Scarlet's steps into the inn.

The parlor was crowded, so he didn't see where Scarlet headed. A few familiar faces met his gaze. The hardware-store owner shook his hand, the mayor slapped his back and he was certain Betty Monk had copped a feel of his butt. It was either her or Grace Lewis. And neither of those ladies had seen their natural hair color in thirty years.

"Adam," the bride said, pulling her dress hem from under the heavy foot of Bubba Malone. "I'm so glad you made the reception. Have you had a piece of cake yet?"

Leave it to Rayne to try and feed him the minute he stepped inside. He shook his head. "Not yet. Sorry I had to miss the ceremony, but someone had to keep thieves and murderers from crashing the wedding."

Along with sexy sisters on a mission to destroy wedded bliss.

But he didn't add that fact.

Bubba shoved the last of his cake into his mouth and mumbled, "I'da liked to see 'em try to crash that wedding. Heads would have rolled, by God."

Rayne laughed. "It's too bad you didn't pull my baby sister over. She almost made it in time to cause even more of a sensation than she did."

"Actually—" Adam said, only to close his mouth when Bubba made the kill slash across his own throat.

"Actually what?" Rayne said, her brow furrowed.

He stared at Rayne for a moment, not sure how to get out of admitting he'd ticketed her sister and did what she'd suggested—held Scarlet up long enough to keep her from crashing the ceremony. He could almost visualize Scarlet blazing into the church and stalking up the aisle with her vibrant hair flaming around her. Rayne was pretty with an angelic face framed by wild red corkscrew curls. But she was nothing compared to the siren who had bent over the back of her car and dared him to frisk her. No comparison whatsoever.

"Nothing," Adam said, looking at Bubba, who looked alarmed. Scarlet's antics must be a touchy subject.

"Oh." Rayne spun around and her hair nearly landed in Bubba's punch glass. "My sister is around here somewhere. I'd like you to meet her. You might want to go ahead and introduce yourself. If she stays any longer than a day or two, you'll run into her. She draws trouble like roadkill draws flies." Rayne laughed as if she'd cracked a joke, but there was an edge in her voice.

As if he didn't already know.

As if Scarlet's naughtiness wasn't exactly what drew him to her. That and her playground of a body.

His mouth watered at the thought of taking a ride on Scarlet.

"She done slipped out the back. Or maybe up the stairs," Bubba said, rotating his large head like a periscope. "All I know is she ain't feeling herself or she'd be down here regalin' us."

Rayne sighed. "True. She's hurt. And angry."

"You know, Hinton, I've been thinking of taking up law enforcement. You got room on that huge force for a man of my statue?"

Bubba's intent was obvious to Adam. He wanted to change the subject. For what reason, Adam hadn't a clue. And he wasn't sure about Bubba being a *statue.* "I might indeed."

Bubba actually brightened at his words. "Heck, I may take you up on it. Jack's pretty sweet on me, but he may let me try my hand at knockin' heads and cuffin' drunks."

Jack Darby, Bubba's boss and a local rancher, evidently heard his words. "I'm not that damn sweet on you. Go ahead, though they better get a tent maker busy on sewing a uniform for you."

Adam moved along as the two men jokingly sparred about Bubba's chances at fitting in a police cruiser. Might not be a bad idea to recruit the big man as a reserve officer. The police force had been shorthanded ever since Sherwood McCann married and moved to Mesquite. Bubba Malone was an established member of the town. Everyone knew the easygoing, loyal-as-a-hound redneck. He'd be a good man to have when the chips were down.

The crowd didn't lighten as he neared the back of the

house. Left and right, people nodded at him or threw a wave of acknowledgment as he approached the porch. But he didn't fool himself. People were friendly to him for good reason. Being Police Chief of Oak Stand may have been a lateral move for him, but it was top dog as far as law enforcement was concerned for the people of the community.

They didn't trust him yet. Didn't know him well enough to call him one of their own. But they respected him well enough. For the moment that was all he needed. One day he hoped to feel at home in Oak Stand, but until then, he did his best to be the man he expected himself to be. Focused, progressive and fair.

And he knew his weakness for women like Scarlet would chip away at any respectability he'd built within the hardworking, traditional-values community. He needed to stay away from her and those like her. He needed to make a date with the mayor's daughter, the perfectly respectable one who had recently moved home to teach kindergarten at Oak Stand Elementary. What was her name? He couldn't remember.

The back lawn was as crowded as the house, and he briefly thought about grabbing a piece of cake and returning to the vacant front porch. But there would be no sexy redhead to keep him company. He couldn't help scanning the crowd for her, even though seconds before he'd told himself to forget about her.

He didn't find Scarlet, but he did find the irascible city councilman, Harvey Primm. Unfortunately.

"Hinton, we need to talk about this upcoming hoopla at the library. We need a plan for how to handle the riffraff that's going to show up."

"Not today, Harvey. Come by my office and we'll talk about it."

"You know they're planning a protest, don't you? Gosh danged liberals. As if we don't have bigger things to worry about in this country. Misguided fools, the whole pack of them." The councilman shook his head, disgust plainly etched across his weathered brow.

Harvey Primm served on the city council as he had for the past twenty-odd years. He was a self-proclaimed pillar of the community. Once a tire salesman, he now worked from home, producing a questionable piece of journalism called the *Howard County Examiner,* which unleashed gossip about his neighbors. Ironically, he also served as a deacon in a nondenominational church on the outskirts of Oak Stand. Adam found the man to be overbearing, insufferable and a little cracked. Supposedly, Harvey had grown increasingly obsessed with stopping evil in all forms ever since his wife had been killed by a drunk driver several years before. Harvey's feverish climb onto his soapbox had him extolling his views on everything from prohibiting the sale of alcohol to this newest cause—the removal of a children's book containing witchcraft from the county library. Adam tired of the man shadowing his doorstep nearly once a week.

"I'm aware, but this is neither the time nor the place. Come by and we'll talk," Adam said, trying to slide past Harvey.

The man's hand clamped down on his arm. "There is no better time than the present. The library board voted. It's done and all the protestors in the state of Texas can't stop us from removing that filth from the shelves of our library. Away from the hands of our innocent children."

Adam removed Harvey's hand. "Mr. Primm, if you

wish to discuss potential problems that might arise as a result of the library board's vote, stop by my office."

With that, Adam turned and plowed through a small crowd of people, many of whom likely overheard the exchange if their silence was any indication.

Harvey didn't follow him, but Adam could feel the hard stare of the man burrowing into his back. A prickle of unease crept up his spine. Harvey, who had wholeheartedly supported Adam's hire as the new police chief, was turning out to be trouble. Adam supposed the man thought a younger appointment would be easier to control.

Guess he hadn't done his research.

Adam was definitely by the book, but he also wasn't a man to be pushed around by the whims of an egotistical, right-wing looney bird.

A flash of red caught his eye.

But it wasn't Scarlet. It was Betty Monk wearing a lavish red sequined dress paired with matching cowboy boots. Not quite fitting with the homespun, earthy decor of the reception. How he knew it was homespun and earthy was beyond him. Must have been something he picked up from the decorating magazine Roz had left in the john at the station.

Time to shake Brent Hamilton's hand, then get out of Dodge. Go to the station. File a report. Drink a cup of Roz Lane's bitter coffee. Forget about buxom beauties and how splendid they looked in black leather and red lipstick.

Betty raised her painted-on eyebrows and started barreling toward Adam.

He slid to the right, ducking behind a cluster of occupied tables. He didn't want to hear about how no one picked up after their dogs when they walked through the downtown park. Nor could he tolerate her incessant touching. She flirted as if she were a twenty-year-old. And seemed absolutely convinced he was into her.

To hell with shaking Brent's hand. Adam would grab cake and head for the hills.

He was a good cop, but he wasn't a saint.

CHAPTER THREE

SCARLET LEANED HER HEAD against the fluffy pillows on the bed and studied Rayne. The last time she'd seen her had been four months ago when she'd come to New York City to meet with producers and TV execs. At that time, her older sister had looked thinner and more stressed. Scarlet had concluded the wear and tear to be caused by her career and dealing with being a single mother. She hadn't known Rayne had been seeing Oak Stand stud-muffin-extraordinaire Brent Hamilton. When Rayne mentioned she'd been seeing the man, Scarlet had nearly gone through the roof of the upscale bar they'd sat in.

It was obvious Rayne had given little credence to Scarlet's warning about how men like Brent never changed, since she sat in a ladder-backed chair, wearing an ivory wedding dress.

Scarlet had to admit. Rayne looked good. She'd gained weight and as she'd glided down the church steps, hand in hand with her new husband, she'd been glowing most radiantly. God, Scarlet hoped Rayne wasn't pregnant.

Now, as the shadows fell and the party-supply workers packed up the tents and folding chairs outside, Rayne looked...uncomfortable, like a kid who faced the dreaded flu shot.

Scarlet crossed her arms and glared at her older sister until their gazes finally met across the room.

"I called you," Rayne said. "I left two messages this past week alone."

Scarlet sniffed and tossed her hair over one shoulder.

"Summer," Rayne said, her words plainly apologetic. "I called and left a message on your answering machine. And I sent you an email. Have you checked your messages?"

"My name is not Summer. Not anymore."

Rayne frowned. "I know, but you'll always be Summer to me."

Scarlet shrugged, dismissing the mushy sentiment. She'd changed her name to Scarlet when she started acting. She preferred it over the misnomer her parents had given her. Nothing light and sweet about her. Especially now that her heart had been broken into a billion throbbing pieces. "You know my cell-phone number. Any thought I might be on the move, since we're on hiatus?" Scarlet drawled. She wasn't buying her sister's story. She had an inkling Rayne hadn't wanted her here for the wedding. Which hurt like hell.

"You never answer your cell. I called the number you gave me. I did." Rayne spread her hands apart. "You never called me back."

"That's not tr—" Scarlet snapped her mouth closed. Okay. She vaguely remembered a call from her sister several weeks ago. She'd been at a party. She'd had two gin and tonics in her attempt to have fun. She hadn't accomplished her mission. And she'd forgotten about Rayne's call. Damn.

"See." Rayne gave her the I'm-always-right older-sister nod. The one Scarlet hated beyond all others. Rayne clung to the power she wielded as the eldest.

"Fine. I remember it now. I was at a party in the Village. The cute guy from that hospital show was there. Sober, but still yummy. I, on the other hand, had a few drinks too many. I forgot about the call."

Rayne closed her eyes. "Good gravy, you are a piece of work."

Scarlet tossed her sister a smart-ass smile. "Why, thank you."

Rayne opened her eyes and leveled her gaze. "Look, I know you have reservations about Brent, but—"

"*Reservations?* Yeah, you could call them that," Scarlet said. "Rayne, he tried to pick me up at a bar three years ago. Slimy pick-up line and he didn't even buy me a beer. He's not the marrying kind. Guys like him don't change."

Rayne waved her left hand in front of Scarlet. The diamond on the wedding band caught the sunlight streaming into the room. "I beg to differ. He *is* the marrying kind."

Scarlet shook her head. Rayne had no clue what she'd done. She'd married a veritable slut. No way would Brent be faithful. Scarlet knew his kind. They smiled, cajoled and had a gal's ankles over her head before she could even get his digits. No way this ended well. "I'm sorry I can't be happier, but this has heartbreak written all over it."

Rayne laughed. "Says the girl who has never been in love. What's your longest relationship? A month? You flit from one thing to the other. *Deep Shadows* is the biggest commitment you've made thus far, so I don't think you're qualified."

Little do you know, big sis.

"I don't have to be in love to know you just screwed the pooch," Scarlet snipped. "And let's not bring me into this. We're talking about you. Wholesome, smart, accomplished Rayne. Butter wouldn't melt in your mouth. You don't know about the big, bad wolves in this world."

The ones that rip out your heart and then tap-dance on it.

"So I have to live in New York City to recognize people for what they are? Jeez, I didn't know. I suppose I should have consulted my experienced, world-weary twenty-six-year-old sister on the steps I should take on falling in love."

"Love?" Scarlet snorted. "I don't think you should call your desire to get into a hunk's undies love."

Rayne flushed. "You wouldn't know love if it slapped you in the face." She usually looked sweet and fragile. She wasn't. She fought dirty and pulled hair. "This is not about sleeping with Brent. I could do that without a ring on my finger. I love him and he loves me…and Henry."

Scarlet shook her head. "I've been around Oak Stand. I've been around him. You want to believe that because you're lonely and Phillip is gone."

Rayne looked as if she might physically lash out at her. "This has nothing to do with being lonely or Phillip. You can't understand, because you're not capable. This is my life. If I make mistakes, they're on me. I don't need you to save me. You have enough on your plate."

Scarlet couldn't disagree. Her life had been tough since she and John had split well over a year ago. What good would it do to toss her pain out for others to see? Her heart still ached, but no one would ever know how broken she truly was. She wouldn't allow it because she couldn't survive in her business by admitting to being vulnerable. To being dumped like last year's fashions.

Her sister rose. "You know, I won't be able to change

your mind. That's obvious. Maybe if you hang around for a couple of days, you might see things differently."

"You're not going on a honeymoon?"

"Not until October, when we go to San Antonio for the Christmas show. Brent has a deadline at the end of September and I'm a working wife and mom. Plus, every day with Brent is—"

"Don't say it." Scarlet knew she sounded like a snotty kid who didn't get the last piece of candy. Her intentions *had* been honorable. She hadn't wanted to see her older sister suffer through more than she'd already suffered after the death of her first husband. Didn't want her to feel the aching emptiness Scarlet felt each time she closed her eyes. Time didn't always heal wounds. "I'll stick around for a few days, but don't count on my changing my mind on lover boy anytime soon."

Rayne opened her mouth to argue, then seemed to think better of it. She kept her hand on the doorknob for a moment, gazing hard at the Tiffany lamp on the nightstand next to Scarlet. Finally she made eye contact. "For what it's worth, I appreciate your caring enough to try to save me from a perceived mistake."

"You're welcome," Scarlet said, trying to keep her stern resolve, but a warm spot pooled in her heart at her sister's words. She'd always craved Rayne's approval. Probably because Rayne had been such a steadfast influence in a world that had rocked arpeggio Scarlet's whole life. From the moment she'd been born, her artisan parents had dragged their children around the country, living in communes, on Indian reservations and sometimes in campers in the middle of huge national forests. Scarlet's childhood had been both magical and discordant. The two little girls had needed more stability than either parent was willing to deliver in their quest for peace, love and rainbows.

Rayne had been the one to braid Scarlet's hair, teach her how to tie her shoes and make sure she had milk money in her pocket. Rayne had sung lullabies, made macaroni and cheese, and helped Scarlet learn how to write her full name on broken-line paper. She'd been Scarlet's angel right up until the day her parents had sent Rayne to live with Aunt Fran.

But they hadn't allowed Scarlet to stay in Texas. They'd chained her to them, declaring her too young to be separated from them. They had bumped from town to town. And it had made Scarlet tough. She learned to take care of herself. To punch bullies in the nose. To connive members of the commune into giving her ice-cream money. To manipulate. To blend. To pretend. Her earliest experiences had been training ground for becoming an actress.

There was little Scarlet wouldn't do for Rayne…even if it meant knocking some sense into her.

But it was too late for such drastic measures, thanks to Officer Tight Ass.

She swung her legs off the bed and padded to the window. The sun sank behind the neighbor's house, thrusting brilliant fingers of light upon the deep green grass. It was peaceful and very, very different from the noisy streets normally outside her window.

Her mind flitted from her sister to the cop who had frisked her. Officer Adam Hinton.

When he'd touched her, she'd felt something that had been absent for well over a year—a stirring of desire. The flicker of feeling had rocked her. For the past few months, she'd been on a mission to feel something, anything, at a man's touch. She'd forced herself to flirt, purposefully drank too much and bore sloppy kisses from strangers in clubs, but to no avail. She'd been dead to desire. Until a few hours ago.

So why now? Why him?

Adam Hinton was not her usual type. Or maybe he was. She couldn't be certain. Until John, she'd liked young, wild and irresponsible in a guy. Now she didn't have a clue what she wanted in a man. But something had been there between her and the cop. Perhaps his refusal to fall prey to her manipulation had poked her inner psyche. Maybe his by-the-book, take-no-shit attitude had reminded her of John. Had to be that. There was no other reason she'd felt anything other than anger at the squeaky-clean Officer Hinton.

She pressed her forehead against the warmth of the windowpane and touched the gold slipper nestled between her breasts.

Her heart felt like tissue paper, so how could she even contemplate being with another man when she still hemorrhaged from the only time she'd taken a chance on love? It didn't seem right.

Still, Adam Hinton was utterly tempting.

Straight as an arrow, honest as a Boy Scout and clean as a… She couldn't think what would be as clean. Not a whistle because spit got in it. Something about Adam made her want to smudge him with her fingerprints, and that baffled the hell out of her.

Because she was still in love with John.

THE COFFEE REMAINING in the pot at the police station looked as if it might cure a bacterial infection, so Adam skipped an evening cup of java and grabbed a bottle of water from the small fridge beside Roz's desk, which she kept stocked.

"Harvey Primm called again," his on-duty officer, Jared Mullins, hollered from the desk he'd set behind a makeshift bookcase to prevent anyone from seeing the colossal amount of time he wasted on the internet.

From over the barrier, Adam saw Jared switch his computer screen from something on YouTube to the screen saver showing his dog, Winchester, holding a duck in his mouth. Jared was a decent person. Mostly. He wasn't, however, a good officer. Because he was the nephew of the mayor, he'd stayed a permanent fixture at the Oak Stand Police Department for the past five years.

"Already saw him at the Hamilton reception. He'll be on our doorstep Monday. Bank on it." Adam twisted the top off the water bottle. "So I'm guessing you found a suspect for the Porky case."

Jared rolled his chair backward and faced him. "Huh?"

Adam indicated the computer screen. "Find the culprit on YouTube? Is that how they got the statue from the parking lot? On a skateboard?"

Jared wasn't smart enough to show shame. "Well, not really. But I've been checking out Facebook in case any of the little punks posted something about it in their status updates."

Adam didn't blink. "Sounds like good detective work."

Jared grinned. "Yeah, I thought so, too."

"Not good with sarcasm, are you?"

"You being sarcastic?"

"Never mind," Adam said, pulling himself from where he leaned against the filing cabinet. "If it wouldn't be too much trouble, head out and question the neighbors next to Porky's. See if they saw any kids hanging out around the joint last night. Whoever took Bud Henry's pig statue didn't waltz out without someone seeing something. It's pretty big."

"It won't be no trouble. I need to grab some grub anyhow."

"Well, don't let actual police work stand in your way of onion rings and a fried-chicken sandwich," Adam drawled, heading toward his small office in the rear of the station. The place had been built over fifty years ago and still smelled like cigarettes. Adam supposed the chain-smoking former chief of police had overlooked the ordinance banning lighting up in public facilities. He'd also overlooked the chest pains that had landed him over at the Overton Funeral Parlor. He'd died in the very chair Adam now sank into.

Actually, not the "very" chair. Adam had purchased an ergonomic model when he first arrived in Oak Stand. But Dan Drummond had died in the office. The greasy fries got to him before the cancer sticks did.

Roz wouldn't even come inside the office anymore. The administrative assistant handed him messages and files when he passed her desk. She said she felt a presence in the office. She believed in ghosts and karma and crap like that.

Adam didn't believe in poltergeists, but he did believe the former chief's influence hung over the station to the point of being stifling. Dan had been the chief for over thirty-three years before buying the farm, and Adam discovered very quickly the other officers and Roz believed Dan's way had been the only way. Which had become a bit of a problem.

The next time he heard another "But that's not the way we do it," he might dock some pay.

Of course, he would never resort to something so

cruel as to take bread from the mouths of his officers' families, but he was damned tired of having every suggestion and order questioned because it wasn't how they'd always done it. Frankly, how they'd always done it had been ineffective. The files were antiquated, the equipment not up to standards and the procedural elements redundant. The department had needed an overhaul for a long time.

Lucky Adam. He got to fix it. Not an easy task.

"You want me to pick you up something at the Dairy Barn?" Jared asked from the open doorway. Adam glanced up and suppressed a scowl at the way the man's shirttail hung out on one side. He'd asked his officers time and again to make sure they looked professional. Jared seemed the most challenged in this area, especially as it seemed his shirt was a magnet for barbecue sauce, mustard and other nefarious condiments. But at least he was generous enough to ask Adam if he wanted a sandwich.

"No, thanks. I'll grab something later."

Jared sent him a wave, and moments later the heavy metal door slammed shut. The small building fell silent.

Adam leaned back in his chair and sighed. He had plenty of paperwork awaiting him, but for some reason, he didn't feel like diving into it. He closed his eyes and was immediately assaulted by the image of Scarlet Rose.

He hated that he couldn't shake the niggling of want that had burrowed inside him and taken root. He couldn't act—

The harsh ring of the phone interrupted his self-admonishment.

Roz had clocked out. No one to answer but him. He should let the machine pick up, but it might be an emergency. He snatched the receiver off the hook. "Oak Stand Police Department. Hinton."

"Well, hello, stranger," the voice purred.

He closed his eyes. "Angi."

"Oh, you remembered what my voice sounds like."

Adam breathed a silent curse. One he'd never say aloud. "How could I forget? I heard it almost every day for the ten months we were together."

"You changed your cell-phone number," she breathed, ignoring his gibe about the length of their marriage. Her voice sounded gravelly from the cigarette smoke of the bar she had likely visited the night before. He could visualize her on the other side of the line. Tight dress, too much makeup with a glass of sweet tea cradled in one hand. She'd be sprawled across the bed on her stomach, likely barefoot, chewing a piece of spearmint gum to give her tea mint flavor. She'd likely taken a break in getting ready for round two for the weekend, where she would probably hit two or three clubs with her girlfriends. He knew her, and he knew her schedule. It hadn't changed with their marriage and it sure hadn't changed with their divorce.

"New life, new number," he said.

Angi didn't respond. A few seconds slipped by.

"That's what you want? A whole new life? You want to just forget about us? About me?" Her poor-me routine was in full force, the one she'd perfected after losing their baby. The one that stirred guilt inside him every time.

He tried to dash away the feelings of sadness, anger and bitterness her words brought forth. "Don't start, Angi. There is no *us* anymore." Adam rubbed his eyes with his thumb and finger. He didn't need this now. Not when he had a report to file on a certain speeder. Not when he had a giant pig statue to locate.

"You didn't think that the last time you were in Houston. It felt very much an us. In fact, it felt like old times." Angi's voice had returned to breathy and teasing. This was the voice she used on him every time she wanted something, whether it was a drink, sex or money. Usually it was all three. And damn his weak hide, he sometimes gave in.

"That night was a mistake," he muttered, wishing he hadn't answered the phone. He also wished he'd shoved her out of his Houston hotel door the last time he'd been in the city. Instead he allowed her to wheedle herself inside for a nightcap. Which had led to sex so hot the hotel manager had called the room and requested they keep it down. Which had led to his writing her a check to cover her rent for the month—money over and above the alimony he paid her on a regular basis. As he'd scribbled his name on the signature line, he'd felt dirty and used. Shame had coursed through him. Didn't matter that she had seduced him. Didn't matter that no one had forced him to write that check. Guilt reigned where Angi was concerned. As it always had.

Their disaster of a marriage had been his fault. He'd forced her into something she hadn't wanted, tried to make her into something she could never be, and they'd both paid for his mistake.

"Somehow I knew you'd say that, darlin'."

"What do you want, Angi?"

"Why do I have to want something? Can't I call my ex to find out how he's doing in his new job?"

"No," Adam said, shuffling papers around on his desk. "I'm pretty busy here, so if you don't need anything, I'll have to let you—"

"Wait," Angi chirped. "I do need one itty-bitty favor."

He slapped down the paperwork. Of course she did. "What?"

"Well, it's not that big of a deal, but this past Wednesday I went out with some girls from the shop. We all thought Sheryl Lynn was the designated driver. It was her turn. But she thought it was Cathy's turn. Well, anyway, I ended up having to drive 'cause Sheryl Lynn had four belly shots and—"

"You got a DUI?"

"Well..." She hesitated, the slightest edge to her voice. "Yeah."

"Nothing I can do about that, Ang."

"But you know people in the department. You can call Chief Ahern and—"

He tried to remain calm. Had to. "I don't work for HPD anymore. Besides, you—"

"But your daddy is the—"

"Do not go there," he said, no longer able to keep the anger out of his voice. He knew who his daddy was. No one had to tell him.

"Please, Adam. I don't want to have to deal with all this. Things have been slow at the store and—"

"No." The anger wasn't because Angi had called him to use him. He'd accustomed himself to her manipulations long ago. The fact she wanted him to use, no, *abuse,* his family's connections to get her out of something she damn well deserved...that snapped something inside him.

"Adam, just this once, baby."

"You deserve the citation. You'll have to take the punishment. You could have killed someone or even killed yourself. You do a lot of stupid things, lady. But that takes the cake."

"I can't believe you won't help me," she cried, all pretense now gone. "You want to play morality police, when you have the power to make this go away. I guess I should expect that from someone like you. You throw your weight around when it benefits you, but you wouldn't deem to spit on me. I forgot. I'm nothing but trailer trash, right? Never was good enough for you. I can't believe you didn't make me get an abortion in the first place. You—"

"This conversation is over. Our relationship is over. Don't call me again." Pain ripped across his chest at her words. They were the same words she'd battered him with every time they fought. She threw up her less than advantageous background. She threw up his wealthy family connections. And she threw up the baby who had never been born. The baby who had slipped away two weeks after they'd gotten married at the courthouse.

"You mean, until you're ready to get busy," she said, her tone low and mean.

"That was a mistake I won't be making again. You're a beautiful woman, Angi, but you were right from the beginning. We don't belong together. We never did. Don't call back."

He pressed the end button before he said anything more. Anger, regret and guilt twisted in his gut, and his fist itched to connect with something. He stared at the silent office before shoving his chair from his desk and grabbing the hat he'd earlier tossed onto the table beside the battle-scarred door.

He felt twitchy and restless. Only one solution for that.

Strip down and go toe-to-toe with someone.

The image of Scarlet Rose with arched back and jutting breasts flashed across his mind. Not exactly what he had in mind.

He needed a fight. Not a woman.

He punched the numbers on his cell phone. The ones that would bring him needed release. Then he'd call Jared back to the station to cover. He needed to pound the frustrations from his body and then he could do another sweep of the town.

If he got lucky, he might find that damned pig.

CHAPTER FOUR

SCARLET STARED AT HER PLATE before sliding her gaze to where her eight-year-old nephew sat chomping happily on Pop-Tarts. "What's the white stuff in the eggs?"

Henry shrugged one shoulder. "I don't know. Probably goat cheese. She likes to put that in everything."

"Bluck."

Her sister's new husband glanced at her before redirecting his attention to the freshly squeezed orange juice sitting at his elbow. "Thought city slickers liked fancy eggs."

"You thought wrong." Scarlet couldn't keep the annoyance out of her voice. She didn't want to talk to Brent Hamilton. She edged one shoulder forward, effectively cutting him out of her world. She scooted closer to her nephew ,who stuffed his frosted pastry in his mouth, though he eyed her a bit warily. Guess he thought she might go after his breakfast. She *was* tempted. "Are you supposed to be eating those? I thought your mom wouldn't allow you to eat anything with chemical crap in it."

Henry slid his gaze to Brent, who had, for the most part, ignored her after her venomous comeback. And she, too, had tried to pretend he wasn't sitting kitty-corner from her, but that mission remained unsuccessful. For one thing, Brent was a good six-three and easily weighed two hundred and thirty pounds. For another, he was the type of guy who attracted attention as naturally as he breathed. With his dark wavy hair, icy-blue eyes and rugged good looks, he'd been popular with the ladies of Howard County for excellent reason.

She wished her parents had stayed at the inn instead of with a friend outside town. Nothing like Moonbeam—or whatever her mother was known as these days—to bring serenity to a table. Her mother preferred silent contemplation during meals.

"Pop-Tarts every now and then won't hurt," Brent said, meeting her gaze. He didn't look afraid of her. More as if he didn't want to bother with her.

"Oh, really?" Scarlet challenged, for no other reason than she was pissed she had to eat goat-cheese eggs with a man she knew was going to break her sister's heart… if not give her VD.

He didn't blink. "Yeah, really."

"At it already, I see," Rayne said as she breezed into the breakfast room. She looked gorgeous in a ruffled skirt and sleeveless lawn blouse with tiny roses embroidered along the neck. Her copper curls tumbled around her shoulders, framing her smiling face. Rayne looked…in love.

"Morning," Rayne said, scooping an arm around her son and dropping a kiss on his head. She snagged a corner off the pastry and popped it into her mouth. "Mmm, strawberry. My favorite."

Scarlet gaped. Her sister never ate anything that wasn't "of the earth." Which certainly did not include anything that came in a box or contained frosting and dyes.

Rayne moved on to her husband, grazing his scruffy cheek with a light kiss. "Morning to you, too. Again."

A devilish light appeared in Brent's eyes. Scarlet wanted to barf.

"Morning, baby," he said, tugging her toward him so he could cop a cheap feel. Okay. Maybe a pat on the bottom wasn't a cheap feel. Maybe it was a sweet display of affection. And maybe Kim Kardashian would win an Oscar.

"You, too, Scarlet," Rayne said with a little smug smile.

Did she think the little display of family bonding would suddenly change Scarlet's opinion on the bonehead decision her sister had made in marrying Brent? Scarlet wasn't that easy. Even if some people thought she was.

"Morning," Scarlet said, pushing a piece of asparagus to the top of the plate in order to make a roof over the family of disgusting eggs. Who in the world ate asparagus for breakfast anyhow?

Rayne grabbed a floral-patterned plate off the buffet and loaded it with asparagus and one piece of toast. Guess that question was answered. Yuck. Rayne sat next to Brent and buttered her whole-grain toast with fresh-churned butter from the farmer's market. She brushed her husband's hand. "So have you decided what you are going to do about the library vote?"

Brent took a sip of coffee. "I'm going to publicly oppose it. Harvey Primm is a jackass."

"Brent," Rayne warned, glancing at her son. Henry laughed behind his pastry.

"What are you talking about?" Scarlet asked, shoving her plate away. "And why the devil are you mixing goat cheese in with perfectly good eggs?"

Rayne blinked. "Huh?"

"The eggs." Scarlet waved a fork at her abandoned plate.

"They're the signature breakfast dish. Organic brown eggs with goat cheese and sautéed baby spinach. Everyone loves them."

Scarlet shrugged. "Okay. Whatever you say. Do I really need goat-cheese breath in the morning?"

Rayne glanced worriedly at Scarlet's half-eaten plate. Scarlet shouldn't have said anything. Her sister would be in the kitchen, trying out a new recipe.

"So what's Harvey up to now?" Scarlet asked. "Didn't he already get the liquor laws changed?"

Rayne nodded. "Yeah. Last year. Now we have to buy liquor outside the city limits. In fact, the inn had to obtain a special license to serve champagne and Bloody Marys on Sunday. This time it has to do with a children's book at the county library."

Scarlet's internal radar received a bleep. "A children's book?"

"Yeah, a children's book," Brent said. "He's hoodwinked the library board into removing it from the shelves."

"Why?" Scarlet asked.

"Because it deals with witchcraft. No different from *Harry Potter* or *The Chronicles of Narnia,* but he's convinced the book will 'rip the innocent veil from the children's eyes.' Ridiculous." He snorted and set his fork on the empty plate before him.

"Have you read it?" Scarlet asked Rayne.

"I have," Henry piped up. He had crumbs on his chin and looked suitably adorable. "*The Magpie's Jewel.* It's really good. There's this ruby that has a curse trapped in the center of it. And this one wizard dude, well, he gets this, um, scroll thing and reads about the jewel.

But then this magpie steals it from the most powerful witch in the world. So these kids have to find the jewel before this crazy dude does or he'll rule the world."

Henry paused for dramatic effect. Scarlet wasn't exactly following the story plot, but he certainly seemed excited about it. "They find it, and find out this bird is really the spirit of their grandmother who was killed by the evil wizard. It's a really good book. I wish they wouldn't make them take it out of the library."

Brent smiled at Henry. It made Scarlet feel uncomfortable because she could see the love in the man's eyes. Rayne's words rang in her ears. *He loves me...and Henry.* Scarlet swallowed her doubt and redirected her attention to Primm and the book in question. "So what is the community saying?"

"They're split," Rayne said.

Brent nodded. "Very splintered, and with some throwing religion into the debate, it's become very polarized with neither contingency giving the other a chance to change minds. It's been frustrating as an author to see people decide the worth of a book without even bothering to read it."

Scarlet had nearly forgotten Brent was an author. When Rayne had revealed Brent's secret career as an author of middle-grade sports books, Scarlet had been as shocked as anyone else who'd met the hunky, all-American former football player. It wasn't as if she didn't think him capable. Okay, she hadn't. So it was a-baseball-bat-against-the-head shocking. "What's going to happen?"

Brent shrugged. "A few people have talked of staging a peaceful protest in front of the library. I belong to several writers' loops online and there has been a lot of chatter about the censorship of the book, with some news networks covering it. Surprised me that a small county like ours would receive so much attention. But something about an award-winning children's book being ripped from the shelves and unavailable to countless children has many people angry and ready to do battle over the issue. And not just in Oak Stand."

Scarlet had loved a good protest ever since she'd watched *Norma Rae* on the rented VCR when she was twelve. Something about the spirit of fighting for one's convictions, of banding together against wrong, made her blood sing. She'd participated in dozens over the past few years. The last one had been over the destruction of historic storefronts in order to build a parking garage. A picture of her, openmouthed, toting a protest sign had made the front page of the city section of the *Times.* John had obtained the original photo and had it framed for her. Pain struck swift and hard as it always did when she thought of John. She shoved her hurt away and focused on the task at hand.

"Has anyone tried a town-hall meeting? They've been pretty successful in many communities when there is serious contention on a subject."

"I don't think anyone has thought of it," Rayne said.

"That's actually a good idea, Scarlet. Not sure if we have time, though. They're removing the book this Saturday. I'm sure Harvey will have something dramatic planned." Brent studied Scarlet. She could sense his thoughts. *Maybe this chick has a brain.*

Yeah, cowboy, she did.

"I participated in one when they were going to tear down some buildings in the Bronx. Of course, it did little good. Seems parking was more important than Saturday-night bingo. We held a protest, too, but if you could arrange a town-hall meeting, it may help people in Oak Stand see another side of the issue."

"Do you think we can make that happen? I don't see a church wanting to get involved, and the library surely won't encourage something like that." Rayne shoved another piece of asparagus in her mouth and chewed thoughtfully.

"A local business place might work if there is room for people to gather," Scarlet said, turning to the tea at her elbow for morning sustenance. She'd have to scour the kitchen later for something normal to eat.

"I'll talk to Nellie Darby. She worked at the library several years ago and has been pretty vocal in her opposition. She just had a baby, but I bet she'll be willing to help. She's definitely got pull with the mayor." Brent picked up his plate, dropped a kiss atop his wife's head and pushed open the breakfast-room door toward the kitchen. "I'll drop by the Darby ranch later, but first I have work to do. Deadlines don't care about weddings or town-hall meetings. They wait for no writer."

"See you later, honey," Rayne said. Henry managed a wave.

Scarlet said nothing, but she had good reason. She was caught in her thoughts.

"I think I'll stick around for a while." She pushed her chair back from the table.

"Cool," Henry said, swatting at the milk moustache above his wide smile. Darn, he was charming…and growing up. How long had it been since she'd spent quality time with her nephew? Too long. "You can come to my football game. We're playing the Horned Frogs this Saturday. Horned Frogs is a funny name, ain't it?"

"Isn't it," Rayne corrected, before leveling her gaze

at Scarlet. "And you're not fooling me. You're staying because of the potential protest. You love the drama."

Scarlet ignored her sister's barb and looked at Henry. "I'd love to see y'all whip up on the Horned Frogs this Saturday. And it is a funny name. Ain't it?"

Rayne punched an asparagus-ladened fork toward her sister. "Watch it."

Scarlet slid her gaze to her sister. "And for the record, I'm sticking around to visit with my family, who I haven't seen in a while. I can stay away from trouble."

"Yeah, right. I know you. You missed out on disrupting my wedding. You're itching for a fight. And then you'll be gone like the wind."

Scarlet snorted. Rayne loved to play upon the name Scarlet had chosen as her stage name. So she liked drama. She *was* an actress. Besides, she knew her sister's words were partially true. She did hate injustice and was quick to jump in where she felt she was needed. Case in point, she'd gotten a driver's license, bought a car and drove over eight hundred miles to stop her sister from making a mistake. Hadn't worked out, of course, but she would never admit to thinking with her heart above thinking with her head. Even if it were true.

The fact was she needed to spend some time with her family. Thanks to Rayne's wedding, both her parents, along with Aunt Frances, Henry and assorted other relatives, were all staying for the next several days within a ten-mile radius. No time like the present for cramming in hot tea on the porch, sifting through old family photos and playing UNO into the wee hours of the morning. She had several weeks' vacation and Aunt Frances had told her the inn was closed for the next few months while they filmed *A Taste of Texas.* Scarlet had a new car, a room in which to sleep and time on her hands.

The French Riviera would have to wait.

"Whatever," Scarlet said, grabbing the plate and following the path Brent had just taken.

"Hey, Sum—Scarlet," Rayne called.

"Yeah?"

"I'm glad you're staying. I've missed you."

Scarlet turned and glared. "Stop doing that."

"What?"

"Saying things that make me less pissed at you."

Rayne's soft laughter lingered in Scarlet's ears as she entered the kitchen.

Brent stood at the sink, drinking from a coffee mug. Damn. She didn't want to have to make nice with him. Not when she didn't trust him. No matter how in love with her sister he looked, she remembered his advances three years ago. He'd been classically smooth, intimately knowledgeable about what it took to get a gal in the sack. His kiss had told her all she needed to know about him…and now he was married to her sister.

She glanced at him as she set her plate beside the farmhouse sink. "Waiting to show me what a woman like me wants?"

"Don't do this, Scarlet."

"What?" Scarlet spun on him and parked her fists on her hips. "Don't remember your words to me that night? The sweet nothings you whispered into my ear while trying to get into my pants?"

"I was a different man."

"Yeah, right."

Brent set his mug on the tile counter. Loudly. She could feel his anger. "Look, I get it. I was an asshole. But I'm not that guy. I never was that guy. I'm no more a man-whore than you are a vampire-queen bitch. Just an act."

"What do you mean by that?"

"I mean that my life was damned empty. I was a shell of a man, but I'm not anymore. I love Rayne. I always have. She and Henry, along with claiming my writing career, have made me whole. Have filled me up. So don't hold my past against me. It's not fair."

Oddly enough, she liked him better pissed than smarmy. "I'll judge what's fair. I don't want you making her believe in love and then leaving her behind when new pastures call. I've seen it before."

I've experienced it before.

Broken hearts were no stroll through a park. She'd be damned if poor Rayne had to endure what she had over the past year. Only now did she feel as though she could creep around and function, no matter what face she wore in public.

"There are no other pastures. I've found my sanctuary." Brent shoved past her to the back door that would lead to the carriage house he leased from his parents. "I don't have to convince you, Scarlet. Don't make Rayne choose. You'll lose, because I'm her family now."

Ouch. His words filleted her heart. She lifted a hand and tugged on the slipper that pressed heavy against her chest as if it could stop the hemorrhaging. It didn't help. She knew there was truth to his words, and that scared her. She couldn't protect Rayne or Henry. Not from the hurt that would come when Brent Hamilton moved on. And she knew he would, no matter what he said. He was too much like John, chasing shiny new things when he tired of the familiar.

She pushed a hand through her hair, allowing the tresses to fall forward and give her a whiff of the coconut shampoo she'd used earlier. For some reason, the beachy smell soothed her.

"He's right, you know." A voice came from behind her, causing Scarlet to jump.

"Jeez, Aunt Fran, you could sneak up on a CIA operative," Scarlet said, shoving her hands into her back pockets so she wouldn't fiddle with the necklace she wore like a personal albatross.

"How did you find out I was in the CIA?" Aunt Frances grabbed a ceramic mug with a picture of a Boston terrier on it and filled it to the tip-top with coffee.

Scarlet laughed. "Wouldn't surprise me a bit if you were."

She took in the aunt who had taught her how to swing by pointing her toes at God and how to look for blackberry vines along ranch fence posts. Her aunt had aged well. Her gray-streaked brown bob framed a lined face that bore a cheerful countenance and wide blue eyes. She smelled of roses and freshly baked pound cake. She smelled like coming home, though Scarlet would be stretching it calling Oak Stand home. She had no home. Rolling stone and all that. Living in New York City for the past four years was as close as she'd gotten to calling a place home.

"Why did she marry him, Aunt Fran? He's a player and I don't see anyone taming a man like him."

Aunt Frances raised the mug to her lips and regarded Scarlet over the rim. Her stare was wiggle-worthy, but Scarlet refrained from squirming. Never could hide much from Aunt Frances.

"Perhaps, you are only seeing what you want to see. Allowing your experiences to color your perspective."

Scarlet shook her head. "You know how he is. You've lived in this town and you know what everyone says about him. How all you need is a ticket and you can stand in line for a ride on Brent. He's—"

"Your sister's husband and a part of this family. You need to remember that and not make her choose between the two of you. Because as much as she adores you, Summer, she loves her husband. And, honestly, he loves her."

"Scarlet," she reminded her aunt.

"Fine. Scarlet. Summer. Whoever you are." Aunt Frances waved a hand. "Your name doesn't change the fact those two have always had a connection."

"How? She didn't live here long enough to fall in love. She was a kid."

"Love doesn't happen when it's convenient, honey. It happens when it's meant to be. Rayne and Brent were meant to be from the first time he pegged her with an acorn to get her attention. He truly loves her…way more than he loves himself."

Scarlet didn't respond. What could she say? No sense in arguing. Not with Aunt Fran, who had obviously had her boots charmed off by the dashing boy next door. "Maybe."

"No *maybe* about it. If you stick around for a while, you might see for yourself and feel better about things."

How she wished those words could be true. Not only for Rayne, but for her, too. How long had it been since she felt truly happy? She knew the answer, of course. It had been a Wednesday and John had taken her to dinner and then a concert in Central Park. They had danced beneath the stars and she'd outlined all the things they would do in Italy when the film wrapped. They would shop for heirloom silver in the piazza shops, hike the trails above deep blue lakes and eat at the trattorias hidden down meandering alleys. It had been the last night they'd made love. The last night he'd kissed her and whispered he loved her.

The next afternoon, it had been over. Nothing but smoldering ashes in what was once her heart. Scarlet caught the tiny charm John had given her between her fingers and directed her thoughts from the pain echoing in her empty heart. She couldn't save Rayne, but she could help the town by speaking up against Harvey Primm and the misguided library board. She ignored the voice in her head telling her she searched to save others because she couldn't save herself. That wasn't true. She was okay and getting better every day.

Hadn't the sexy police chief jump-started her with his touch, with his warm—okay, sizzling—regard?

Still, a town meeting and a protest would be just what she needed to make her feel productive. Useful. Powerful.

She had less than a week to help organize opposition to the censorship of *The Magpie's Jewel.* Her blood roared with purpose. She'd fight the good fight.

No man could stand in her way.

Not even the memory of the man she loved still.

CHAPTER FIVE

SIX DAYS LATER, Scarlet wiped her brow with the damp cloth she'd stored in the ice cooler at her feet and lifted her sign with purpose.

"Children have rights!" she shouted, circling the flagpole and World War II memorial centered in the front of the Oak Stand branch of the Howard County Library. Other protestors joined her in her cries for justice. There were more than twenty of them. All from different walks of life, all gathered with purpose—to protest the library board's removal of *The Magpie's Jewel* from the shelves of the children's sections of the seven library branches.

"It's hotter than hell today," Meg Lang grumbled, tugging her long skirt up so air circulated around her pale legs. "Wish I'd worn something cooler. Thought the black emo look would stage well for the cameras. I'm paying for my stupidity."

Scarlet smiled. Rayne's assistant had likely let vanity get in the way of practicality. The Texas sun played no favorites as it bore down upon the shoulders of the protestors. Meg wore a tight T-shirt that declared Protest This! with a not-so-polite gesture below it, along with a long, tight black skirt and combat boots. Her short hair stuck to her head, making her look as if she were a silent-screen goddess. Well, it would have if not for the silver ring piercing her nose.

"Yeah, I don't think I could wear any less without getting arrested." Kate Mendez groaned, fanning herself with a now pudgy hand. She was way too pregnant to be out in the sun. A fact her husband, Rick, complained about every five minutes on the dot. Currently, her husband stood on the sidewalk with the yummy Oak Stand Police Chief.

Scarlet eyed Adam as he watched attentively from the sidelines. He stood with several townspeople who had gathered as news cameras whirred, capturing the sweating but determined protestors. "Bet he'd do it, too."

"Who? Adam?" Kate brushed away a trickle of sweat. "Maybe. He's a by-the-book kind of guy, but he hasn't taken our signs away and made us leave even though technically we don't have a permit. Although, I think I might let him cuff me if it means spending some time in the AC."

Scarlet thought she might let him cuff her with or without air-conditioning.

Kate's husband appeared at her elbow. "Okay, babe, I've let you do this for an hour. Now I'm ordering you to put that sign down and think about our unborn child." Rick crossed his arms over a phenomenally muscled chest. Tattoos peeked out from beneath the snug T-shirt he wore and his golden skin seemed to soak in the rays of the sun, empowering him in his quest to remove his nearly eight-months-pregnant wife from the library memorial.

"No one orders me to do anything," Kate responded, rubbing her back in spite of her fierce words.

"Kate, I appreciate your passion, but your husband is right. You can't endanger yourself or your child for this." Scarlet said, resting the sign on her shoulder.

Another news van pulled aside the curb, joining several others lining the downtown square. A larger crowd had gathered on the sidewalk and the buzz of their conversation provided energetic background music for the showdown between the protestors and Harvey Primm, who had not yet showed his yellow-bellied self to the townspeople lacing the grounds of the historic library.

"I have an obligation to make this a better world for him, Rick. We've got to make sure ignorance doesn't prevail in this matter. Not here. Not now." Kate crossed her arms over her baby bump.

"How about I take up the sign and you go over to the Curlique and put your feet up?" Betty Monk, the co-owner of the town's only true salon, interrupted. "We'll do shifts."

Kate slid her eyes toward the wispy-headed older lady who wore an outlandish pair of silk parachute pants and long tunic. She looked like an older, plumper, very much whiter version of M. C. Hammer. "Can I get my toes done while I'm there?"

"What would it matter? You can't see them, can you?" Meg drawled.

Kate narrowed her eyes. "Just because you can't see something doesn't mean you don't want it painted bada-bing cherry, smarty-pants."

Meg took a swig of water and sauntered off to get on camera. The van that had pulled up moments ago already had a reporter and cameraman in place. She turned and said very seriously, "Spoken like a true romantic."

"I can't believe *you* called *me* romantic. I'm not the one who wore a Victorian gown on a picnic with Bubba Malone," Kate said.

Meg scratched her forehead with the very same finger depicted on the front of her T-shirt. Kate rolled her eyes and toddled down the steps leading to the brick street of the town square. The Curlique hair salon sat several businesses down from the library. Scarlet half wished she could head over and put her feet up, too. It was roasting and the sweat rolling down her back caused her tank top to cling a bit too provocatively. She needed to fall into an ice bath or stand beneath a glacier waterfall. Or maybe fall into a snowbank and make snow angels or—

"Hey, Scarlet." Brent snapped his fingers.

"Huh?"

"Where did you go? You looked miles away and your sign hit Mrs. Monk in the head." Brent toted the largest sign of the protestors. It read Censorship Kills Democracy in bold red-and-blue letters. Honestly, the protest couldn't get much more American.

Scarlet turned to Betty. "Sorry, I got caught up in imagining a blizzard sweeping through."

Betty waved off her apology. "Share it with me. I'm sweating like a preacher on revival night with not a soul saved."

Brent nodded toward the opening library door. "Speaking of deacons."

"I wasn't—" Betty's words died as all eyes shifted to the front of the building. A hush descended over the crowd as Harvey Primm emerged from the one-hundred-and-twenty-year-old cypress door of the library. In his hand, he bore two books. He paused, taking in the crowd before him. It seemed as if he savored the moment, soaking up the power or the glory or whatever he imagined he received in the face of carrying out the removal of the book. Slowly, he walked down the wooden stairs toward Scarlet and the rest of the protestors where they stood in a circle around the flagpole.

Scarlet girded herself with both the sign and a vow not to sink to the man's level. But he didn't pause in front of her. Instead he bypassed them with a small smirk playing about his mouth and stopped in the center of the walk. Scarlet's trained eye caught the man's intention. His spare figure, clad in somber black, would be framed by the American flag hanging limply in front of the stately building. The staging was perfect for the cameras.

"You see this book?" Harvey called out, hushing the sudden burst of chatter sparked by his descent. He lifted the copy of *The Magpie's Jewel* into the air. The black bird on the cover swooped in his hand, as if it were in actual flight.

"Make no mistake, my neighbors, this book is the handiwork of the devil. It does not belong on the shelf where innocent children can read of witches, spells and dark wizards. Where our precious ones can be preyed upon by the evil power that seeks to grab hold and make mischief. This town is a fine upstanding community, and we pride ourselves in teaching our children to turn away from evil."

With that declaration, Harvey threw the book upon the ground.

"And instead seek this book."

Harvey raised his left hand, which clasped a copy of the Holy Bible.

"Amen!" someone called out. Several people standing around clapped their approval.

Scarlet shoved her sign into Brent's hand and scrambled in front of Harvey. She lifted the discarded book from where it fell and waved it. Anger, fast and furious, gathered in her belly and flooded her. How could he? How could this man use the Bible to manipulate those around him? "Have you even read this book?"

Harvey glared at her. "I don't have to see evil to know it exists, young lady. You will do well to heed the power of Satan."

"This isn't about religion. It's about censorship. About refusing citizens the right to make their own choices. This is America, not some communist country. We have the right to decide for ourselves."

Several members of the crowd pressed toward where she and Harvey faced off. Scarlet felt Brent move behind her. She also noted Adam heading her way.

"Are you accusing me of being a communist?" Harvey cried. "You're a presumptuous, misguided fool. This is about protecting our community from filth."

Scarlet shook the book. "This is not filth. It's a book about good overcoming evil, about sacrifice and love. You are making this about religion. It has nothing to do with faith, you old crackpot!"

A woman at her elbow hissed. "How dare you call him such a name. You're nothing but a heathen, prancing around on the television set with no clothes on. You aren't fit to breathe the same air as Brother Primm."

The woman tugged at Scarlet's arm.

"Don't touch me." Scarlet got the words out from between gritted teeth, pulling away from the older woman's grip. But the woman was country strong. She held fast and tugged Scarlet away from the smirking Primm. Even as her feet slid on the smooth concrete of the walk, Scarlet knew she'd played into the man's hands.

Someone else grabbed at her hair, but Brent pushed the angry hands away and pulled her to his side. "Enough."

Her brother-in-law's words fell on deaf ears. Before Scarlet could tell Brent to jump in a lake because she didn't need his help, a scuffle broke out between one of the protestors and what was obviously Harvey's hoodwinked sheep. Several women shrieked as the two men struggled over one of the placards Betty had been toting.

A sharp whistle pierced the air. Once. Twice. Three times. Then the siren from the police car wailed.

Several people tussling over the signs broke apart and moved to the perimeter. Harvey watched the ongoings with satisfaction.

He must have planned this. Scarlet seethed as she pulled her sign loose from a pimply teenager who wore a T-shirt advertising Harvey's gossip rag. "Give me that."

"Witch!" he yelled, eyeing the police officers swarming up the steps.

"Wrong," she growled. "I'm a vampire. Don't make me bite you."

The kid dropped the sign and retreated. She'd freaked him out. Good. She picked up the sign and turned to where the protesters squared off with some of Harvey's people. Meg looked ready to stomp the Hush Puppies of one of the men, and Betty laughed as Brent tried to soothe the older woman who had latched on to Scarlet moments before. The elderly lady had tears coursing down her grooved cheeks. Obviously the older woman was even more of a drama queen than Scarlet ever dreamed of being. But it made her feel bad anyway. It shouldn't have come to this.

Out of the corner of her eye, Scarlet caught sight of Harvey and his simpering, self-satisfied smile. He'd manipulated people into being his winged monkeys, doing his dirty work, while he remained in the center, seemingly serene and in control. A martyr for his misguided brand of justice.

Scarlet stormed toward him. "You did this on purpose."

Harvey lifted a woolly eyebrow. "I did nothing but what was required, madam. I suggest you disperse your group before you end up in the back of a police car."

"You take your people and leave." Scarlet jabbed a finger at him. "You turned this into something it wasn't supposed to be."

"Scarlet," Adam said, his low voice somehow comforting. "Step away and let it go. Nothing can be done."

"Do as he says," Harvey said.

For a moment, Scarlet felt a burning in her gut. It was as if she were caught between two impenetrable walls, walls that were closing in on her. "No."

"Scarlet," Adam said, gently grasping her shoulder in effort to turn her from Harvey.

"Stop," she said, shrugging away from his touch, a touch that stirred, a touch that oddly enough made her feel safe. But his plea wasn't enough to make her step down from the ass clown standing before her, looking condescending and smug. "I'm not leaving. We have the right to protest."

"But not the right to disturb the peace," Adam said, his voice more firm. He raised his voice above the melee. "Okay, folks, that's it. Time to move on. Go home."

A grumbling emerged at his words, but most people stepped away from the area surrounding the flagpole. The law was respected in Oak Stand. Adam meant authority. He meant business.

Brent clamped Adam on the shoulder. "Thanks, man. We didn't want it to turn into this."

Adam nodded. "You, too, Primm. Take the book and go."

Harvey frowned. "Very well. Justice has triumphed and it is done. Good day to you."

"Wait!" Scarlet shouted. "You can't leave. This is a protest!"

Betty shook her head. "We did our best, honey. We'll have to let it go for now."

"No, I won't leave," Scarlet declared. "This is unfair. I can't. I can't let him win."

"Baby doll, come on. Let's have some sweet tea and pound cake on my porch. We'll brainstorm and come at this in a different way." Betty rubbed a hand down her sticky back.

Scarlet spun around and picked up the backpack she'd dropped beside the cooler. It held packages of crackers, a packet of gum, a brilliant script by an upcoming Broadway writer and…a pair of handcuffs. Strong, rimmed in red faux fur, they would just fit around the smaller flagpole that flew the Texas state flag.

Scarlet sat and clicked one cuff on her right hand and the other she fastened around the hot steel of the pole.

"What are you doing?" Adam called. "No. Don't."

She clicked the cuff shut.

"Honey," Betty groaned. "No call for that."

Harvey had been moving toward the street and his large black car. He turned. "And she called me a crackpot."

Reporters moved from Harvey and swarmed toward Scarlet.

Brent crossed his arms. "I knew she was trouble, but this beats all I've ever seen. Better call Rayne."

Adam stared at her. The censure in his eyes burned her and she felt her chin droop slightly. But she refused to be shamed. She had every right to protest the removal of the book from the shelf. She wasn't misguided or irrational. She was…she was…patriotic.

Her forefathers and mothers had fought for the right to speak out. To protest. To chain themselves to flagpoles and other unmovable objects.

She wasn't trouble or a drama queen.

She was a champion of the cause.

She was—

"Get the bolt cutters, Jared. We'll cut her out of her handcuffs and then put her in ours," Adam said.

About to be arrested.

Scarlet was going to jail.

CHAPTER SIX

PULLING AWAY FROM THE CURB of the library, Adam aimed the car toward the station and snuck a peak in his rear-view mirror at the woman in the backseat. Color suffused Scarlet's cheeks and the dark red hair escaping her ponytail clung to her sweaty neck. She wore no makeup or jewelry. Only a halter top that showed the lacy straps of a camisole, shorts and a pair of flip-flops. He was almost certain the crazy woman hadn't even bothered with a bra, something that made his mouth go dry to think about.

"Are you cool enough?" he asked, pointing the air vents toward the steel-mesh barrier that separated them.

"Huh?"

"Cool enough?"

She nodded. "You are quite solicitous. Most police officers don't bother with the comfort of their prisoners."

The word *prisoners* sounded harsh in his ear. It wasn't as if she were Roy the Can Man, whom Adam sometimes picked up for ransacking curbside garbage cans, or the occasional rowdy oil hand he cuffed at the local bars such as Cooleys or the Rocking Rooster. None of his former passengers had been mouthwateringly hot. None had made him think about naughty things he really shouldn't be thinking about. "Wouldn't want you dying of heatstroke on my watch. Couldn't handle the flack we'd get over that."

She sighed. "Such concern."

He swerved around Clyde Riggs's toy poodle. Picking up the CB, he buzzed the station. "Hey, Roz, put in a call to Clyde Riggs. Bruiser's out for the third time this week. Tell 'em next time they're getting a ticket."

"Ten-four, Captain," Roz's voice squawked over the static.

"Oh, the dangerous life of an Oak Stand police chief," Scarlet drawled.

He nearly flushed at her sarcasm. Sure, his job wasn't dangerous, but it could be. If Bruiser bit ankles. "Yeah, it's a rush."

She snorted. It was cute.

"So am I, like, the biggest bust you've made so far?"

"Nah, we busted the kids who stole Bud Henry's pig statue yesterday. Pig-statue thieves trump disorderlies every time."

He glanced in the mirror again. Scarlet managed to smile. "So that's what I've been arrested for? Being disorderly?"

"Officially, you have three charges against you. Disturbing the peace, unlawfully gathering and resisting arrest."

"I didn't resist," she said.

He eyed her in the rearview again. She looked worried. She should be.

"When you handcuffed yourself to the flagpole, technically you resisted arrest."

"But I didn't know I was going to be arrested. That was before the fact, so technically I didn't resist."

"We'll let the judge decide."

He heard her slump against the vinyl seat.

"There was no cause for the drama. There are better ways to get what you want than handcuffing yourself to a flagpole."

"Like handcuffing myself to a bedpost?" Her voice was mocking but that didn't stop the hot flash of desire from broadsiding him.

"Well, I guess it's too bad I had to destroy your little sex-toy handcuffs in the arrest. You could have checked to see if they would have worked."

"On Harvey Primm?"

No. On me.

He shifted in his seat to relieve the stirring of desire making itself known in his tight motorcycle pants. Why he reacted so strongly to her baffled him. Well, no, it didn't. Scarlet Rose was emphatically the kind of girl who roused his libido. He merely pretended to be surprised by the need building low in his pelvis. "Somehow I don't see Primm being into kinky things."

"Oh, don't let him fool you. It's always the quiet, straitlaced guys who are the sickest," she said, tracing a finger down the squeaky clean window. She tilted her head and met his gaze in the mirror. She arched an eyebrow. "Right?"

"I wouldn't know. I'm into missionary position exclusively."

Scarlet seemed to choke on a laugh. "You say the damnedest things."

"When I shouldn't," he muttered.

"Yeah, but sometimes it feels good to be bad."

He turned onto Tucker Street just off the town square. The station squatted like a gnome next to the fire station. Scarlet must have spotted the brick building, for she grew still and quiet. Nothing like an ensuing incarceration to chase away sunshine. The gravity of the situation struck him.

Damn.

She *was* a prisoner.

He'd forgotten himself. He wished he could reach out and catch the flirty words he'd exchanged with her and take them back. Thank God there wasn't a camera and recording equipment installed in the cruiser. He'd hate anyone seeing his lack of professionalism. He swung into his designated spot, precisely even between the freshly painted yellow lines. It was small pleasure, but he loved all things equal. All things balanced.

He climbed from the car and threw a cautionary wave at the news vans parking at the curb. Arresting the up-and-coming star of a Thursday-night headliner was big news. No doubt the tweets or whatever they did nowadays were blowing up on the internet. He'd have more reporters on the station's doorstep by the end of the day. Of that, he was certain.

He opened the back door. Scarlet blinked up at him before extending one long white arm.

He looked at her hand and then at her.

She sighed. Then she wiggled her fingers.

Where did she think she was? The Golden Globes? This wasn't the red carpet. This was a booking.

He ignored her hand. "Out."

She glanced at him. "For the cameras?"

"No."

"Oh, come on. It'll make good copy and you'll look debonair."

He reached into the car, grabbed her upper arm and jerked her from the depths of the cruiser.

"Ow! Watch it. I bruise easily."

"Then be glad I didn't make you wear the cuffs," he

muttered, pulling her to her feet. He'd placed his hand on her head to make sure she didn't collide with the door frame. He'd done nothing less than what was expected.

"Police brutality," she trilled. He couldn't tell if she was serious or joking. He hoped the latter. He didn't need the hassle of having to explain himself to a jury.

"Come on. Let's get inside before the reporters swarm you again."

"I don't mind," Scarlet said, tossing her ponytail and a smile toward the cameras that moved their way. She raised her hand and gave a cheerful wave. "It's actually perfect. When the free world hears about Harvey Primm and my heroics in trying to keep the book on the shelf, there will be a public outcry. It helps my cause."

He didn't smile. Her words reminded him that he had no business engaging in fantasies about a woman like her. She was trouble. She was self-involved. And she would rip him to shreds if he gave her the slightest opening. In fact, he wondered if she weren't much better than Harvey. Had Scarlet used the protest as a way to gain attention for herself? To garner the spotlight? Help her own career?

He wouldn't put it past the star of a glorified soap opera.

He steered her toward the brick building. Roz met them, swinging the tinted door open wide so they could escape the heat and the infernal cameras.

"Hi, Roz," Scarlet said, giving an air kiss toward the older woman's cheek. "Love the blond streaks in your hair. They make you look ten years younger."

Roz beamed. "Thanks. Carly talked me into doing them down at the Curlique. She's a really good stylist."

"Little Carly Patterson?"

"Yep. My niece ain't so little anymore. She'll be twenty-one next month."

"I can't believe—"

"Lock the door, Roz," Adam barked a bit too harshly. This wasn't a social visit and the two women standing in front of him needed to remember that.

"Oh. Right." Roz twisted the lock as the first reporter reached for the handle.

Adam tugged Scarlet around the long stretch of counter toward the empty metal desk in the center of the office. "Sit here, please. I've got to get the processing kit from the back."

Scarlet sank onto the chair and crossed her legs. "So are you going to frisk me again?"

Roz paused at the coffeepot. Her eyes grew wider. "You frisked Scarlet?"

"Yeah," Scarlet drawled. "He's got good hands, if you know what I mean."

Roz's mouth dropped open and she turned accusing eyes on him.

Adam felt something terrible rise inside him. He knew what it was. A crack in the surface of his calm. One that could untether his self-control and fling it to the four winds, allowing him to bounce around with no constraints, no rules, no goal. "You know damn well I never touched you inappropriately. To say any different—"

"Got you," Scarlet said, giving Roz a wink. "You're so easy."

Roz tittered. "I was wonderin'. Our Adam here is a follow-the-rules sorta fellow. He even makes us punch in on the time cards."

"The horror," Scarlet cried dramatically.

The woman really was too much.

He spun on one newly polished boot and stalked to the rear of the station. He hoped Jared had returned the fingerprint kit and camera to the cabinet next to the extra toilet paper. Last time it had taken everyone three days to discover he'd put it in the box with the Christmas lights.

Adam would process her, put her in the holding cell until she posted bond, then give himself another lecture on pretending the blazing-hot Scarlet was just another criminal. Just another woman. No one who would interest the professional, responsible leader of a police force. No one who made him fantasize about the various ways to use a pair of red furry handcuffs.

He stomped on that thought.

He would lie to himself. He had to. Had to believe she was not an option because the alternative would make him weak. He had to be able to say no to desire. To accept anything else was to admit he couldn't do the job he was hired to do.

He was the chief of police.

It was expected that he would do his job and that he would do it well.

He wasn't his father.

He had integrity. He had control. He had morals.

So he absolutely could not, would not fall prey to his desire. He would pretend like hell he didn't burn for the woman talking to Roz about Jennifer Garner's favorite face cream. He would deny to the hilt that he wanted to cuff her to his bed and spend the better part of an afternoon getting acquainted with her delicious breasts and taut stomach. He would rather cut out the tongue that he wanted to dip in her navel before feasting on the delicate beauty of her ankles…and all the splendor in between.

He would do it because Adam Hinton was a stand-up guy. He was not a horny buzzard looking for fresh meat.

He couldn't allow himself to be.

SCARLET STUDIED her fingernails. The polish was chipped on her pinky nail. Guess she couldn't repair it, since it seemed unlikely they would allow a manicurist in the town jail. "I really shouldn't tease Chief Hinton so much."

"Oh, the man needs it, honey," Roz said with a twinkle in her brown eyes. "He tries so darn hard to do everything right. He's all rules and hard corners. It's almost sad to see a man wound up that tight. I swear, you could shove a piece of coal up his butt and have a diamond in a week."

Scarlet smiled. "Maybe I'll try that. I'm partial to diamonds."

"Aren't we all?" Roz laughed and filled the coffeepot with bottled water. "He's a good fellow, even if he has all kinds of crazy ideas about the way to do things. He loves gadgets and newfangled police stuff. He wants paperwork done yesterday."

Scarlet nodded. "Nothing wrong with progress, though, huh?"

Roz shoved a filter into the basket before looking up. "But nothing wrong with doing things the way they've always been done."

"As long as they make sense," Scarlet said. She glanced around the station. It looked as if the soft gray color had been recently applied to the walls. All the desks were cleared and large healthy plants framed the glass door she'd stepped through not five minutes before. Everything was clean, neat and orderly. Much like the man who had parked her in this chair.

"Guess you're right about that. Just been tough since the chief passed. He was here so long and we was used to him, you know?"

Scarlet knew. Her thoughts flew immediately to John. She hadn't wanted to give him up, either. In the end, that hadn't been an option. John had ended their relationship without any consideration for what she wanted. But time marched on. For the Oak Stand police department. And for Scarlet Rose. She should let go of the pain, the love she still clung to, but her heart wouldn't let her.

"Mr. Don was a good man. I know you miss him, but Chief Hinton seems like what the doctor ordered. New blood brings new opportunities." Scarlet picked at her fingernail again and wondered why she rose to Adam's defense. Maybe because it seemed to be true. Maybe because he seemed to be a good person trying to do the right thing.

"So, you still getting it on with that yummy Karakos?"

"Stefan?"

"Oh, yeah. His real name. I heard rumors he's gay."

Scarlet forced out a laugh. "He is *so* not gay. Actually, we're living together now."

Roz's jaw dropped. "Really? He's so sexy. Those dark eyes and that cleft in his chin. Gives me the shivers."

"You should sleep with him," Scarlet said, heavy on the innuendo but leaving out that when she'd slept with Stefan it had been on the couch. In their jammies. With a bowl of popcorn between them. And the man snored.

"Got it," Adam said as he reentered the large room.

"This time Jared actually put the kit back where it belonged."

Roz frowned as she poured a cup of fresh coffee into a chipped ceramic mug. Obviously, she had wanted more scoop on Stefan. "Well, at least he's learnin' something."

Adam set the kit on the desk next to Scarlet. "Maybe so."

Scarlet glanced at the briefcase. "I'm guessing you don't arrest too many people?"

"Not lately," Roz muttered, bringing Adam the coffee. "Chief Hinton has all the lowlifes scared. Ever since he busted Tullis Jones making meth in his daddy's old barn. That takedown made state news. Everybody in Oak Stand is mindin' their p's and q's."

"Thanks, Roz." Adam accepted the mug. "Well, someone should have told that to Christian Harvey. His old man nearly had an apoplectic fit when he found his pig in the football stadium. I thought Bud was going to have me arrest the boy and his friends."

Roz laughed. "Boys will be boys."

Scarlet watched as Adam laid the items from the kit on the desk. Everything was aligned perfectly. Side by side, one inch apart. Strange.

"I hated to arrest you, Scarlet, but you didn't leave me much choice. People watch me closely. I can't give them an inch or they'll take a mile and string me up with it. Let's do the fingerprinting, then we'll take the picture." Adam took her hand. The one she'd been scraping off the polish from. His touch startled her.

"Sorry if my hands are cold. Roz keeps this office like a meat locker."

"You go through menopause and see how you like

it," Roz quipped, heading to her desk, where a phone lit up like the town Christmas tree in December.

Adam smiled and took Scarlet's index finger between his, rolled it on a small machine that looked like a photo dock. No messy ink on her fingers. Nice. She, for one, could appreciate Adam's purchase of a gadget.

"Don't I get a phone call?" Scarlet said, enjoying the feeling of her hand in his, despite the fact he was processing her for a crime. She still couldn't figure out why this man created a stirring in her belly. Why she wanted to turn her hand over and clasp his, sliding her fingers through his so they met palm to palm.

He lifted his gaze to hers. "Of course. I'm sure your sister will post bond, and we can release you. Your arraignment will be Monday. You'll go before the judge and state your plea."

Scarlet peered toward the front door. Reporters pressed against the glass. She could see a man wearing a Texas A&M ball cap peeking through the shades of one of the side windows. "What judge? Maybe Judge Monroe? I babysat for his daughter once."

He shook his head. "Judge Monroe's in Hawaii with his wife on an anniversary trip. Most likely Judge Cleveland. He's up for reelection. Or maybe Sharon Kent."

Scarlet closed her mouth. She'd handcuffed herself to the flagpole for many reasons, the most important of which was to get national press for the protest. But the reality of the situation pressed down on her. She didn't know Judge Kent nor Judge Cleveland. If Cleveland were up for reelection, would he be tougher on her? Would she have to serve time? For handcuffing herself to a flagpole? Surely not. The last time she'd gotten arrested at a protest it had been a misdemeanor and she'd had to pay a fine.

"What if I can't make bond? How does all this work?"

His green eyes seemed to be slightly sympathetic. "Your sister may be mad, but I don't think she'd leave you here."

Adam lowered his head and punched something into the fingerprinting machine. His hair was so alluringly golden she almost lifted a hand to touch the swirl at the crown of his head. Which would have been way weird. She shoved her hand beneath her thigh.

"You don't know Rayne very well, do you?" Scarlet said, worried that Rayne might refuse. She was likely pissed Scarlet had done something so…so…true to form. Who else could she call? Her parents had left for California and an art show the day before. Maybe Aunt Frances? Maybe Scarlet would simply call the Inn. Whoever answered would come get her. They were probably on their way right now. After all, her family and friends wouldn't leave her in jail, would they?

She wasn't prepared for that. For heaven's sake, she wore flip-flops and hadn't put on a bra, a fact she knew Adam had discovered in the overzealous air-conditioning. She'd caught his gaze sliding lower. She was a pro at catching guys that way.

His voice interrupted her wayward thoughts. "Rayne? She's a sweetheart."

"You're not a good judge of women, are you? Rayne is one way on the surface but tough as nails underneath. She can fight dirty."

"If no one comes, don't worry. The holding cell is clean, and I'll turn down the AC when Roz leaves." He glanced again at her breasts. Scarlet felt her nipples tighten even more at his sneaky perusal. She hunched her shoulders a bit, but it didn't help. She knew her girls were at attention.

"Would I stay here alone?" She hated to sound like a chicken, but being locked up in a cell alone in the building would be creepy. Apprehension tickled between her shoulder blades. She didn't want to be alone. She hated being alone.

"We don't get much traffic in our holding cells, so we trade off. I'll take this one."

The trepidation melted away, only to be replaced with a new tingling. One that pecked at her thoughts. It tapped out, *You. Adam. Alone. No bra.*

She couldn't stay here. Rayne would come through. She was Scarlet's older sister. Accustomed to bailing her out, although never before in such a literal sense.

Scarlet needed to make bail.

Her apprehension made her angry. Rayne better bail her out. "I bet you'd love having me at your mercy. Love seeing me locked up. I've been a thorn in your side since I came to town."

In his eyes, she could see a small measure of truth of her words before he shuttered his emotions. "That's absurd and you are being overly dramatic. Again."

Yeah? She didn't think so. "I'll take that phone call now."

He lifted the receiver. "Have at it."

CHAPTER SEVEN

ADAM STUDIED SCARLET as she sat on the lone bunk in the holding cell.

Rayne hadn't been such a sweetheart. In fact, Scarlet's predictions about Rayne had been true. She was more than willing to let her sister stew in lockup. Honestly, it surprised him, but he sort of understood. This was her way of giving Scarlet time to think. Or so he thought. He really didn't know Rayne, and as Scarlet had said earlier, he wasn't a good judge of women.

From the time Scarlet had slammed down the phone with an impassioned "Fine!" to the present, she'd confused the hell out of him.

Currently, she looked like someone who didn't give a damn that she sat in the middle of a jail cell.

He looked up from the desk in the holding room. Her bare feet swung to a silent rhythm as she leafed through a battered copy of a March 1997 *Glamour* magazine he'd found tucked under a pile of *Field and Streams* in the waiting area.

"Wow, this look really never took off the way they thought," she said to no one in particular. Or maybe she was talking to him.

He grunted and continued typing the incident report.

"Yeah, raccoon eyes aren't attractive on anyone, especially skinny pale girls. It's so corpselike, but I guess some can't resist the attraction of looking like death."

"What are you prattling about?"

"Heroin chic. A fashion trend in the nineties. The women were all skin and bones and wore dark eye makeup."

He tore his gaze from the report and glanced at her again. Nothing skin and bones about Scarlet. She was full-on fleshed-out woman. No more swinging bare feet. She'd tucked them beneath her bottom, leaning over so her breasts fell against the thin material of the top. He had turned the air-conditioning down a bit. But not too much. He'd battled with himself over that, telling himself he hated being hot. But deep down inside, he'd pictured the way her nipples had stood out against the thin material and held the thermostat at a chilly sixty-seven degrees. Guess he wasn't any better than his dear old dad after all. "Why would anyone want to look like an addict?"

She shrugged. "Why would anyone ever wear overalls and think they're sexy? But women did it. Fashion appalls me sometimes."

He shook his head and tried to focus on the words on the computer screen. It was hard with Scarlet's scent filling his nose. She smelled like a woman. Floral, sweet and innocent. Three things he figured she wasn't. He liked that oxymoron.

"So do I get a meal or a bathroom trip?"

"Huh?"

She cocked her head. "Or are you gonna shove gruel under my cell door then make me use the empty bowl for my toilet?"

Adam saved the document, then spun in his chair. "Maybe that's part of your punishment. No meal. No potty."

She rolled her eyes and tossed the magazine onto

the blanket at the foot of the cot. "Seriously. Protesting gives me a high and makes me ravenous. Do you still have my cooler and bag? I have crackers in there."

"That's evidence."

She snorted. "Really?"

He nodded. "Don't worry. I'll get you something."

"I'd prefer it now."

He stood. "I'll get it when I'm ready to get it."

"You really do like having power, don't you?" The teasing smile and light words were gone. "No reason to lord over me. I've been a model prisoner, haven't I?"

"Define *model,*" he said, stretching his arms back. "You've been annoying, demanding and an absolute diva since I met you. If that's your definition of *model,* then we're all in trouble."

"I'm not a diva," Scarlet muttered, shifting her legs and clasping her arms around her knees. "Sure, I can be dramatic, but that's my job. Comes with the territory."

She was about the sexiest thing he'd ever seen this side of the Rio Grande. She'd released her hair for the mug shot, flipping upside down and fluffing it. She'd also pinched her cheeks and given him a winning smile when he positioned her against the white background they used for taking the photos. He was surprised she hadn't asked for a feather boa and better lighting. She hadn't put her hair back up, so it lay in soft waves, framing her face. The top and shorts left little to the imagination, and her bare toes wiggling atop the bunk sent hot, tight darts of desire to his gut. He wanted to touch her.

Instead, he reached for the telephone and dialed the number he knew by heart. When Drake Marciano said, "Mamma Mia's Pizzeria," Adam recited his usual order.

"Be there in twenty, Chief," Drake said, after repeating the order for accuracy.

"Fine," Adam said, his stomach already growling at the thought of the feta-and-grilled-chicken pie covered in Roma tomatoes. He was hungry for more than Scarlet.

"I don't like tomatoes," Scarlet said.

"So pick them off. And be glad I'm letting you have a piece."

"I only get one piece?"

"You'll have to be a good girl to get an extra piece," he quipped, walking toward the cell.

"If I'm a bad girl, can I get three pieces?" She smiled. It was a wicked smile. He should retreat. Not move toward her. But he couldn't seem to stop his feet from taking him toward the cell where she now stood at the bars.

"Don't tempt me," he said.

"Why not? It's fun." Scarlet ran her fingers lightly over the aged bars of the cell. "Don't you like when women flirt with you? Bet a lot of women around here do. How many have you let out of a ticket?"

"None."

She raised one eyebrow. "None? I don't believe you. You said you would have let me slide."

"I say that to everyone. It's a strategy I use in order for the subject receiving a ticket or citation to view me as magnanimous or sympathetic. Take your pick."

A crinkle marred her forehead. "That's deceitful. Manipulative."

He felt a burning heat through his groin. He stepped closer. Couldn't help himself. He inhaled, breathing in her scent. "Maybe it is, but you believed me."

"Kiss me."

He jerked his head. "What?"

"Kiss me."

He grabbed the bars on either side of where she stood. "I can't kiss you. That would be—"

"Unprofessional?"

"Yeah, something like that." He hadn't expected her to be so forthright. It seemed out of character. She was a smooth talker, not plainspoken. Why the devil had she asked such a thing? "Why do you want me to kiss you?"

"Because *I* can't very well kiss *you* with these bars in the way," she said. Her words were matter-of-fact, but her attitude was not so light.

He sensed she was testing him. Honestly, he wanted to taste her on his lips. To delve into the sweetness that beguiled him, but the angel on his shoulder said, "Step away. Forget about it."

He needed to listen to the angel and not the devil who whispered, "Unlock that cell and have your way with that hot piece of ass."

He gave the devil a mental shove. "I can't."

She slumped against the bars. "And I was so close."

"To what? Seeing if you could reach my keys while I tangled in the bars with you?" He said it half-jokingly, but a little piece of him wondered if she would actually try something that silly. She was an actress. No doubt she'd seen—or starred in—some caper that showed a seductress using her wiles to trick a stupid man to coming close enough to be hoodwinked into giving up his keys.

But she looked strangely serious. "Of course not."

He didn't say anything. Simply watched her as she ran a greenish-blue painted nail up and down the steel bar, making a screeching sound.

"More like to see if you could make me feel again." She'd nearly whispered the words.

Adam stiffened. "Make you feel again?"

Scarlet's head dropped forward so it was braced on a bar. She looked so not herself. Nothing kittenish about her. No sexy vixen. Not even a smirk or grin. She looked…depressed. "Never mind. I think the sun got to me. Or the fact I've been arrested and sitting for several hours in a jail cell. Maybe I've already gone stir-crazy."

"I don't think a person goes stir-crazy after only two hours, twelve minutes and thirteen seconds."

She raised her head to meet his gaze. "Then maybe I was crazy to begin with."

"That's more than likely."

She didn't smile at his teasing words. Just lowered her gaze with a sigh.

What was the matter with her? He liked her moxie, her snippy comebacks, her energy. This woman had deflated in front of his eyes.

"Hey," he said.

"What?" The shiny curtain of red hair hid her face.

"What did you mean by *make me feel again?*"

"Nothing."

"Okay, I know how this works. I'll have to pull it out of you. Women love this game."

She looked up. "I'm not playing a game."

"I think you live to play games."

"You don't know me at all. You don't know what I live for. You can't look at this—" she waved one hand up and down her splendidly curvy body "—and think it defines me."

"Very true. I don't know you. I only know what I've seen. I've seen a woman use her body and her fame to get the results she wants. If you dance the tune, you've got to pay the fiddler."

She frowned, but didn't say anything.

Silence sat between them, fat and stifling.

After a moment, he broke it, offering the only explanation he could. "It is a logical assumption. Your asking for a kiss is merely a way to manipulate the situation."

Her expression looked fierce but tinged with sadness. And at that moment, he saw beneath the shiny veneer she wore so well. "You really aren't a good judge of a woman's character, are you?"

It was his turn to frown.

"You wanna know why I wanted you to kiss me? Fine. I'm in love with a man. A man who dumped me thirteen months, one week, three days ago. For the past year, I've felt absolutely nothing. Zip. Zero. Nada. I'm like a frozen tundra with no hope for warmth."

He didn't know what in the hell to say to that. Hadn't expected that much honesty from anyone, especially not a flamboyant actress who seemed to enjoy pulling on various masks to suit any given situation. What could he say to those very honest words?

He couldn't think of a damned thing.

"Right." She sighed, obviously seeing his total loss for how to deal with what she'd laid on him. "I feel a little different with you. Like a slight buzz or stirring. I wanted to see if it was something more than irritation or the damn Texas heat. Maybe, just maybe, I'm capable of feeling again. Maybe I can get back on that bicycle and ignore my bleeding knees and scraped palms. I thought maybe you could help me find out if I can survive heartbreak."

Her words pierced him. Her sincerity stung. He felt a little like lint and about as useful.

"Well, I can't really. What I mean to say is there is protocol and I'm responsible for representing myself as the…" He trailed off. There was nothing he could say to make her feel any better. Nothing he could do but—

He stepped toward her and reached a hand through the bars, effectively trapping her head.

Her eyes flew open and she reflexively pulled back.

But he didn't let her.

He was strong and she was soft. Her hair felt like angel wings. Not that he knew what angel wings felt like. But he could imagine.

He lowered his head and caught her gasp of breath with his lips.

And the crack in his control became a chasm. He tumbled through it without compunction.

He had no choice.

He had a mission. To protect and serve. And at that moment he needed to serve the queen of the vampires.

SCARLET CLASPED THE STEEL bars in front of her. Adam kissed her like a thirsty man, clasping her head with both of his big hands. For a moment she felt absolutely nothing.

Her heart sank.

Then something changed.

His tongue dragged across her bottom lip, direct, bold and very, very sexy.

Liquid heat poured into her belly, swirling, bathing her in a wonderful, sweet pool of desire. She closed her eyes and kissed Adam back, sliding her own tongue against his, tasting him, drinking him in as though he was sweet tea. Or full-bodied wine. As though he was life-giving elixir.

He tasted so good.

She moved her hands to his shoulders, sliding them up to the rasp of his jaw then to the nape of his neck. His hair had been trimmed short, yet it was soft against her fingertips.

Like a tidal wave, desire crashed over her. She climbed onto it and rode it, opening her mouth even more, pressing her forehead against the unyielding bars. Adam stroked her jaw with the pads of his thumbs, drawing a hum from deep inside her.

He answered her with his own groan.

"Hey, Chief." The voice came from the front of the station. And sounded so far away. But it grew closer. "Chief?"

They broke apart.

She grabbed the bars so she wouldn't conk her head against them. She felt drugged. Out of it. That's how strong the wave of desire had been. And it had beached her. She felt wrung out and dazed, lying facedown on the sand.

Adam looked much the same way. He took one step backward. Then another, blinking once. Twice. Three times before spinning toward the door of the holding room.

"Hinton? Where are you?" the voice called.

Adam cleared his throat and returned his gaze to where she clung to the cell bars. "Back here, Drake. In the holding room."

Scarlet straightened, dragged the back of her hand across her lips and whispered, "Holy guacamole."

Adam shook his head, as if he were denying what had occurred between them. He stepped to the desk, then fell into the chair and tucked himself under the surface so his lower half was hidden. She almost laughed, but it wasn't quite funny.

She wasn't sure what it was. The door to the holding room flew open.

"Whatta you doin' back here?" the man said, entering the room, holding a pizza box. He had dark hair that brushed his shoulders, a craggy profile and a small beer belly that pooched out beneath the T-shirt emblazoned with a Mamma Mia's logo. He swiveled his head like a hawk and caught sight of her. "Oh. I see."

Adam managed a smile. "Hey, right on time."

"Yo," Drake said, dumping the pizza on the desk and sliding her way. He literally slid in the checked slip-on Vans he wore. The legs beneath the ragged cutoffs were peppered with dark hair and hadn't seen much sun for mid-August. "If I commit a crime, can I get locked up with her?"

His words were for Adam, but his dark eyes never left hers.

"Do you know how to do nails? 'Cause I could use a manicurist," Scarlet said, raising her hands with presto-change-o flourish. She wiggled her fingers. She'd peeled off more teal polish as she leafed through the magazine. She gave him a teasing smile, hoping like hell he bought her light tone and flirtatious manner. She still felt a little shell-shocked from Adam's kiss.

The man smiled back. "Oh, the things I could do to those hands."

Adam cleared his throat. "How much do I owe you, Drake?"

"You're not going to introduce me to the lady?"

"Since when have you ever taken interest in my work?" Adam said. He sounded irritated. Or maybe it was jealousy that laced his words. Or perhaps it was anger. He'd lost control. He'd done something very non-chieflike. Something a little naughty.

And thank goodness he had. Scarlet didn't think there was any way to repay him for what he'd done. For what he'd given her back. Finally, she'd felt desire again.

She moved one hand to finger the golden slipper, but it wasn't there. It was in an envelope along with her red watch and hoop earrings. Her personal effects.

"Since you started hauling in sexy vampire queens." Drake grinned and waggled his bushy eyebrows at her. He was cute in a Big Ragoo sorta way. "Lady Veronica, I'm at your disposal."

Scarlet held her smile. "Now, darling, you don't want to get put in here with me. I bite."

"Oh, God," Drake said, clasping his chest. "Don't worry about paying, Hinton. I'm off to rob Oak Stand National."

Scarlet laughed. Adam didn't. Instead he stood, pulled a twenty out of a shiny leather wallet and slapped it against Drake's chest. "Keep the change."

Drake took the twenty. "Man, you never let me have any fun."

"That's my job," Adam said drily.

Drake extended a hand toward her. "I'm Drake Marciano. I own Mamma Mia's. That pie is my specialty. I hope he lets you have a piece."

Scarlet clasped his hand. It was a little sweaty. Or maybe *yeasty* would be the word. She would be willing to bet he was the type of guy who tossed the pizza dough in the air with acrobatic energy. "I think he owes me three pieces."

A smile twitched at Adam's lips, but the rest of him remained stoic.

"Enjoy." With that Drake turned, popped Adam on

the shoulder then disappeared through the door, whistling “That’s Amore.”

Adam studied the pizza box, before finally looking at her. “I’m sorry. That was a mistake.”

“Not to me.”

CHAPTER EIGHT

SCARLET WALKED OUT of the Oak Stand police department, wearing the exact same clothes she'd had on the day before when she'd been processed, booked and jailed. The only notable exception was she wasn't wearing the tiny golden slipper pendant on a chain around her neck.

And not because she'd put it away like some schoolgirl boxing up her corsage, love notes and the locks of hair of a former love.

No.

The damn police department had lost it.

Or someone had taken it.

She tapped a finger against her breastbone and gave a jaunty, not so heartfelt wave at the journalists clustered in the shade of a giant silver-leafed maple tree. They looked hot and not so alert. They jerked to attention, every cameraman hoisting a camera to his shoulder, every newsperson running a hand over her updo.

"Scarlet!" they shouted.

She double-timed it toward the beat-up construction truck idling at the end of the sidewalk, wrenched open the unlocked door and said, "Hit it."

The reporters and cameramen disappeared in a blur of color.

"Your sister is still pissed at you," Brent said as he whipped a U-turn and gave the media a wise-guy smile.

"Duh," Scarlet said, running her hands over her face. She hadn't slept well. Not after kissing Chief Tight Ass and wolfing down three pieces of pizza. She'd had heartburn to go with the heartache she bore like a cross. What had she been thinking, asking for a kiss like some desperate geekazoid? How could she still love John and feel so turned-on by a virtual stranger?

Brent didn't say anything for the next minute or so.

"Thank you," she said, breaking the silence in a small voice she usually reserved for scenes requiring contriteness. "For coming to get me."

He didn't look at her. Simply kept his eyes focused on the faded yellow line dividing the road. He turned off onto a neighborhood street.

"You're welcome. Couldn't leave you there no matter what Rayne said. She talked Frances into leaving you there, too. But if someone hadn't posted bail for you by noon, Adam would have had to take you to county lockup." He turned his head to look at her. "You wouldn't have wanted to go there."

She swallowed a lump of guilt and stared straight ahead. A shaggy dog stood at the base of a tree, presumably barking at a squirrel. Fred Harp shuffled toward his car, wearing his Sunday best and grasping a Bible. A mockingbird swooped at a cat hunkered in the faded lawn of Brent's parents' house. All things normal. A typical small-town Sunday morning. Even the bells in the Presbyterian-church bell tower pealed the all-familiar call to worship.

"No, I wouldn't have, so thank you."

He nodded and gave Fred a wave.

Fred waved at Brent, but scowled when he saw Scarlet sitting beside his neighbor.

"Is Rayne mad at you, too? I mean, am I gonna cause

some problems between you two?" Scarlet asked as Brent pulled into the graveled drive of Serendipity Inn. A week ago she would have been pleased to be a thorn in her sister and Brent's relationship, but now it felt self-indulgent. Maybe yet again, she'd rushed in where no one should have tread and fallen on her face. Maybe she'd been wrong about Brent.

Brent shrugged. "I think she's secretly pleased I took the initiative to get you out. She wants us to mend some fences."

He shut off the engine, but made no move to exit. "You know Rayne loves you, right?"

Scarlet pushed her hair back. "She has to. I'm her sister."

"No, she doesn't. Family is family, but you can choose not to love them."

Scarlet looked at him. He seemed earnest. Sincere. Not slimy at all. "I know she loves me, but sometimes she doesn't like me. She doesn't understand me."

"But that's okay. She doesn't understand me sometimes, either. That's part of loving someone."

Scarlet lowered her head slightly. "I didn't give you a chance. I took what I thought I knew and pinned it to you. I wasn't very fair. To you. Or to Rayne."

"No, you weren't. But that's okay. I understand."

She licked lips that were suddenly too dry.

"No, I do," he continued. "You were trying to protect her and you screwed it up. I know exactly how you feel right now. Like gum on the bottom of a shoe. Been there." He patted her thigh. Any other time she would have assumed he was hitting on her, but now she knew he wasn't. "We all make mistakes."

"That's a platitude. And it won't work with Rayne. I'm sure she's damned tired of the drama I bring."

"But it's a platitude that's true."

She sighed. "Okay, it's true."

"And Rayne might get tired of your drama, but it's who you are. You don't really look before you leap, do you? That gets you in trouble, but it's also a great strength in a person. Rayne's the opposite. She measures three times, dips a toe in, sends off for test results, puts on her jumping shoes and double knots them before she even thinks about taking a leap of faith."

That was definitely Rayne. "Yeah, guess you got her pegged."

"That I do."

"You love her," Scarlet said. The idea didn't feel as bad as it had.

"Don't go into detective work anytime soon. You'll starve." He climbed out of the truck and headed around to her door. Like a gentleman. Like his mama had raised him.

Scarlet shoved the door open before Brent could reach for the handle. She noted reporters driving up the street and parking. They were like cockroaches scurrying when a light switched on. "Don't worry. I'm planning to stay as far away as I can from the police."

Yet as the words slipped from her mouth, she knew them to be false. There was one police officer she didn't want to stay away from. In fact, she felt quite the opposite. He'd awakened a fire in her, and she wanted to feel its warmth again. To bask in the flames. Even as she resented the hell out of his meddling in her emotions. She wanted to keep her armor in place.

She reached for the necklace that wasn't there. Maybe losing the golden slipper was for the best. Maybe the weight of it against her heart allowed her to cling too hard. Perhaps it prevented her from healing, prevented her from getting on with her life. She should have taken it off months ago. She would try not to miss it pressed against her chest. Try to put it—and John—away. For good.

As Brent turned and waited for her on the first step of the inn, the image of John appeared. There was something of her former lover in Brent. The confidence, the charisma, the curl of the mouth. John wore a sardonic smile like a weapon, and his salt-and-pepper hair was his trademark as an actor, along with dimples on his rough-hewn cheeks. Wicked brown eyes and wicked sense of humor. And a warm embrace. John Hammerstein had taken care of her the way no other man ever had. With John, Scarlet had been safe.

And now she wasn't any man's concern.

"Just a minute," she said, shaking off the memory. "I need to address the press, or they will be on the lawn all day long—something I don't think Rayne or the neighbors will appreciate."

Brent eyed the clamoring pack of media heading up the drive as if they were a pack of stampeding triceratops or hungry T. rexes. He looked fascinated and repulsed at the same time. "You sure?"

Rayne appeared at the door. She looked at Scarlet, then at Brent. She didn't say a word.

"Scarlet!" one reporter shouted in a nasally voice, before shoving a microphone at her.

"Give me a little space, and I'll address all of you," Scarlet said, tucking a piece of hair behind her ear and wishing like mad she had worn a bra. She knew she looked tired and worn out. Like someone who had spent a sleepless night on a narrow cot in a cell. The mirror in the bathroom of the police station had not lied.

She climbed onto the porch and held up a hand.

"Scarlet, how was your night in jail?" one reporter shouted. She looked familiar. Had someone from *Star Access* come all the way to Oak Stand?

"Okay, here's my statement. Yesterday, I stood up for a cause I believe in—giving Americans the right to choose what they read. Most of the time, censorship of books like *The Magpie's Jewel* is a result of ignorance and fear. I don't regret my decision to protest the removal of the book. I do, however, regret thinking with my heart and not my head. I never should have broken the law in my quest to make my opinion known. It was irresponsible. For that I'm sorry."

"Scarlet, what has the network said about this?"

"Have you talked to any cast members?"

The questions flew at her, left and right. She shook her head. "That's all I have to say for now."

She whirled around, dodging the questions still being shouted, pushing away the microphones being shoved in her direction. Brent stepped in front of her and crossed his arms, a six-foot-three-inch barricade, while Scarlet slipped into the house beside her sister.

Rayne wrapped an arm around her. "You okay?"

Scarlet shrugged. "I'm surprised you care. Aren't you the person who left me in jail so I could learn a lesson?"

Rayne dropped her arm. "Okay, I was angry. Dealing with you is like dealing with Henry. You don't think. You act—"

"But I'm not your child. I'm your very grown-up sister. Your family." Scarlet stepped into the parlor, where Aunt Frances sat, looking a bit shamefaced as she pretended to read a daily devotional book. "Thanks, Aunt Fran."

Aunt Frances looked up. "Maybe you needed to think

about what you did. Rayne is right. You have to start thinking about other people and how your actions affect them. Your sister has a lot riding on this show. The whole town does, and the audience who will tune into *A Taste of Texas* is not the same audience who will overlook over-the-top antics."

Scarlet felt anger bubble inside her. "So it's the inn and the TV show you're worried about? Not me. Or the injustice that occurred yesterday. Just your reputation."

"No. Of course we care about you. You were safe. Likely safer than if you'd come back here. We've had reporters camped out on the curb all night long."

Rayne appeared at her elbow. "We shouldn't have left you there. I shouldn't have let my anger get the best of me, but Aunt Frances is right. You were safe with Adam."

"You left me in jail! There is no excuse for that. Make up whatever you want, but that's the fact. I wouldn't have done that to you—" Scarlet pointed her finger at Aunt Frances before swinging it toward her sister "—or you."

With that, she turned and ran up the stairs, feeling a little childish but absolutely justified. Her sister and aunt were wrong. What she had done had not been that bad. She'd handcuffed herself to prove a point for a noble cause, not embarrass her family, not get attention. No, she hadn't thought, but that didn't make her a bad person. It didn't make her someone who should have spent a single night in a jail. No matter how clean it was.

She flew into the pristine guest room that had once been her uncle Travis's trophy room for wild game. Once, it had been painted deep green with mounted deer head and boar snouts covering the walls. Now it was soft blue with antique china plates hanging by satin ribbons. The coverlet was chenille, draped with a soft, minky dot throw. The pillows were fluffy, the curtains were lace, and Scarlet Rose didn't belong here any more than the baby gazelle once had.

She pulled her suitcase from the closet. She was not staying. There was a cheap motel on the outskirts of town. She'd sleep there, even if there were bedbugs the size of Dallas. Then she'd show up for court, pay her lousy fine and get the hell out of Oak Stand.

"Scarlet," Rayne pleaded from the open doorway. "Don't."

"Don't what? Leave? Why the hell would I stay?"

Rayne entered the room. "I was wrong."

Scarlet wiped tears from her eyes. She reached for the gold slipper, which wasn't there. Somehow her missing necklace made everything worse. "Not good enough."

"Please, Scarlet, everyone makes mistakes."

She wadded a T-shirt into a ball and tossed it haphazardly onto the growing pile of clothing. "Yes, we all do."

"Don't leave. Please. I'll make you a grilled-cheese sandwich."

Scarlet sat on the bed and wiped the dampness from her cheeks. The last time she'd cried real tears had been the afternoon John had told her they were through. She didn't cry real tears easily, though she was pretty decent at the actor kind. "I don't want a grilled cheese. I want a sister who supports me."

Rayne sank beside her. "I do support you. I said I was sorry. I let my anger get the best of me."

Scarlet didn't respond. She was too tired and didn't want to sleep on a lumpy hotel bed anyway. Especially if there were bedbugs. "You left me in jail."

"I know. I'm a crappy sister."

"Not always," Scarlet said.

Rayne bit her lip and looked as though she, too, might cry. "I'm really sorry. Don't go. Okay?"

"Okay. I'll stay. I'm a big girl and I get it. We both allowed our passion to overcome logic."

Rayne opened her mouth, then clamped it shut. "Right. So what next? Do you have to pay a fine or something?"

"I'll have to see what the judge says tomorrow. Adam said they do arraignments on Mondays. The last time I got arrested for a protest, it was a misdemeanor and I paid a fine. I figure it's the same here. After I'm through with it, I'll head to New York. Maybe the coverage of the protest will be enough to pressure the library board into changing their stance about the book."

Rayne took her hand. "Sure you won't stick around longer? Even though I'm filming the show, it would be good to have you here."

"Don't you think I've done enough damage? Trying to stop your wedding and handcuffing myself to the flagpole is probably enough drama to last a lifetime."

"When you put it like that…" Rayne said in a teasing voice.

Scarlet pushed into her sister with her shoulder. Rayne pushed back. It only took a moment for them both to start smiling. Then Rayne laughed. And Scarlet could do nothing else but join in, falling back onto the bed, knocking half the pile of wadded-up clothing onto the floor.

Rayne shoved the suitcase to the foot of the bed and joined her. "The fan needs dusting."

"If you keep it turning, no one will notice."

"Only you would think like that."

Scarlet shrugged and yanked one of Rayne's curls. "So I'm lazy."

"No, you're not," Rayne said, jerking her hair from her sister's grasp. "But you could use a shower."

Scarlet lifted one arm and sniffed. "I don't stink."

"But you don't smell good."

Scarlet couldn't be insulted. After all, Rayne had taught her how to shave her legs and how to use tampons. Wasn't much sisters didn't share. She sat up and reached for her toiletry bag. "Okay, shower it is."

"Where's your necklace?"

"Huh?" Scarlet said, kicking off her flip-flops and pulling the top she'd been wearing for more than twenty-four hours over her head.

"That necklace with the golden shoe. You're not wearing it. What is that thing anyway? Some kind of jewelry for a cause?"

Scarlet shook her head. "No cause. And it's not important."

A small wrinkle appeared between Rayne's cinnamon eyes. She opened her mouth, then shut it, something that seemed to be becoming a habit with her. She was a smart older sister. Always had been. "Okay, I'll fix you lunch. I'm sure you didn't get breakfast."

But she had. The officer on duty when she woke this morning had dug around in the break room for a good ten minutes before returning with an overripe banana and a package of cheese crackers. He'd paired it with a Tab soda. She didn't know they still made Tab. "No goat cheese, right?"

Her sister spun and grinned. Rayne was so feminine and pretty, not exactly the opposite of Scarlet, but a gentler version. Rayne's face was softer, her frame slighter, her carriage ladylike. Scarlet was, well, supersize in a sexy way. This she knew, this she used to her advantage.

Rayne saluted and left the room as Scarlet's cell phone vibrated on the dresser where she'd left it the day before. She left it behind often, a bad habit for an actor.

She glanced at the caller ID. It was her agent.

"Hey, Bert. What's up?"

"Making quite the splash, aren't we?" Bertie said, his British accent more pronounced than usual. A fake British accent. She'd learned from a tipsy, withered socialite at a charity function that Bert had been born and raised on the Jersey Shore, but he did a helluva good northern British accent.

"I try."

"I'd rather you make nice with the Texans and scoot your rather gorgeous behind over to L.A. I've got you a read next Thursday."

"With who?"

"Sparrow."

"Shut up!" She sat down on the bed. Hard. "Tell me Brad Pitt is lead."

"Male lead hasn't been cast. It's a bit part, but substantial enough. You've built buzz with *Deep Shadows.* Strike while the iron is hot, love. I pulled a string or two, but the casting director thinks you're ideal."

"What movie? What part?"

"*Angel Dust.* And your role is a bisexual prostitute."

"A bisexual prostitute? Do they have those?" Yikes. Talk about a meaty role. Maybe too meaty. But working with David Sparrow would be phenomenal. His films made people sit up and take notice. In a big way. Even a small part could fling her career in a whole new direction. A direction dreamed about by nearly every actor pounding the pavement for roles or smiling winningly while scrubbing out the ring around the collar in commercials.

"Doll, there's a prostitute for everything. You'll be a good fit."

"Gee, thanks. I'm not sure whether to thank you or break your Armani glasses with my fist."

She could hear his smile. "Try the former and get to L.A."

"I'll head out as soon as I pay my fine tomorrow."

"Brilliant. I'll let Macy Flores know. She's pulling casting on this one. Ciao."

Scarlet pressed the end button and shimmied out of the North Face shorts she'd slept in last night. A chance to work with David Sparrow. Her heart beat twice as fast in her chest. It could be a dream come true. An absolute coup. But first she had to get to California. Like, fast.

As she padded to the bathroom, a momentary pang of regret struck her. Adam had awakened something in her she thought she'd lost. He'd virtually glued a part of herself that had been broken. Tomorrow would be the last chance to double-check that stirring of desire. If he even showed up to court. She supposed he had to. After all, he was the arresting officer.

She wondered if she could pay her fine for the broken taillight and the speeding ticket, too. Hopefully. Two birds with one stone. Or rather one check.

It was time to dust Oak Stand from her shoes. She had two more months before she had to be back in New York for production on *Deep Shadows.* A month in California sounded dandy to her. Sunshine, sand and shopping on Rodeo. Plus her parents were in San Francisco. So who needed France?

She hummed "I Love L.A." as she adjusted the faucet in the shower.

Maybe she'd find someone there who could finish what the straitlaced lawman had started. Someone to unzip her dress while mending her heart. Someone with golden hair and a quizzical smile. Someone who didn't look a thing like the man in New York who had ripped her to shreds and made her doubt her ability to ever find passion again. She didn't need love. She needed a good time.

Yes. Exactly.

Time to move on.

CHAPTER NINE

THE RHYTHMIC THUNK of the glove connecting with the body bag soothed Adam. He punched the bag, rattling the chain that secured it to a beam in the garage. Right jab, right jab, block, feint left, left hook. Repeat.

Sweat rolled down his back, coated his arms. He blinked the saltiness away, doubling his efforts as if the leather bag were the bundle of trouble that had fallen in his lap.

It was the worst sort of trouble—one that had bee-stung lips, curvaceous hips and an inclination for drama.

Scarlet Rose.

This afternoon, she had received forty hours of community service for her disorderly conduct. And he was assigned as her supervising officer.

Wasn't going to be easy. He had to prepare himself for trouble. For three reasons.

First, Scarlet was royally pissed. During the sentencing, everyone from one side of Oak Stand to the other had learned she "couldn't stay in their Podunk town." She had to audition for a role of a lifetime. In California. "For the hottest director in Hollywood." She'd nearly been held in contempt for her dramatic, pleading performance. Hell, if he'd been an Academy voter, she would have had his vote.

Second, Judge Sharon Kent had given an atypical sentence—a community-service project.

And third, did he mention he'd been appointed her supervising officer? Even though he was the chief? That meant he'd be required to check on her. Which meant he'd have to see her. Which meant he'd be tempted to touch her. To kiss her. To bend her over his cruiser and run his hands over her spectacular ass.

He punched the bag harder, making it swing erratically.

"Shit," he said to the empty garage, dropping his arms to his sides. He tilted his head back and panted, taking shallow breaths that smelled like hot asphalt and burnt oil. "I mean, shoot."

He tried not to swear. Or drink. Or kiss sexy actresses with legs a mile long and breasts that made his mouth water. He also tried not to talk to himself.

Battle lost on all fronts.

He tossed the gloves on the workbench welded to the garage wall and opened the fridge he kept stocked with water and beer. He grabbed a Heineken, wrenched the top off and took three long swallows of the icy beer. His body needed water. His mind demanded the beer.

No way he could keep his hands off her. Worse, he'd screwed up and got caught doing something highly unethical on video tape. That little tidbit hadn't crossed his mind until he'd left Scarlet eating pizza and escaped to the outer office. The minute he'd opened the door, his gaze had landed on the locked cabinet holding the surveillance tapes they kept numbered and dated. He'd broken out in a cold sweat. He and Scarlet had been kissing right in front of the damn video camera.

He'd felt about as stupid as a cow.

He wiped away the sweat dripping in his eyes and

stared out the open overhead door at the darkening Texas sky. Brilliant pink trimmed the rich blue that pressed upon the earth. It was a nice sky as far as skies go. And the sun was a flaming orb sitting on the horizon.

"Got one of those for me?" his friend Rick Mendez said, strolling into the garage.

"You don't drink beer."

Rick shrugged. "I'll settle for water."

Adam opened the fridge, grabbed a bottle of water and tossed it Rick's way.

Rick caught the beverage with one hand. "Wanna come out to the center and rid yourself of whatever demon's riding your ass?"

"Who says I have a demon?"

His friend propped himself against the metal slide of the roll-up door and smirked. "We all got demons, man. They ride us harder sometimes more than others."

Adam nodded. Rick knew his story. He was the only person in Oak Stand who did. Adam had known from the very beginning he and the former gang member would hit it off. Most would have thought differently. Rick was dark, dangerous-looking, with gang ink spiraling onto his neck and an almost permanent scowl etched on his broad face. Adam was the antithesis. One of the girls on his swim team had once declared he looked like her Ken doll. Give him a pair of seersucker pants, a sweater tied round his neck, and he became as country club as Skipper Doyle, his father's golf partner.

But, yeah, Adam had demons.

And a persistent one had just attached itself to him.

Desire…for the absolute wrong kind of girl.

"Not this evening. I've sweated enough beating out all the frustrations of the day."

"Summer, huh?"

"Yeah, she's going to be a problem." Adam took the last two swallows of the beer and tossed the empty bottle toward the recycling bin.

"Huh?"

"She's gonna—"

"Oh, you mean Scarlet. Or Summer. The actress. I meant the heat, but, yeah, that one's trouble. I told Kate to not meddle. But that's like telling a nun not to pray."

Adam straightened. "This was Kate's idea?"

"She's always trying to bring new things to the guys. She hates the boxing ring. We need *culture* she says. Those muchachos think culture is drinking Hennesey at a strip club."

He tamped down the aggravation. Kate meant well, but having Scarlet teach acting classes at Phoenix, the gang-rehabilitation center that Rick operated, was a disaster waiting to happen. Mostly because if Scarlet showed up wearing a halter top without a bra around guys who hadn't seen any action in months, an all-out riot could occur. Plus, gang members studying Shakespeare? Acting out emotions? Not going to work. And when he showed up to check up on her? Suffice it to say Adam wasn't a crowd favorite at the center.

"It would be easier if she had to pick up trash on the highway." He sighed.

"Not if you don't want a pileup. She'd still be smoking-hot in an orange jumpsuit."

Like Adam didn't know that. "Dude, you're married."

"But not blind."

He nodded. "Scarlet is a problem, no matter which way you look at her."

"Yeah, but at least she's something to look at."

He opened his mouth, but Rick held up a hand. "I know, I know, I'm married. But Kate's driving me nuts. I'm on an ice-cream run. Rocky Road. Not the store brand. But Ben & Jerry's. And I can't forget a bag of pretzels. She crushes those and sprinkles them on top."

Adam smiled. If there was a man in love with a woman, it was Rick Mendez. "How much longer?"

"Less than two months till the baby comes. Then I will be at the beck and call of two forces of nature." Rick pulled keys from his front pocket. "I better run before she starts calling me. Just saw the garage door up and thought I'd make sure no one was stealing the 'Vette."

Adam walked to the other bay in the garage and patted the muscle car beneath the padded cloth. "If anyone touches Farrah, I'll rip his face off."

Rick's bark of laughter followed him toward his own fine piece of machinery—another passion that drew them together. Rick's cherry-red '66 Mustang made the driveway look classier. "See you tomorrow, gringo."

Adam held up a hand in a farewell gesture. Rick always called him *gringo,* which might seem derogatory, but Adam knew it wasn't meant to be. Yet, he didn't dare call Rick anything slightly offensive. He'd been raised to mind his tongue. Having a family in the spotlight made a person cautious with his words, but not necessarily with his morals. His father had proven that, serving on the church building committee while screwing a member of the altar guild. Morals? What morals?

He pulled the door down and secured it with the padlock before entering the small house he rented. The place had been built in the twenties, and though it could use a fresh coat of paint and new doorknobs, it radiated charm. Age sat upon it well, giving it the faint odor of mothballs, lemon furniture polish and years of home cooking. It was normal. Regular. Nothing special. And it suited Adam fine.

That was all he'd ever wanted in life.

To be normal.

Not be Hal Hinton's kid.

Not be Daphne's boy.

Just be plain ol' Adam Hinton. Small-town police chief living on Hickory Street. In a plain white house with black trim and a green lawn.

Because the first half of his thirty-one years had been a torture to be endured. Huge brick mansion. Mercedes Benz. East Coast boarding school. And lots and lots of time alone. Sitting alone in his childhood suite of rooms—called *the nursery* by his mother, which annoyed him to no end—he'd been surrounded by the latest and greatest toys, video games and gadgets while dreaming of eating fried baloney and fishing in a creek with a bunch of siblings. Adam didn't want to be a wealthy, influential Hinton. He wanted to be a struggling, happy Hinton. A regular kid on a normal street with a simple, salt-of-the-earth mom and pop. Mayberry. Mayfield. Pleasantville. Anywhere but River Oaks in Houston.

His wish had not been granted. He *was* a Hinton. His great-grandfather had dabbled in real estate, buying, selling and building a huge financial empire. His family owned chains of furniture stores, a handful of shopping complexes and fifty gas stations. He had millions languishing in a trust fund. His family owned a jet, a yacht, a villa in Italy and more land per square foot than in all of Howard County. Adam wasn't only rich, he was loaded.

He switched on the light in the kitchen and set about making a sandwich for his dinner. Plain ol' baloney.

SCARLET STUBBED HER TOE on a root that peeked through the grass at the side of the Hamilton house. "Ouch!"

It was insult added to injury.

She was grounded in Oak Stand for the next three weeks. She wouldn't be able to make the audition. How would she tell Bert? He'd be annoyed. Maybe furious. Probably would out-diva her in his temper tantrum. The only thing that had saved her was the possibility of sending in a tape as her audition. She'd phoned the casting director earlier and was awaiting the return call. Thank goodness, Rayne had a production company at her beck and call.

So much for making contacts in L.A. For soaking up sun. For catching a wave.

Scarlet's toe started throbbing.

"Yeah, I've hit my toe on that root before. It hurts," Henry said, tossing the ball to her despite the fact she hopped on one foot.

"Well, thank you, Mr. King of Obvious."

Henry smiled, the two big teeth that had recently grown in making him look like a miniature beaver. "You say that a lot. That's sarcasm."

"Again, I crown you King of Obvious," Scarlet said, hopping to where the uncaught ball had rolled.

Henry laughed. "You're funny."

"So they tell me." She pitched the ball toward her nephew. He caught it easily and threw it back.

"Are you mad you have to stay here?" Henry asked, his brow wrinkling, making him look like a small thundercloud. "I heard you talking to Stefan."

Her roommate had encouraged her to leave Oak

Stand and pay the consequences later. The man thought a big check fixed everything. Sometimes it did, but she doubted the judge would look favorably on bribery. Stefan didn't get small-town values. He'd grown up in Miami and it showed. His tastes were sophisticated, expensive and sometimes vulgar. "He's outraged for me, but I'm not skipping out or breaking the law. I did something wrong and I have to pay for it."

Scarlet gave herself an invisible pat on the back for being Aunt of the Year. She might be good enough to be a mother someday. Maybe.

"Well, I think it's cool you're staying for a while. I'll go to Phoenix with you if you want. I've been there before. They have a dog named Banjo. Dad says he's the ugliest dog he's ever seen, but I think he's kinda cute."

Dad? So Henry had taken to calling Brent his father. Weird. But maybe not. She'd watched the two of them eat ice cream and watch the Rangers play on TV last night. They were pea podish. Brent seemed to love the boy, and the feeling was returned. A flash of shame flickered in her subconscious a moment before she dashed it away. She *had* apologized to Brent.

"Hmm, maybe you can go with me once or twice. If your mom says it's okay." She wasn't sure if an eight-year-old belonged at a gang rehabilitation center. She was a little uneasy herself. She had experience teaching acting classes. But that had been to Jewish grandmothers with unnatural hair colors at a Brooklyn YWCA. Come to think of it, those women were tough. They could probably reduce Hispanic gang members to a passel of kittens in ten seconds flat. She might be A-OK.

She pushed her bangs out of her eyes and caught sight of someone lurking behind the sweet olive bushes lining the side yard. Reporter? Likely.

She sidled closer. She tired of flashbulbs and microphones. Sure, she knew it was her fault. She'd brought all of their attention upon herself when she'd picked up the picket sign and joined the protest. But, still, she needed a bit of peace.

She purposely overthrew the ball. It sailed over Henry's head and smacked the siding of his new grandparent's house.

"Jeez, Aunt Scarlet. You suck."

She clamped down the strange impulse to fuss at him for his colorful language and darted toward the shrub.

"Get out of there!" she hollered, tugging the arm of the Peeping Tom.

It was Harvey Primm.

"You!"

He glowered at her but said nothing.

"What do you think you're doing sneaking around, spying on me?" Scarlet felt her limbs shake with adrenaline. The good deacon was beyond creepy. Most thought him harmless, but there was something a little unhinged about the man. Something about the passion he brought to unearthing dirt on the people who lived in this sleepy community.

"You think you can turn people against me? You can't, missy. What you've done is a mortal sin. You oppose God. You support the devil's work."

"You have a lot of nerve coming on my family's property, lurking in bushes and throwing accusations at me. Accusations you know nothing about. For the second time, this is not about religion. This is about taking away people's right to decide for themselves. Stop judging me. It's hypocritical."

Scarlet crossed her arms and glared at the stooped

older man. She might have felt sorry for him if he had not been so bitter.

"I'm no hypocrite. I stand on my principles and oppose presenting innocent children with filth."

He held up a newspaper. Looked like a Dallas one. The Local/State section showed a picture of the protest. "You're trying to make me look crazy. Trying to turn people against me, using your fame. Well, it won't work. God is on my side."

"I doubt it," she said.

Harvey lurched toward her. "You better think twice about who you go up against, girl. You may have the liberal media on your side, but good people know what is right."

"What is right? Trespassing? Harrassment? Bullying? Is that what you preach? Is that your example of good living?" Scarlet stepped closer. She could smell his breath, see the spidering of red veins rimming his cold eyes. "I'm not scared of you, Mr. Primm. I know plenty of good people who don't agree with you. Isn't there a saying about throwing stones when you live in a glass house?"

"You better watch yourself, girl."

"Are you threatening me?" Scarlet felt the slightest tremor of fear mingle with the anger inside her. She'd lived in New York City long enough to build strong self-preservation instincts.

"No, I'm warning you."

As Scarlet studied the embittered man in front of her, something poked her psyche, and suddenly she could see what had caused Harvey to hit the warpath. She'd known his late wife. Mary had smiled often, loved theater, the arts and wearing flowers on her hats. She would not have approved of her husband's crusade.

"What would Mrs. Mary say about what you're doing, Mr. Primm?"

Harvey paused, seeming momentarily taken aback. "I'm doing what's right."

"Maybe in your mind, but I knew your wife. I'm not sure she'd approve of yanking a children's book off the shelf the way you have. And hiding in the bushes?"

He took a step away. "I wasn't hiding. I was..." His words trailed off.

Scarlet didn't retreat. He needed to hear her words. Someone needed to show him he'd colored his beliefs and shaded his world with grief. "Maybe you should take a hard look at what you're doing. At your intentions. You can't fix the world. That won't bring Mrs. Mary back."

"Don't say her name. You don't know anything about her. A redheaded Jezebel like you couldn't hold a candle to my wife. No matter how you cut it, witchcraft, wizards and magic is wrong."

"So quick to judge. Maybe you should do some reading. Either of the books you held up would do."

Anger caused the man's face to redden. "Watch the way—"

"Aunt Scarlet?"

Scarlet turned her head. Henry stood, holding his glove and ball. He'd been listening to their conversation and he looked worried.

"Mr. Primm was leaving, Henry."

Harvey gave her one last hard look before slinking toward a late-model Lincoln Continental parked down the street. Scarlet shoved her trembling hands in the pockets of her shorts. She didn't want her nephew to know how affected she'd been by the exchange.

"What was he doing here, Aunt Scarlet?" Henry jogged over to her, as if he could sense her unease.

"I don't know," she said, curling an arm around his neck. "But I bet that's the last we see of him."

"He's kinda scary. He always wears black and he never smiles. He's like a bad guy in a movie."

Scarlet steered him toward the inn. "I don't think he's a bad guy. He's scared."

Henry stopped. "Of what? He's a grown-up."

She paused for a moment, trying to recapture her Aunt of the Year vibe. "Well, all people are scared of something. Mr. Primm is afraid of the world he lives in, so he tries to control it."

"I don't get it."

"The world around us constantly changes. We have to learn how to change with it. But that's hard for a lot of people. They want to have their own version of how the world should be. Mr. Primm wants to go backward, to rewind, but he can't. None of us can go back. Gotta remember there are plenty of things wrong with the past, and there are things—"

Henry's eyes took on a glazed appearance as he zoned out. She'd rattled off coffee-shop philosophies to an eight-year-old. What was she thinking?

"What I'm trying to say is people need to be able to choose. Mr. Primm wants to take that right away because he's scared of where it may lead. He doesn't have faith in other people, and that's no way to live."

Even as she said the words, she wondered if she'd done much the same. Hadn't she clung to the past, holding fast to empty love for John? Hadn't she lost faith in people? People like Brent…or even Adam?

"Oh," Henry said, scratching his head. "I get it. It's like making someone play a position without giving him a chance to play what he wants. Like when Coach Armbruster made Hunter play on the offensive line just 'cause he's big. That wasn't fair. I like giving people chances. I like being fair."

Scarlet wasn't sure her nephew completely got what she meant. But whatever. "Yeah, something like that, Tiger." She ruffled his close-cropped hair and withdrew a damp hand. Boys sweated. A lot.

"Okay, let's head in. And, Henry, if you see Mr. Primm hanging around again, don't talk to him. Go inside and tell someone. Okay?"

"Sure," he said, pounding up the back steps of the porch. Not only were little boys sweaty, but they were loud, too.

"Mo-om!" Henry called as he banged open the door that led to the kitchen. "Aunt Scarlet got in a fight with Mr. Primm!"

Oh, no, he did not.

Scarlet sped up the steps, hoping to do damage control. Little boys were sweaty, loud and had big mouths.

Rayne met Scarlet at the door. "What's he talking about?" Rayne had braided her hair and wore a snug polka-dot apron with a ruffle at the hem. Her label. She also wore a frown.

"Oh, nothing. Harvey stopped by to give me his regards."

"Was he harassing you?" She slapped a wooden spoon against her palm. She looked like a mob boss ready to mete out justice to anyone crossing her or hers. It made Scarlet smile. "What are you smiling about?"

"Nothing. You. What are you going to do? Whack him with a spoon? I think you being arrested for assault will do more damage to your show's reputation than your passionate sister handcuffing herself to a flagpole during a protest."

Rayne rolled her eyes. "I'm not going to hit anyone. Yet."

"He's upset I'm destroying his credibility or whatever. He waved a Dallas newspaper at me. The picture of him holding the book and pointing a condemning finger wasn't very flattering."

"We better watch him. I don't trust him. No one does. A man like that digging up dirt on his neighbors and then sitting on the pew beside them every Sunday, holier-than-thou. Something's wrong with him." Rayne went back to the sauté pan on the huge Viking range.

The kitchen smelled like bacon. And cake. Two tantalizing smells that oddly complemented each other.

"I'm not worried. He's a bitter, grieving old man. Not a criminal."

Brent came in. "Man, I'm starved. Writing about swim meets gives me the munchies." He nuzzled Rayne's neck, sneaking a hand down to her bottom.

"Um, hello? I'm sitting here," Scarlet said from a stool on the other side of the kitchen island.

Brent snatched his hand away from his wife's tush. "Oh, so you are."

Scarlet slid off the stool and headed away from the two lovebirds. They could have their moment together. She would rather not imagine her sister getting it on with Brent. Shudder.

But she could imagine herself getting it on with tall, blond and tight-assed.

The only silver lining to having to stay in Oak Stand was the judge putting Adam in charge of her case. If she had to perform community service, at least she could do it under him. Or she could do it on top of him.

She was flexible. Literally.

Her dirty thoughts made her giggle.

It was unlikely she would act on anything. Adam was the chief of police, a position he obviously took very seriously. After the kiss in the jail cell, she doubted he would allow temptation to overcome professionalism again. Even if temporarily losing their heads had been mutually pleasurable.

Kissing Adam had accomplished what she'd been searching for. He'd unstuck her. Given her back the piece she thought she'd lost when John had abandoned her. For that, she'd be grateful. And she would try to behave herself.

Try being the key word.

CHAPTER TEN

PHOENIX WAS NOT what Scarlet had expected. The large structure that appeared when she drove between the two stone pillars didn't look like a gang rehabilitation facility. It looked like a mountain lodge with its cedar-planked siding, huge wraparound porch and stacked stone columns. Ornamental grasses softened the stone base upon which the structure was built. An ugly dog waited for her on the porch.

She guessed Banjo was the welcome committee.

Scarlet stepped from the black convertible and pushed her sunglasses atop her head. She'd dressed in her standard uniform for acting classes—snug black pants, black T-shirt, hair pulled into a low ponytail. She was a blank canvas, awaiting the opportunity to morph into whatever character she needed to become. Improv was her favorite. She hoped it would work with her new students.

"Yo," a voice called from her left. "You bringing sexy back? Or is this more of a back-in-black sorta thing?"

Scarlet spun and met a smiling face, attached to a startlingly plump physique. "More of a Black Magic Woman. I'm Scarlet and I'm the new acting coach."

The man smiled and extended a hand. "I'm Georges. I'm a counselor here at Phoenix. One of the first graduates, too."

Scarlet shook his hand. It was slightly sweaty. Like

Henry's, but the smile the man gave her was charming. "Nice to meet you, Georges. Now, where am I to go? You know, to work my magic. Or as some call it, my community service."

Georges grinned and beckoned her to follow him toward the front door. "Right this way, Black Magic Woman."

The dog rose, stretched and trotted down the steps to greet her. She reached down and scratched him behind the ears and received a sloppy doggy kiss on the back of her hand for her effort. She could see the appeal of the scruffy mutt, and it occurred to her Henry needed his own pet. She'd missed his birthday, so maybe…

The dog lifted his leg and peed on a potted plant next to the door.

Maybe not.

Scarlet stepped inside the center behind Georges into a large rustic room. Rick and Kate Mendez sat on the leather sectional, drinking lemonade.

"Welcome, Scarlet," Rick said, rising. He gestured for Kate to remain seated when she tried to struggle to her feet. "Lemonade?"

"No, thanks. Wow, what a fabulous place," Scarlet breathed, taking in the wagon-wheel chandelier, arched wood ceiling and huge moose head hanging above a stacked stone fireplace. Fans whirred above and the concrete floor was softened with Navajo rugs and an animal-skin rug, which was enclosed by the sectional.

"We like it." Kate patted the plush leather beside her. "Have a seat. We'll talk first and then take you around to meet the staff and the clients."

Georges disappeared with a salute as Scarlet sat.

"That sounds good. I didn't know what to bring. Back in New York, I teach at a community theater adjacent to the YWCA. We have a stage, props and sound equipment. I'm afraid this will be a little basic."

"We like basic," Rick said. "This room is our communal room and it's probably the only space big enough for your class. Unless we move the games out of the recreation room."

"This should be fine if you don't mind my moving the sectional a bit." There wasn't much privacy for shy actors, but for the hours she was here it was her job to teach them to become someone other than themselves.

The door opened, interrupting her thoughts.

"Ah, right on time," Rick said. Scarlet turned her head and watched Adam stroll their way. Though he wore a pristine, pressed uniform, his gait was lazy and rolling. Almost seductive. Something fluttered in her belly.

"Afternoon, ladies." Adam set his hat on a sofa table, unveiling golden hair that glinted in the late-afternoon sunlight pouring through the unadorned windows. He was altogether yummy, yum, yum.

"We were about to go over the center's protocol with Scarlet. Do you have anything first?" Rick asked Adam.

Adam glanced at Scarlet. She hadn't spoken a word to him since he'd ripped himself away from the cell bars and paid the pizza guy. After Drake had left, Adam had handed her a loaded paper plate, another can of soda, then moved his center of operations to the front of the station. When Scarlet awoke the next morning, stiff from attempting sleep on the narrow bunk, another officer had greeted her and led her to the bathroom. She'd seen Adam briefly in the courtroom where he'd remained silent, only nodding his head at the judge's directives.

"I have a few papers for you to sign, mostly stating

you understand the conditions of the sentence," he said now, waving a manila folder before setting it on the low coffee table.

Scarlet picked up the folder and leafed through it as Rick began explaining how the center worked. With half an ear, she learned the clients were well-screened and held to a certain standard of behavior. She read on the forms she couldn't drink alcohol or carry a firearm without violating the terms of probation. Well, there went her Saturday night.

After Scarlet scratched her name on the appropriate lines in the documentation, Kate took her on a tour of the facility, which included classrooms, sleeping quarters and a separate building outfitted with all the supplies necessary to run an auto-detail shop along with a...boxing ring?

"What's that for?" Scarlet pointed toward the ring.

Kate smiled. "Oh, that. Well, Rick swears the clients like to take out their anger by beating the crap out of each other. But I think he really bought it for himself. And Adam."

"Adam?"

"Yeah, he and Rick box at least once a week."

"Box?"

"What are you? A parrot?" Kate said, waddling toward the rear of the metal building. Fans were mounted in the corners and a miniature gym lurked behind the boxing ring, complete with weight benches, an elliptical machine and a treadmill.

"Nope. I'm a vampire queen," Scarlet said.

Kate snorted and continued her tour. "So this is where the guys work and work out. On Wednesdays and Saturdays we run an auto-detail shop. We make enough money to cover entertainment costs, equipment and give them some money to send home to their families. The guys like the ring and weights. Guess it does give them release. This program can be extreme, digging into a lot of stuff they don't want to talk about. Intensive therapy about relationships, guilt and things no one should suffer through." Kate rubbed her lower back. Scarlet had nearly a foot on the diminutive Kate, whose distended belly jutted forward. The woman had to have perpetual backaches. Probably spasms, too.

"So what do you think?" Georges said, materializing at Scarlet's elbow. She squeaked. For a big fellow, he had an incredible talent for stealth.

"It sounds like a program that works."

Kate nodded. "It does, for the most part."

"So?" Scarlet said.

"So what?" Kate asked.

"What do I do now?"

"Oh." Kate snapped to attention. "Georges, let's take Scarlet to meet the guys."

He saluted yet again, making Scarlet wonder if he'd been in the military. He led her out to the long back porch of the main building. There was a nice flagstone patio with Adirondack chairs and a fire pit. Adam stood waiting.

"Can I speak with Ms. Rose before she gets started?" he asked. It hadn't really sounded like a question. More of a command.

"Sure," Kate said, before turning to Scarlet. "Come on inside when you're finished."

Scarlet nodded and Georges and Kate left her alone with the sexy cop who kicked off weird sensations inside her a mere four days ago. Part of her was pleased she would have time alone with Adam. Part of her wanted to get everything over with so she could move on. Go to L.A. Or back to New York. Anywhere but this little Texas town treading water.

For a moment, Adam didn't speak. He seemed captivated by the way an old wooden fence zigzagged the property. Finally he turned to her. "This won't be easy."

"Not much in life is," she responded, kicking the weather-worn footstool sitting in front of a chair.

"About that night in the holding cell—"

"Think nothing of it." She waved a hand. "It was no biggie. A moment of insanity. One we can't repeat."

"Exactly."

"And about what I told you. About being in love with a man who dumped me—" She paused, looking away from him. Something about connecting with his eyes felt too raw. The man stripped her defenses. Obviously. Why else would she have told him about John? No one knew about their split. Maybe her roommate, Stefan, had an inkling, but even he didn't know Scarlet had been dumped. Heart-trampled. Abandoned. "I'd appreciate you not mentioning that information to anyone. I shouldn't— It was a strange moment. I'm sorry I asked you to do…um…what you did. It wasn't fair of me."

She could feel his stare and forced herself to meet it.

"Who are you? And what have you done with Scarlet?"

"What?"

"That was…heartfelt." He crossed his arms over his chest, which caused his shirtsleeves to pull tight over his muscled arms. His skin was as golden as his hair. He was an all-over golden boy. No, not a boy. A man. She swallowed. Hard.

"You weren't acting out a scene in your head, were you? Because when I first met you, I got the idea that you acted out stuff going on in your mind. It was as if you listened to an inner voice directing you."

Scarlet blinked. How in the hell had he known? It was a bad habit, seeing everything as a director might, carefully orchestrating responses as if she were in front of a camera. But she'd tried really hard since she'd been in Oak Stand to step out of acting mode and be more herself. "I'm not acting."

He arched an eyebrow.

"Seriously. I'm sorry. I can see how much your job and your reputation mean to you. I shouldn't have put you in an awkward position, especially knowing you want me."

His eyes widened slightly, but he regained composure quickly. "That's pretty egotistical even for a soap star."

"My show is not a soap opera. It's a drama. And you do want me. I've been around men long enough to recognize the signs. You—" she pointed at him "—want me." She pointed to herself.

Something crackled between them. Static electricity building like an imminent storm.

"I don't want you."

"Yes, you do," Scarlet said. "Hey, it's okay. I want you, too. So we're attracted to each other. Big deal. We're young, single and not ugly. It's natural. But don't worry. I won't act on it."

"You mean, *I* won't act on it. If I were a betting man, I'd say self-control is not one of your strong points. But it *is* one of mine. So I won't wig out and lose all sense just because you walk by in a tight pair of pants and don't bother to wear a bra." He glowered at her, uncrossing his arms and propping them on his lean hips.

"Hey, I'm wearing a bra today. And did you say *wig*

out?" She didn't think she'd ever heard a man use that particular expression. He looked so cute when he was angry. So sexy when he was defensive. She wanted their banter to go on and on, culminating in—

No. She wasn't going to provoke him. Wasn't going to let the spark of attraction go anywhere. She still loved John. Still dreamed about him. At least she wanted to dream about him even if he faded more each day.

Adam bristled like a dog guarding its turf. "What? No. I mean, yes. What does it matter? The important thing is what happened at the station isn't going to happen again. I don't make many lapses in judgment, and I damned sure don't repeat them."

Scarlet smiled inside, though she presented him with a calm demeanor. She *was* a good actress. "I'm sorry. Of course. And I've made you angry enough to curse. Sorry about that, too."

"I'm not angry."

"You sure? Because you look angry."

He spun on the heel of his perfectly polished boot and stalked up the flagstone path to the porch. "Report to me after this first session. I have your email address and will send you the time I expect you to come to the station. Behave yourself," he called over his shoulder.

Then he disappeared into Phoenix.

"And goodbye to you, too," Scarlet said to the emptiness surrounding her. For a moment she felt lonely. Which was stupid. She wasn't any more alone than she'd been ten minutes ago. But something about Adam did things to her. Confused things. Things she'd rather not think about.

So she wouldn't.

She followed the path and prepared herself to meet

the men she would be working with. Teaching acting to gang members. Should be a piece of cake.

ADAM WAVED TO RICK, then stepped outside. Scarlet had gotten to him with her very honest and very true words.

Yes, he wanted her. But did she have to bring it out in the open? He didn't want to admit it to himself, much less say it out loud. Now it was out there. Floating. Waiting to fan the flames of need that burned inside him.

Yes, he wanted Scarlet.

But he couldn't have her.

To take what he wanted from Scarlet would be unethical. Illegal. Misconduct. And even if no one found out, those actions would only lead to disaster. Better to imitate his mother's approach to life. Close eyes and ignore what's right in front of you. Don't acknowledge. Don't respond. Do nothing. Life is easier that way.

Even as he thought about avoiding truth, he knew it was no way to live. At least, no way *he* wanted to live.

Scarlet was braver than him. She'd said what she felt, what she knew to be true. He'd denied and ran. He didn't feel too proud of himself, even though the final result was what he'd been after. He and Scarlet were totally platonic and they had to remain that way.

His phone buzzed as he opened the door to his cruiser. He pulled it from the holder clipped to his belt. No ID.

"Hinton."

"Oh, Adam, you answered," the voice said with a nervous giggle.

"Yes."

"This is Sophia. Sophia Waters, Mayor Waters's daughter."

"Of course. What can I do for you, Miss Waters?"

Another nervous giggle. “Well, this is going to sound very forward. I wondered if you had a date for the Labor Day picnic next weekend? I haven’t met too many men in Oak Stand. Or should I say single men. Um, single men who are nice men. Oh, I’m so botching this—”

“No, you’re not botching anything—”

“Oh, but I am.” She gave a self-deprecating laugh. This time it didn’t sound as nervous. “I’m not really good with being an aggressive, modern woman.” She paused. “I called to ask you to attend the picnic with me. I make a good lemon pie and I’ll even be naughty and sneak in some wine.”

What could he say? Sophia was the right kind of woman. She’d said so herself. With her bright blue eyes, subdued makeup and nicely padded bra, she was exactly the sort of girl he should be dating. Sophia taught Sunday school at the Methodist church, she whipped up brownies for the firefighters’ bake sale and she painted her fingernails the lightest shades of pink. She was refined, polite and cheerful. Everything a man could hope for in a partner.

“I’d love to go with you, Sophia. I have Labor Day off, so I can lose the uniform and wear jeans.”

Sophia laughed again. “That sounds wonderful. And, please, call me Sophie.”

“Okay, then, Sophie, shall I pick you up?”

“Well, sure. I guess. If you’d rather not, I can meet you there.”

Adam thought she sounded as if she’d rather him make it an official date and pick her up. “The picnic starts at noon, so I’ll pick you up at eleven forty-five.”

“Great. See you then,” she murmured. He could hear pleasure in her voice. Something about it made him feel uneasy. The way he’d felt at the dozens of debutante balls his mother had forced him to attend when he was in college. He felt…hunted.

"See you," he said, pressing the end button and returning the phone to its holder.

He ducked inside the cruiser, firing the engine as Scarlet appeared on the porch. She stood, one hip cocked, arms akimbo. She watched him for a moment before raising her hand and wiggling her fingers, which he took to be a wave.

He felt his groin tighten. Damn it.

He didn't wave as he reversed out of the gravel parking area and turned toward the highway that would take him to the town he served. He wasn't being rude. Simply childish. Damn Scarlet for making him want her so much. Damn her for making Sophie Waters seem like taking a bath with his socks on.

Then it struck him. What he faced was a test.

Nine months ago, he'd left Houston and all that it represented. He'd left behind being his father's son. Left behind Angi and a failed marriage. Left behind using his name to get ahead. He was done being Adam Hinton, heir to a large fortune, ne'er-do-well, seduced by big-breasted women in honky-tonk dives. Instead he set out to be who he'd always wanted to be. A policeman. A citizen. A friend. A neighbor. A regular Joe.

So the desire Scarlet Rose evoked in him was a test.

Would he revert back to his old ways?

Or stick to his guns about being a changed man?

Much depended on holding to the latter. He had no choice. He had to ignore the lust humming in his blood and look toward a future with someone who would stay in Oak Stand. Who would have his children. Who would balance a checkbook. Who would head a committee. Who would conduct herself in an orderly fashion.

This was a test he had to pass.

CHAPTER ELEVEN

Two days later, Scarlet pushed through the glass door of the police station, relieved no reporters lurked outside. Seemed as though her stint as news item of the week was over. They were on to drunken heiresses who had face-lifts and child actors getting out of rehab, then wrecking their expensive rides while driving under the influence.

"Hey, Scarlet," Roz called from her desk behind the faux-wood front counter. "How are things at Phoenix?"

Scarlet shrugged. Not good. But she didn't want to admit she'd utterly failed to engage the guys' interest in acting. They were way more interested in the way her butt filled out her tight black pants. Very different from her Jewish matriarchs. Tomorrow night, she would wear a gunnysack. "Fine. Just takes some getting used to."

"That bunch has been there for only about two weeks. Sometimes they need a sort of decompressin' time before they open up. Or that's what Trudy Cox says. She teaches GED there. You met Trudy yet?"

"Not yet."

Roz opened her mouth, but Adam interrupted her. "Scarlet, come into my office and we'll talk." He turned into his office like a dictator. Guess she'd play the part of obedient subject. She was, after all, under his authority…which pissed her off. She shouldn't have to toe the line for any man.

"Coming, dear," she called, giving Roz a wink before heading toward Adam's office. Roz chuckled.

"Close the door." He didn't bother to shift his gaze from the computer screen. He seemed grumpy, which should have made him less appealing. It didn't.

She nudged the door closed with her foot and settled onto one of the standard-issue office chairs in front of the shiny teak desk. "You sure that's a good idea?"

He gave her his attention. "Why not?"

She arched an eyebrow.

"Good God, I'm not going to rip your clothes off, throw you over my desk and have wild sex with you."

She didn't say anything more, mostly because the scenario he'd painted made her pulse race. Desire snaked low in her tummy, uncurling and spreading its warmth. She shifted on the chair. "So you say."

"Not a chance."

Her desire fell apart and disappeared. Instead a little dart speared her heart. What did he mean *not a chance?* He didn't want her anymore? Of course, they'd agreed to not doing any sort of sexual hokeypokey, but to be so brutal about it…

"Tell me about yesterday." He resumed his preoccupation with the computer, moving the mouse, clicking and scrolling. His eyes narrowed in concentration.

Something about his easy dismissal annoyed Scarlet. "Well, after I passed out joints to get us in the zone, we took turns acting out scenes from our favorite porno flicks and then I left. They loved it. I must commend the judge on finding such a *fulfilling* community-service project for me."

No response. Not a flicker in his eyes or a jerking of his chin. Oh, he was a cool customer.

"Maybe I should give the class a whirl. Sounds… educational and…stimulating."

Scarlet shrugged. "A sure thing."

Adam slid the keyboard beneath the desk, pushed his chair back and gave her his full regard. "Okay, so really, how did everything go?"

"Badly." She crossed her arms as she crossed her legs. Today she wore a strapless denim number by D&G that hit her upper thighs with a cute flounce. She'd paired it with strappy sandals and a cheetah-print scarf at her neck. She'd left her hair down, and the deep red waves brushed her collarbone. It was a hot look. She'd hoped to have Adam with his tongue lolling out.

Obviously it hadn't worked.

"Why?" he asked, folding his hands across his flat abdomen like a principal addressing a student he'd caught cheating.

"Because they couldn't stop staring at my ass long enough to do any of the exercises I wanted them to try. They looked at me blankly before giving me a once-over and making come-jump-on-this expressions. One even made kissing faces."

Adam lifted his eyebrows and then his gaze raked her, much like her students had. "Maybe you should wear a sweater. Cover yourself up."

"I wore what I always wear to teach acting classes. Every inch of me was covered. In black."

He unclasped his hands and spread them apart. "Perhaps something baggy. Make it professional."

She rolled her eyes. "It wasn't that they were being sexist pigs. They were uncooperative. They snorted every time I demonstrated what I wanted them to do."

"I know you might not want to hear this, but not very many people are open to acting classes, especially gang members who've spent their whole lives putting on a tough face for the world. I don't know much about acting, but I do know you have to strip away who you are to create who a director wants you to become."

"True. I like to think I'm a blank slate awaiting the direction, waiting to be swept up in the moment."

"That may be easy for you, but not for these guys. They're not very tuned in to their inner, emotional selves."

A niggling of an idea seized Scarlet. "You."

"Me?" Alarm appeared in his eyes. "What about me?"

"Will you come to my next class? All I have to do is show them a rugged, manly man going through the technique. Who is more macho than a guy with a gun strapped to his waist?" It would be perfect. She and Adam could start with a repetition exercise. If she could show her students how easy it was to bond and respond to a partner in the moment, they would be more apt to see acting as a serious discipline.

But Adam looked horrified.

"First of all, I don't wear my gun at my waist. It's not a fashion accessory. It's on my hip. And second, I'm not taking part in your class. I'm supervising you, making sure you don't violate the terms of probation—"

"I'm not." Scarlet stood, shoving her hands in the baggy pockets. She paced as she worked through the idea. The students at Phoenix needed a role model, needed to see another man abandon his inhibitions and immerse himself in portraying a feeling. Yeah, having Adam there would be perfect. He was as buttoned-up and conservative as a guy could get. Not nerdy. No, with that body and his sense of humor, he was way beyond geek chic. But his reserved demeanor held him apart. If a guy like Adam could stand up in front of everyone and engage in acting exercises, then anyone could.

She stopped pacing and whirled around. "Say you'll do it. Not for me, but for those guys."

"No. Use Rick. He's—what did you call it?—macho. He's their leader. Much better to use him than—"

"I want you."

"You can't have me."

"Please."

"No."

What was wrong with him? "Are you chicken?"

He bristled. Men. Always the same. Double dog dare them and they jumped right into your hand, every time. She closed her hand to seal the deal. "I think you are. I think you're scared they will think you're girly if you do a simple acting exercise. You're afraid of getting in touch with your inner self. Typical man."

"I'm not afraid. I simply don't want to be there. Doing that." He stood and crossed his arms over his chest, concealing his badge. But Scarlet knew body language. He was defensive. Protecting himself. His masculinity.

She smiled and tilted her head. "I see."

"What do you see?"

"I see a man who has a chance to make a much-needed impression on guys who are scared and angry. Who hate police officers and see them in only one light. This is a chance for you to let them see the man beneath the uniform. To see you are more than the law. But you're afraid it will make you weak."

His eyes narrowed.

"Don't worry," she said, shifting her gaze to the

ceiling and sliding her tongue over her top lip in an I'm-thinking gesture. "Maybe I can get Drake to come. He seems fully in sync with his emotions."

"Fine. I'll do it." The way he almost growled the words revealed more than he was probably comfortable with.

Yes. Scarlet clapped her hands. "Perfect."

"Anything else going on I should know about?"

Other than dreaming about sliding her hands over his chest and licking his neck? "Nothing else. I'm in bed by ten o'clock every night and I'm eating my veggies."

He smiled. Finally. Something about it warmed her to her recently polished toes.

"Good."

For a moment, silence hung between them. Adam studied her. Then his eyes dipped a smidgen. To her décolleté. She peeked surreptitiously and saw that her neckline gaped a bit. His observation didn't feel the way the gang members' ogling her had. Adam's notice felt...welcome.

The air became supercharged, crackling with unfulfilled desire. Scarlet swallowed and tried to find a smile. She failed. She pressed her lips together and tried to avert her gaze from his broad shoulders, from that small sprinkling of hair at the base of his throat, barely visible above the T-shirt he wore beneath his dark uniform. Tried to pretend he didn't have lean hips, a tight stomach and long, lanky legs.

"Um, guess I'd better go. I told Rayne I would pick up Henry from school. They're doing preproduction stuff today and start filming tomorrow."

His gaze met hers. "Oh, yeah. Good. I'm logging two

hours in for you as time served, and I'll see you tomorrow."

Silence fell again. Scarlet didn't move. Just soaked him in. Want burgeoned into beast mode. It clawed its way out from beneath the boulder of reason. She couldn't stop it. "I really want to kiss you right now."

"Shit," he breathed, closing his eyes.

"But I won't. I promised you I wouldn't jeopardize your integrity. Still, I think you should know that I really, really want to kiss you."

"Stop saying things like that. Please. I'm trying—"

"Never mind." She moved toward the door. "My mouth gets me in as much trouble as my actions. This office isn't bugged, is it?"

"No." He sank into his chair, a pained expression on his face. "We have to ignore this thing between us. Giving in to temptation will bring only temporary satisfaction and it can lead to disastrous consequences… for us both. This is a test of our resolve, Scarlet. If I did what I want to do to you, people would find out. The press would find out. I'd lose my job and you'd be painted as—"

"A scarlet woman?"

He smiled. "Is that why you picked the name?"

She shook her head. He was right, but she didn't like it. For the first time since John, she felt something for a man, and she couldn't pursue it. So not fair.

"It's too bad, isn't it?" she said. "To play together would be so mutually beneficial. But it can't happen because of who you are. And what I did."

"Even if I weren't the police chief and you weren't serving out community service, it wouldn't work between us. I'm not looking for a good time. I'm looking for a woman who will make a good wife."

"A wife?" She widened her eyes. Not a role she wanted to audition for. She couldn't see herself like Rayne. No setting a perfectly prepared dinner in front of a man at the end of a long day. No wiping babies' bottoms or decorating Christmas trees. *Wife* was a shoe that did not fit.

"Well, yeah. I can't spend my life having one-night stands and avoiding the noose. I need a partner, a helpmate, someone who will sit on the porch with me and grow old. I want the American dream. And, no offense, but you don't fit that—"

"No, I sure the hell don't." Another dagger of hurt lodged in her heart. Which was dumb. He'd out and out stated she was wrong for him. But at least he had been honest about what he wanted. He wanted a Stepford wife, something she could certainly portray on film but would never do in real life. This was for the best. "So we'll ignore this thing and stay totally platonic. Outside of that one kiss, we've done nothing wrong, so you have nothing to worry about. Right?"

He didn't look convinced.

"Well, see you in a few days." She slipped out the door. Her inner child stamped her foot and screeched, "It's not fair," at the top of her little lungs, but Scarlet knew Adam was right. Indulging in a fleeting, but likely pleasurable, horizontal tango would open a can of slimy, icky worms. She didn't like worms. She liked Californian sunshine. So she needed to get this thing in Oak Stand done and get herself to the West Coast.

After all, she had a bisexual hooker to portray.

ADAM STARED AT THE CLOSED DOOR for a good three minutes before sliding his hand into his desk drawer to check for the videotape.

You have nothing to worry about.

In the words of football analyst Lee Corso, "Not so fast, my friend."

He had cold, hard evidence of his inappropriate behavior in his desk drawer. Misconduct with a prisoner.

If anyone caught wind of it, Adam would be toast.

He'd lose his job.

His reputation.

Everything he'd worked so hard for over the past year.

He closed the drawer as guilt crowded his mind. The tape belonged in the locked cabinet in the outer office, but he couldn't bring himself to put it there. He'd told the department he'd locked it in his desk because of the celebrity of the prisoner. Everyone had agreed upon the idea, and it was likely no one would ever view it. But, Scarlet *was* a celebrity. No doubt there were many who would love to get their hands on footage of the vampire vixen in lockdown. He could see it now, rolling across his TV screen on *Star Access.*

He could see himself, threading his hands in her hair, covering her fabulous lips with his own. He could imagine the heat that would radiate from them. All the pent-up lust he had for Scarlet would be right there for everyone to see.

He didn't know what to do with the tape. If push came to shove, he'd turn it over to a judge or another law agency. He'd have to. And because of his job, he couldn't erase it or damage it.

So he kept it safe. It could stay in his desk until things died down. Until Scarlet left, taking the nosy reporters and the trouble she caused with her.

A nudge of regret reverberated in his chest, but he ignored it. The way he had to ignore his libido.

"Hey." Roz stuck her head in his door, swiveling her gaze left, then right as if the ghost of her former employer would rampage upon her and deport her to the bowels of hell. "You got a call on line two and Harvey Primm is out front. He missed Scarlet by a minute. Thank God."

She shut the door before he could respond with a dirty word. He'd gotten his filthy mouth under control before Scarlet hit town. Now every other thought included a colorful obscenity.

Harvey appeared at his door as the light on his phone stopped blinking. "Hello, Hinton. I need to talk to you about this Scarlet Rose gal. She's causing all sorts of problems in this town and, as police chief, it's your job to curtail problems."

Adam closed his eyes and gestured Harvey to take the chair Scarlet had vacated. He locked the drawer and tucked the key into his pocket. Primm narrowed his eyes and Adam wished he'd waited. A man like Harvey would read into such an action. He could probably sniff out Adam's guilt, too. "What can I do for you, Mr. Primm?"

"This girl is harassing me. I caught her spying on me the day before yesterday. Trying to catch me doing something she can take to all the big papers."

"Scarlet Rose?"

"She's waiting for me to mess up so she can expose me. That's harassment. Think I don't know that?"

"Mr. Primm, I hardly think the woman would bother. She doesn't seem the type to stalk an older man—"

"You've been hoodwinked by a pretty face. Her sinful body has you in its grasp, doesn't it?"

If only you knew.

"Beware falling for the sins of the flesh." Harvey pointed a bony finger at Adam.

"Now, wait a minute, Primm. I don't like what you're accusing me of. I have not been taken in by anyone, and you can't make accusations against the woman without backing them up."

"So you want proof?"

Adam knew the old man was a bit of a crackpot, but had no idea he had such delusions. He couldn't imagine Scarlet dashing behind buildings and digging through trash cans in order to get dirt on Primm. But Primm? Definitely. He would wade through raw sewage to get the scoop on someone. "That's usually what we need in order to arrest or issue a citation against someone."

"I want a restraining order. I don't want that woman near me. And I'm thinking of suing her for slander. She can't go telling people things about me that aren't true."

"No, she can't. What exactly has she been saying?"

"That I'm crazy," Harvey shouted. Flecks of spit flew out of his mouth and christened Adam's desk.

Adam wanted to tell Harvey it wasn't slander if the comments were true. Instead he donned a patient face and waited for Harvey to finish. "And that's all?"

"No," Harvey said, opening his jacket pocket and reaching in.

Adam's senses tightened. He set both feet flat on the linoleum and leaned forward. His reaction was instinctual, born of years of police training.

Harvey revealed a newspaper. "See. Right here. Look at this picture. Look at the way the press is slanting their accounts. They're making me look like I'm fanatical, instead of a crusader intent on protecting our community from that abomination of a book."

"Mr. Primm, as a journalist yourself—" though

Adam thought that was stretching the truth by a good mile "—you must understand the tone a writer takes is his prerogative. I can't issue a restraint against Ms. Rose based on the opinions of a journalist in Dallas."

"Bull feathers!" Harvey's voice shook with rage. "This girl is trying to ruin me. Make people in my town think I'm insane."

Adam stood. "Now, see here, Mr. Primm. You have no proof Ms. Rose is out to destroy your reputation, and you have no business making accusations against her or this journalist. People have the right to think whatever they wish about you. Nothing I can do about that."

His office door crashed open. "Adam, there's been an accident on Highway 71. State patrol requests assistance. Looks bad. Seven miles out, mile marker one forty-two."

"Excuse me, Mr. Primm," Adam said, grabbing his hat and holster.

"But—"

"No time to talk." He rounded the desk and exited his office. "Call all units, Roz, and escort Mr. Primm out."

Roz saluted and picked up the dispatch radio.

Adam pulled the keys from his pocket and pushed through the front door, glad to be away from Harvey. Glad to be doing something more useful than ticketing people for not picking up dog poop. He never wished for anyone to be in harm's way, but damned if it didn't feel good to be useful. He missed this. The adrenaline. The urgency. The knowledge he could make a difference in a life-or-death situation.

Everything he'd been worrying about—Harvey, his ex-wife, his date with Sophie, the damning tape of him kissing Scarlet and the crazy desire he had for the redhead—disappeared.

This was what he was made to do.

And he wouldn't let anyone get in his way of fulfilling his purpose.

CHAPTER TWELVE

SCARLET GLANCED DOWN the hallway of the Longview hospital, wondering which way the emergency room was. Rayne had called her about an accident that had occurred earlier that afternoon—a car had been hit broadside by a logging truck and the people inside the vehicle had been gravely injured. The mother and her friend had been flown to Shreveport, but the two teenage daughters had been sent to Longview Regional. The two thirteen-year-old girls had non-life-threatening injuries and were stable. A state trooper had called the inn after noticing the *Deep Shadows* shirt one of the girls had been wearing.

Scarlet had been going over notes for teaching the acting class when Rayne had popped her head into the room.

"Scarlet, I have something you need to do," she'd said.

Scarlet glanced up. "What? I'm kinda busy working on a few scenes using *The Magpie Thief*."

"There was an accident outside town. Two girls were taken to the hospital. One of them was wearing a shirt from your show, so a state trooper called to ask if you would be willing to visit. They're not sure if the girl's mother is going to make it."

Scarlet tossed aside her pen and notebook and

searched for the flip-flops she'd kicked off earlier. "Wanna come with me?"

"Can't. Henry has football."

Scarlet found her keys and purse, then grabbed a cereal bar before making her way to Longview. Now that she was here, she had no idea where the emergency room was. She'd followed the signs, but she was lost.

A lady stood beside a sliding-glass window indicating Scarlet was in Radiology. "Excuse me, could you point me toward the emergency room?"

The woman, clad in mauve scrubs, turned her head and droned, "Down the hall, take the second right."

"Thanks," Scarlet said, stepping around her.

"Oh, my gosh!" the woman said. "You're an actress. I've seen you on *Ghost Whisperer.* No. What was it?"

Whoever the woman had been talking to inside the office poked her head out the window. "Veronica! Holy sh—" She caught herself, obviously remembering she was in the workplace.

Scarlet smiled. "Hi."

The woman leaned farther out. "I love your show. Never miss it, and I can't wait for next season. Oh, gosh, you've got to tell me. Is Gina really pregnant with a werewolf?"

Scarlet bit her bottom lip to keep from laughing. "I honestly can't tell you. It's, like, in my contract. But let's just say she won't need a winter coat for that baby."

The woman shrieked. "I knew it! I knew Romero had attacked her in the woods and she'd be forced to bear the shame of a werewolf's child. Oh, my gosh, I can't wait to tell Sally."

Scarlet shook her head.

"Not Romero? You're joking. Who's the father?"

Scarlet made the lock-and-key motion over her lips,

throwing the imaginary key over her shoulder. "Sorry, you'll have to watch."

The woman in scrubs, who hadn't stopped staring at her for the entire conversation, finally spoke up. "I can't believe you have kissed Karakas. Your lips have touched his lips. That's so sexy."

Scarlet stepped back because she was afraid the woman might ask to kiss her in some weird attempt to transfer the effect. If only the woman knew. She'd lanced blisters on the bottom of Stefan's feet last year after he'd run the Boston Marathon. And the man left used Q-tips around the bathroom. So not sexy. "Um, yeah. If it's any consolation, he sometimes has garlic breath."

Both women laughed.

"Well, it was nice talking to you. Better find the E.R."

She waved as they called out how much they'd liked meeting her. Having fans was cool sometimes…and yet sometimes freaky.

Scarlet followed the directions and found herself in the middle of the E.R. She headed to the triage desk.

"Hi. I'm looking for the two young ladies who were brought in earlier from a car accident near Oak Stand."

The older man looked up. "You a relative?"

"Um, not exactly. One of the state troopers called and said one of the girls was a fan." She glanced around, looking for someone in a uniform. Maybe the guy was still around and could vouch for her.

"A fan of what?" the man said, narrowing his eyes at her. He took in her T-shirt, shorts and flip-flops before focusing on his magazine.

"My television show," Scarlet said, pushing her bangs back and giving the older man a smile. "*Deep Shadows.*"

"Never heard of it," he said, not bothering to look up. "What's it on? Cable?"

Scarlet bristled. He made it sound as though her show was a fly-by-night production. Televisions shows on TBS, HBO and AMC were perpetual Emmy winners. Cable had become desirable to even big-name actors. "Yeah, it's on cable."

"Well, if you're not a relative, I can't let you in."

"It's okay, Charlie," a voice said from over her shoulder.

She saw a burly man in uniform coming her way. His name tag read Barlow. He held out his hand. "Thanks for coming, Ms. Rose. I appreciate your taking the time."

She shook his hand. "No problem. I'm glad to be able to do something."

Charlie rolled his eyes. "Go on, I guess."

Scarlet gave Sergeant Barlow a secret smile. "He doesn't believe I'm on a television show."

Charlie snorted. "I've seen the crap on cable."

Scarlet sighed. "Okay, where are the girls?"

"Charlene is in X-ray, but Destiny's down here. She's the one who wore your show's shirt. I didn't know you were in town, but one of the other officers at the crash site did. He suggested I give your sister a call."

Scarlet wondered if it was Adam. The wreck had been close to Oak Stand, so it stood to reason he would be on the scene. "I'm glad you did."

"Okay, she's back here. She's a little scratched and a lot shaken up."

Scarlet nodded and he pulled back the curtain of the emergency-room bay. Lying in the bed was a teenage girl wearing a hospital gown. She had short dark hair and a small elfin face that looked as if it had been peppered with glass on one side. She looked very much alone and scared. Scarlet didn't have many maternal instincts, but she felt as though she could scoop up the child and hold her in her arms.

"Destiny?" Sergeant Barlow said softly. "I brought a friend to say hello."

The girl shifted her gaze to Scarlet. Her eyes widened, but she didn't say anything.

"Hi, Destiny. I'm—"

"I know who you are," Destiny said. "You're Veronica Collins."

"Well, I play her. My real name is Scarlet. Mind if I sit with you for a little bit?"

The girl shook her head. "That would be cool."

Scarlet stepped in front of Sergeant Barlow and pulled up one of the chairs sitting in the corner of the bay.

"I'll leave you two, if you don't mind. Need to make some calls," Barlow said, before leaving.

"How are you?" Scarlet asked.

"They think I broke my collarbone. I'm waiting to go up to X-ray. My friend Charlene is there now. She was crying. I think she got hurt bad." Destiny studied the sheet covering her lower half. She bit her lip and looked at Scarlet. "I don't know where my mom is."

Scarlet knew the girl's mom was critical. "I don't know, either. Do you have some other family?"

"My dad, but he's offshore working until the end of the week. My brother lives in Galveston. He works at a bank there. I told that policeman to call my gran. She lives in Gilmer."

The poor girl looked so terrified. "Hey, they'll call her. I bet she'll be here before you know it. Does your shoulder hurt?"

"Yeah." Destiny sniffled and tears trembled on her dark lashes. "I'm so scared. What if my mama dies or something? She looked real hurt. She was bleeding bad."

Scarlet took the girl's hand, the one that lay uninjured beside her. "It's okay to be afraid, Destiny. I'd be afraid, too. But you're not alone."

The girl nodded even as the tears fell. "Thanks for staying with me. I mean, no one is going to believe that Veronica sat with me in the hospital."

"Well, we'll prove it."

Destiny wiped her nose. "How?"

For once, Scarlet had her cell phone. Since she was a novice driver and not familiar with the East Texas roads, Rayne had forced it into her hand as she stepped out the door. Fortunate because she had Twitter on her phone.

"Let's tweet about it, using my account." Scarlet pressed the bird icon. "That will be your proof. Cool?"

Destiny smiled for the first time. "Cool."

"Now, I'm not real good with this. Should we do one of those little hash-mark things?"

"I don't know. Um, how about *#atthehospital?*"

Scarlet shook her head. "No, let's use *#destinyisawesomesauce.*"

Destiny giggled. "You're calling me awesome sauce?"

Scarlet tapped in the tweet. "You wanna see?"

Destiny nodded and Scarlet passed her the iPhone. The girl smiled at the retweets and responses from followers. "This is so cool. Oh, wait. Patrick Bailey just tweeted. OMG! He is so cute!"

Patrick was the youngest cast member. Twenty-two years old, he looked fifteen, so he played her youngest cousin. He'd been on the cover of *Tiger Beat* magazine three times since the show debuted last October. "He's funny on Twitter. Do you follow him?"

The girl shook her head. "I don't do Twitter. My mom won't let me have a phone yet."

At the mention of her mom, she lowered the device. "Do you think you could find out about my mom? I'm worried about her."

Scarlet nodded and took the phone the girl held out to her. "Of course I can. Will you be okay alone?"

Destiny nodded. Then she sniffled and dragged a thin arm across her nose.

Scarlet slipped between the two curtains and nearly stepped on Adam's foot. His gaze met hers and she knew he'd been listening. It should have offended her. It didn't.

"What are you doing here?" She retreated a step.

"I worked the wreck and followed the ambulance here after they loaded the two women into the copter."

"Oh." She rubbed her arms to chase away the sudden chill. Or maybe she felt guilty about the pleasure that welled at seeing him. "Do you know anything about her mother? She's asking."

He shook his head. "It didn't look good. She'd lost a lot of blood, but they have a good trauma team in Shreveport."

Scarlet felt her heart sink. "I told her I'd try to find out."

He took her elbow in a comforting gesture. "Let's go to the nurses' desk and see if we can sweet talk one of them into checking for us."

She allowed him to escort her toward the triage desk. Charlie wasn't in sight, but a plump brunette wearing a sequinned hair clip and holding a *WeightWatchers* magazine was.

Adam propped one elbow on the edge of the desk and leaned toward the nurse. He must have startled her, because she gasped as she reared in her chair.

He gave her a toe-curling smile. Damn. Even Scarlet felt like bowing before him and inquiring after his pleasure. "Hey, Lori." Clearly he'd checked out her name tag. "Can you do me a favor?"

The woman looked at Scarlet, then back to Adam. She visibly warmed to his smile. "What would that be?"

"The girl, Destiny. She's asking about her mother. Any way we can find out how she's doing?"

"The trauma department in Shreveport is always busy. They wouldn't bother with me." Lori glanced around as though searching for someone. "But Doc Grabel put in a call to them ten minutes ago. Let me check with him."

Adam's smile deepened, his green eyes looked warm, almost a caress. Double D-yamn. He was really good at getting women to do his bidding. To prove the point, Lori picked up the phone and punched in a number.

"Thanks, Lori," Adam said softly, with the right amount of intimacy.

He walked a few steps away. Scarlet followed. "Did I see what I think I saw?"

"What's that?"

"You hypnotized that girl into doing your bidding."

"I know how to get things done, Scarlet."

His words teased. And they heated. Which was wrong. She had come to visit an injured girl. Not play flirty games with the man who had told her that very afternoon she was the wrong kind of woman. "So I see."

He stopped smiling. "How's the girl?"

"She's terrified her mother's dead. She's hurt, but doesn't seem to care about her own injuries. I should go sit with her."

He nodded.

She turned toward that section of the E.R. Adam stopped her with one touch. "Hey, Scar?"

She looked over her shoulder at him.

"It's really decent of you to do what you're doing."

"Why wouldn't I? I may play a vampire-queen bitch on TV and I may be a drama queen in real life, but I have a heart."

Before she got too far away, Lori hung up the phone.

"Her mother is still in surgery," she said. "They'll call when she's out."

ADAM WATCHED SCARLET disappear behind the curtain, his eyes taking in every square inch of her retreating form. He hadn't expected such generosity from the beautiful actress. He'd typecast her as self-centered and shallow based on her looks and persona. He'd been wrong. And he was an ass.

His past experience with stunners like Scarlet had colored his perception. Sure, Angi and a bevy of honky-tonk heartbreakers like her had given him good reason. He'd taken one look at Scarlet with her too-high heels, glossy red lips and obvious cleavage and lumped her into a category where she didn't belong. It was a classic case of judging a book by its cover before taking time to read the pages within. And there was little doubt he wanted to read Scarlet's pages.

He just couldn't risk it.

"She's something, huh?" Barry Barlow said, sneaking up beside him.

Adam nodded. "I didn't think she would come."

"She's easy on the eyes even without that smokin'-hot catsuit and those black boots she wears on TV. If I weren't married..." Barry trailed off, leaving Adam to draw his own conclusions.

Something close to jealousy ripped through Adam. Barry was a stand-up guy—tough, fair and brimming with integrity. Yet Adam still curled his hand into a fist. He made himself relax. He had no right to be offended by the man's offhand remarks. Scarlet *was* a babe—a fact no man from age five to ninety-five could deny. "But you are."

Barry grinned. "Ellen will thank you for reminding me."

Adam managed a smile. He'd been to Barry and Ellen's a few times for barbecues. Ellen was short, feisty and liable to brain her husband for ogling another woman. "I'll collect the ten spot she owes me the next time I see her. She told me money was to be made for keeping you in line."

Barry snorted. "She would."

They stood a moment, watching an orderly roll the other girl who had been extracted from the twisted Toyota through the automatic doors of the E.R. The girl still had tears coursing down her cheeks. A young nurse walked beside her, patting her arm and murmuring comforting words.

"That was a bad one," Adam said, shaking his head. He'd seen fatalities, and though no one had died as a result of this wreck, he thought it a miracle they'd been able to pull the women and girls from the wreckage. Gasoline had poured from the logging truck's fuel tank and the smaller SUV had burst into flames seconds after the unconscious driver was cleared from the vehicle.

"I heard a few moments ago the truck driver woke

up." Barry dropped his voice. "He told another trooper he hadn't slept in over thirty hours and had fallen asleep."

"Let's hope both women pull through or he'll be facing negligent homicide." A charge like that would all but end the guy's career.

"Thanks for your help on this one. I couldn't get units dispatched from the sheriff fast enough. Glad you were close, or things could have been much different."

"No problem. I'm here anytime you need me."

"The next time we need to get someone out of a burning vehicle, you'll be at the top of our list." Barry stuck out his hand and gave Adam's a brief hard shake. "Later, Hinton."

Adam watched his friend walk out the automatic doors into the Texas twilight and wondered if he should have become a trooper. Troopers didn't build the relationships Adam had built with the citizens of Oak Stand, but they didn't have to listen to old crazies like Harvey Primm. State troopers dealt with danger and adrenaline. Not parking tickets, property disputes and dog poop.

"Chief Hinton?"

"Yeah?" Adam turned to face the desk nurse, Lori.

"We got word from Shreveport that Destiny's mother pulled through surgery. She's still critical, but alive. Do you mind delivering the news? I've got to take a bedpan to someone in the waiting room. Stomach virus."

Adam made a mental note to wash his hands. Thoroughly. "Sure."

As he approached the bay where Destiny lay, he heard the murmur of voices and paused to listen.

"And then that cute cop?" one girl said.

"Chief Hinton?" Scarlet said.

"Yeah, the guy that looks like an Abercrombie model? Well, he set me on the grass and ran back. The door was stuck and he kept pulling at it, using his foot against the side of the car and everything. I could tell things were bad, you know? 'Cause he kept looking at the ground—"

"I had blood all over my face, but I saw what he was looking at." He thought that was Destiny's voice. "I could smell it, too. It was gasoline. It freaked me out because my mom was stuck in there."

"Yeah, he'd already got my mom out from the other window," the other girl, Charlene, said.

"So then he kicked the glass out, reached in and rescued my mom. It was crazy, because a few minutes later, our car caught on fire."

He heard Scarlet's intake of breath. "Are you serious?"

"He, like, totally saved my mom's life," Destiny said. "Really cool."

Nothing was said for a moment, so he pulled back the curtain.

"Hey," Destiny said, "we were talking about you."

Scarlet glanced at him. He wondered if he detected a newfound respect in her eyes. "The girls told me about your heroics. You saved them."

"Maybe." Destiny's quietly spoken word deflated the mood.

Adam stepped inside, careful to leave the curtain slightly open. There was no family member with the girls and he didn't want to make either of them feel uncomfortable. "The desk nurse got word from Shreveport. Your mother is out of surgery and is stable."

Destiny sank against the bed with a near sob and a wince. "Oh, thank God. I— I—"

Charlene patted her hand. "See? I told you, Des, she's okay."

Destiny cried harder and Scarlet stroked the girl's bangs from her eyes. "No tears now, Destiny. This is very good news."

The girl nodded and clung hard to her friend's hand.

Scarlet met his gaze, her uncertainty obvious. Her look spoke volumes. *Do something.*

He approached the other side of the bed where the two young girls held hands and awkwardly patted Destiny's uninjured shoulder. "Ms. Rose is right. This is good news."

The girl calmed at his touch. He didn't know why. He was damned uncomfortable. He'd had no experience with teenage girls. They were like holding a loaded weapon with a hair trigger. Likely to go off at any moment.

Scarlet didn't look much more capable than he. They were both fish out of water, hoping for someone to save them. At least Scarlet had the benefit of being female.

Their gazes met, and for a moment the absolute lunacy of the situation they found themselves in struck him. He could see the same revelation in her eyes. A sort of awareness of being ill at ease with two girls who were virtual strangers and a sort of determination to put their own discomfort aside for those two frightened children. He didn't know how he knew her thoughts. He merely did.

"Destiny!"

The shriek came from the doorway.

"Gran!"

Scarlet and Adam had been saved by Gran, the rotund woman with platinum highlights and sunglasses the size of small saucers. In short order, introductions were made, thanks given and goodbyes said.

He and Scarlet slipped out of the bay and left the emergency room. He took her elbow as they headed down the main hall. “I’ll walk you to your car.”

She tugged her arm free. “I’m not sure that’s a good idea.”

“Why?”

“Because I’m feeling highly emotional right now, and you’re looking pretty damn good in my eyes. I might not keep my promise. I might toss you into my convertible, drive to the nearest motel and teach you not to go around playing the hero. It’s a real turn-on for cheap girls like me.”

The hurt in her voice gave him pause. Damn. He’d wounded her today when he told her she wasn’t the right kind of girl. Why had he said anything to her about what he’d been looking for in a woman? Why had he allowed an abstract ideal to overshadow the spectacular real person right in front of his eyes?

The florescent lighting was harsh and he knew he looked wrinkled and weary, his uniform and boots smudged with dirt. Scarlet didn’t look much better. Her dark red hair hung scraggly around a face that looked paler than normal. Her T-shirt was wrinkled and her toenail polish was chipped. And he’d never seen a woman look more desirable.

“Maybe I don’t want you to keep your promise.”

“Yes, you do.”

He stared at her. Didn’t she understand? Couldn’t she feel how much he wanted her? Couldn’t she see how the shallow version of her he’d built in his mind, the one he’d been clinging to, had crumbled, leaving a woman who was so lovable it scared him?

She brushed her bangs from her eyes. "This afternoon you were quite clear about the type of woman you want."

He didn't respond.

She gave him a slow, sad smile. "And I'm not that woman." She walked away.

He didn't follow. Why should he? He'd hurt her and misjudged her...and she was right. No matter how much he wished she was the right girl for him, she wasn't a realistic candidate for wife or girlfriend. She wasn't sticking around Oak Stand to make him pork chops, sit on a pew at Oak Stand Methodist with him or pick out trim colors for his shutters.

There was no future with Scarlet Rose.

Scarlet might be Ms. Right Now.

But she would never truly be Mrs. Right.

CHAPTER THIRTEEN

"WE DON'T WANT to do those exercises again. They're stupid," Marco said, dropping into one of the chairs gathered around the communal area of Phoenix, as if he were a sack of grain. He dared her to challenge him.

Scarlet pushed up the sleeves on the navy shirt she'd found at the only dress shop in Oak Stand. It was loose and blousy. She felt like her grandmother Rose. She might as well have worn horn-rimmed glasses and Daniel Green gold lamé slippers. "Then don't. Sit there and be a prop."

She surveyed the other five men still standing before her. They were a motley group. One, Juan, was whip-thin and sallow, with amateur tats covering both arms. Julio was plump and ill-tempered. Tito had yet to speak. There were two Miguels. Miguel I talked too much, yammering innuendos about her in Spanish and making inappropriate gestures. Miguel II made the kissing faces. She didn't like the Miguels.

Marco was the only one with real potential. And the only one who refused to participate at all.

"Okay, then," she said, looking at the clipboard she held. Nothing much on it, but it gave her the feeling of a security blanket. As though it would give her a veneer of professionalism. Make her look as if she knew what the hell she was doing. Jewish grannies were so much easier. At least they had wanted to be in her acting class. "Let's start with a stretch. We're going to be using the Meisner technique for acting, which is essentially focusing on the truth of the moment."

"Yo, let's do some moments from *Going Down on Mr. Brown.* That's my favorite movie," Miguel I said, sliding a sly smile her way. "I'll play Mr. Brown."

"Fine, your friend Mr.—" she scanned the names on her list "—Jaurez can act with you."

Several of the guys laughed.

"Yo, I ain't no homo," Miguel I said. He moved away from her, his posturing defensive.

"I believe there are rules here regarding the use of derogatory language, Mr. Rodriguez. That's inappropriate."

"So?" He crossed his arms. "What you gonna do about it? Spank me?"

"No, but I might load you in my squad car, take you to the next county and beat the crap out of you." The new voice came from the doorway.

All heads swiveled to where Adam stood. He wasn't wearing his uniform—wore jeans and a short-sleeved shirt instead—but his authority couldn't be questioned. It had been several days since she'd seen him. Since she'd left him in the hospital hallway, looking confused and hungry. Walking away had been a smart move because, regardless of whatever attraction sparked between them, Adam was right. They were nothing but Police Chief and Crazy Actress on Probation.

The room grew still; the air taut.

Scarlet watched the former gang members. They didn't like Adam. They looked wary. Hunted. Perhaps even scared.

Marco broke the silence with a nervous chuckle. *"Ay viene la jura."*

"Yeah, the cop is here," Adam said, closing the front door behind him. "And I'd hate to have to bust some heads."

"He's kidding," Scarlet said, waving Adam into the area she'd created to serve as their stage. She was surprised he'd shown up. She'd half expected him to bail. She'd forgotten that he was a man of his word.

"No, I'm not. Ms. Rose is performing community service. Key word *service.* She's giving her time and expertise to you and deserves your respect."

Marco leaned forward. "Yo. She wouldn't be here if she didn't have to."

"Yo. Doesn't matter." Adam's gaze flickered over the group with a toughness Scarlet hadn't seen before. "She's a lady, she's a professional and she's here to instruct you."

Everyone was on edge. Wasn't the ideal environment to encourage opening up. She needed to break the ice. Bring the focus back on the art of acting, not the differences between the gang members and the sexy lawman standing alert beside her.

"Well, thanks, Chief Hinton, for setting everyone straight. These guys are very new to acting and it's hard to summon up enthusiasm for something unfamiliar." She directed her next words to the guys. "And this is the reason Chief Hinton is here."

Marco snorted. "Yeah, he's here to harass a bunch of chunties. That's what cops do in their spare time."

"Derogatory." Scarlet wagged her finger at Marco. "The chief is here to be a guinea pig for the evening."

Adam shook his head. "Not a pig."

The guys laughed and the mood lightened with Adam's jest.

She joined the laughter. "Okay, not a pig. An example. I thought if you could see someone like the chief setting aside his reservations, it might be easier for you to do the same."

"Why would we do that?" Tito asked.

Huh. So apparently he wasn't mute.

"Because Chief Hinton is a leader in this community, much like some of you may be one day."

"Who wants to be a *sucio cochon?*" Miquel II sneered.

"No one like you." Adam's stare was hard, his eyes flinty, unyielding. "Rick has rules. Follow them."

"Okay. Um, stretches." That sounded a bit lame, but she needed to get them to focus on something other than a who's-tougher-than-you contest. "Let's warm up our bodies."

Scarlet led them through a series of stretches. The guys complied with little enthusiasm but they followed her instructions.

"Now, we're going to do a repetition exercise. In this exercise one person makes an observation about his or her partner. For example, one may say, 'You look happy,' or 'You look sad.' Then the other person will respond in the same way. You use the phrase to bounce off the other person and try to garner nuances in the other person's character. The goal is to establish a bond and, through the bond, to allow a moment to be created that catches the actors and transports them to a more truthful existence. So, essentially, though actors take direction, all actors strive to achieve this truthfulness."

She looked at Adam. He looked uncertain. And uncomfortable. He wasn't the only one—the other guys looked as though she'd asked them to recite an entire encyclopedia.

"It's not hard. I'll demonstrate with Chief Hinton."

She waved Adam over. "Now, come stand next to me and pretend we are alone."

He arched an eyebrow. She could almost hear his thoughts. *You sure you want to do that?*

She repeated the gesture and added the tiniest of frowns as extra incentive. She needed his help. Needed him to treat what they were about to do seriously.

"Okay, would you like to comment on me? Or shall I start?"

"I'll comment on you, *gringita.*" Miguel I snickered.

Adam's responding glare caused Miguel I to drop the hand he'd held up to Miguel II for a high five.

"I'll start," Adam said, turning to meet her gaze. "You look nervous."

"*You* look nervous," she replied, with a slight bob of her head.

"But you *look* nervous," he said, emphasizing her twisted fingers.

She shrugged. "You look nervous."

"I'm not nervous. I'm irritated."

He'd veered off course. The focus was on reading each other's external and internal cues. He now conversed. Not part of the exercise, but she would keep things a little loose with this crowd.

"I'm nervous because this is important to me," Scarlet said. "You look...uncomfortable."

"Not really, but I don't want to do this."

"Why not?"

"Because I feel stupid." His gaze flickered to the men watching them. Someone laughed.

"It's not stupid to want to keep the mask you wear for the world to see in place. More like it's stupid not to get real with yourself. Are you being real with yourself?"

"No. Are you being real with yourself?"

She hesitated. "No."

His gaze probed hers, creating a cocoon of intimacy. It was as if the men in the room had disappeared. It was only Adam and Scarlet. She could feel the magic start. The tentative bond form. But it was more than acting. "So why can't you be real?" she asked.

"Because being real could get me into trouble. It could cause me to lose everything I've worked for. If I follow what I want, I'll trample my honor. I'd hate myself if I became that man. A man like my father, who takes what he wants and forgets consequences."

Scarlet tilted her head. She couldn't believe how easily he'd shed his reservations. His words were genuine. And now she knew something more about him. His hang-ups had to do with his father.

He closed his eyes for a moment. Then opened them. "So why can't you be real?"

The expression in his eyes was soft, like the sticky sweetness of new spring growth. She knew he wanted her. Knew that if he could put away his convictions, they would end up in a tangle of limbs, sated from marathon sex. But Adam did have a conscience. He wanted to do what was right. And he wanted an ideal fantasy woman. A woman she'd never be. She stepped closer to him. "I can't be real, because I'm afraid. I'm afraid to surrender a burden I've carried for a long time. This hurt has been my constant companion. I'm used to it."

"Burdens sometimes refuse to leave us."

She wanted to shutter herself from him, but the moment wouldn't let her. "I don't know how to make it go away."

"You have to want to move forward." His voice was

as soft as his gaze, like the stroke of a mother's hand on her newborn's back.

"Maybe. But moving forward means letting go of something I thought I wanted. Someone I thought I loved." Suddenly emotion overwhelmed her. Tears hovered in the back of her throat, making her voice husky.

Adam moved closer. "You can't be afraid. And you can't make love work with someone who doesn't want it to work. Can't build something on sand. It'll crumble and fall apart. Sometimes you can't fix it. You have to walk away."

Scarlet nodded, reaching for the necklace that was no longer there. Her fingers brushed her chest and dropped. Adam picked up her hand and squeezed it. "So walk away from what can't be fixed. Move toward someone new. Someone worthy of your love. Move toward—"

"This is some serious shit," Marco called out, breaking the bond Scarlet had created with Adam.

She blinked and focused her attention on Marco. "You're not supposed to interrupt."

"Oops. My bad," Marco said, looking around at the other guys sitting around him. A few of them looked annoyed. Tito frowned.

Adam stiffened beside her. What had he been about to say? Move toward…him? With all defenses, all the restrictions and rules, stripped away, maybe deep down inside that was his true desire. Something awakened in her at that thought. What if this thing between them was more than sexual attraction? What if there was some cosmic force at work, drawing them together, creating bonds, tugging them toward each other until there was no other recourse? Until they both accepted everything that had happened thus far had happened to push them together.

The thought paralyzed her, so she tucked it in the recesses of her mind.

Adam looked extremely ill at ease. As in, forgot-his-pants-this-morning uncomfortable.

"Apology accepted," Scarlet said to Marco. "But that's a good point. Things can get deep when you do a repetition exercise. Allow yourself to get caught up, as Chief Hinton and I did. This is not therapy, but tapping into the truth of the moment. If you are given a scene of about a murder, you must be truthful under imaginary circumstances. If you have not had a person close to you murdered, you can still allow yourself to feel what a person who has would feel."

"What if you've had a friend murdered? Right in front of you," Juan said. Anger laced his words. Real emotion. Not fabricated.

"Then you already know, don't you? You know what it feels like. You won't have to dig deep to feel angry, lost, desperate for revenge," Scarlet said.

"No, I won't," Juan said.

"But remember, this is an acting class. We will use repetition exercises to bond us to our partner. You may say, 'You look angry,' but you can't act on it."

"Why not?" Tito asked, "We're in acting class."

"Because you can't," Adam said.

Scarlet sighed. This wasn't going how she'd planned. She'd studied Meisner for years, adapting some of the legendary drama teacher's techniques, fusing them with some of her own. She gave leeway, but she didn't want too much flowing between guys who might have grudges against one another. "Let's try something different."

The guys gave her their full attention.

"I ended up in here because I stupidly refused to leave the scene of a protest."

Adam arched an eyebrow.

"Okay, fine. I handcuffed myself to a flagpole, but what's important is I took a stand on an issue I feel strongly about—censorship."

"What's that mean?" Julio asked, scooting his folding chair closer.

She explained a little about the children's book and the reactions in the community about such books, citing the Harry Potter books as another example of debate over what children should be able to read. Then she told them her thoughts. "I want to get copies of the book for each of you to read."

"Aw, man. That's like homework," Marco complained.

"Well, if you don't want to read it, then don't," Scarlet said. "But I thought we might focus on a few scenes from the book and work up a sort of screenplay. Any of you like to write?"

Six blank stares met her query.

"Okay, I'll work up the scenes. Then we can use some of the emotions you delve into tonight to portray what happens in that book. Any objections?"

More blank stares.

"Can we act them out in front of Ms. Cox?" Julio asked. "She'd like that. She likes books and stuff."

"Who is Ms. Cox?"

"Our teacher," Tito said.

"Of course. That's a great idea. And we can invite Rick and Kate, too. Maybe a few other members of the community who protested the removal of the book."

"I don't know about standing up and acting out shit," Juan said, looking more like a kid than a gang member.

"I won't force you, but I bet you'll like it." She reminded herself that, as tough as these guys were, most of them were little more than kids. "Let's take it slow. I've got three weeks to spend with you and you'd be amazed at what we can accomplish in that time. We could make it our last performance. Maybe even put up signs and charge a small admission fee."

"And have, like, cakes and punch afterward," Tito said, his expression showing a smidgen of excitement. "My grammar school did that one time. It was cool."

Marco shrugged. "Whatever. Let's get this over with. I want to watch TV before lights-out."

Scarlet looked at Adam. He'd remained silent but attentive during the discussion. Unlike the center's clients who all wore gray, black or white—no hint of gang colors was allowed—Adam wore a deep green button-down shirt that enhanced his eyes, making them more prominent against his tanned skin.

He gave her an encouraging nod. "Sounds like a nice conclusion to this class."

"Would you like to participate? Maybe do a scene or two with us?" Scarlet asked, hoping he might agree. She knew she'd gotten him here tonight by appealing to his sense of duty, his need to make some tenuous connection with the clients of the center, but maybe—

"I don't think so. This is your thing. I came tonight for moral support as your—"

"*Jura* can't hang with *la mara,*" Miguel II said. "We don't need him."

"What do you mean I can't *hang* with you? You still in a gang? You still breaking the law?" Adam crossed his arms. He didn't seem defensive, merely inquisitive.

"No, dude," Marco said, sinking into his chair. "But it would be *majareta* to do that. Crazy, man."

Adam gestured between himself and Marco. "It's crazy for me and you to be in a play together?"

"Sí," Tito said.

Adam looked at her. "Well, in that case, count me in. I've learned that if someone doesn't want you around, there's usually a good reason. I'd like to find out what that reason is."

"Dude, we ain't doing nothin' wrong. We're in this program. Doin' what it takes," Marco said. His muscular shoulders bunched beneath the white Phoenix T-shirt he wore, his posturing defensive, angry. It struck Scarlet at that moment that while these guys were scared boys, they were also dangerous. They'd seen and done things she could only imagine. It would make for interesting acting.

"Again, we're off task," she said. "Chief Hinton can join us for a couple of scenes. I see nothing wrong with trying to improve community relations with the authorities. I'll stop by tomorrow and talk to Kate and Rick about what we're doing. I might even visit my first drama teacher, Mrs. Nolan, to see if she might be interested in helping with the production."

Adam nodded, but didn't move. Marco shrugged and the other guys followed suit.

"Good, now pair off for the repetition exercises. Just don't leave this room."

As the clients paired off, Scarlet motioned Adam toward the door. He gave a perfunctory glance about the room as the guys started the exercise with comments such as "You look like a dog's ass," then followed her to the door.

Scarlet stepped onto the porch and clasped her hands behind her back. "I wanted to thank you for coming tonight. I know it was—"

"No problem."

"Don't interrupt me. I'm trying to be—"

"And you are dressed more appropriately," he said.

She considered the blousy navy shirt and loose cargo pants she'd borrowed from Meg. She looked stupid, unattractive and fashion-challenged. "If you want to call this atrocity to the eyes appropriate. I'll be lucky not to end up in the back of the *US* magazine in the What Not to Wear section."

He shrugged. "It's got more mystery. Makes a guy wonder what you're hiding underneath there."

"That sounds like something a father might say," Scarlet groused. "Just not my father. He never gave a flip what I wore out."

"Well, maybe it would be best if I stuck closer to that kind of role with you. I'm your probation officer, after all."

All her earlier thoughts about *meant to be* and fate pushing her in his direction came back to her, and she realized she'd been fooled by the honest moment between them. She and Adam weren't on some crazy karma ride. Hadn't he basically told her he wanted to sleep with her, but wouldn't? Hadn't he basically said she wasn't the type of girl he wanted in his life?

Her focus should be on serving her time in Oak Stand and getting gone. She needed to get back to her life.

After all, she still loved John, didn't she?

Adam Hinton was nothing more than a Podunk police chief. She couldn't have a future with him, could she?

Yes answered one question and no answered the other. But she wasn't certain which question.

Damn.

She shouldn't have encouraged Adam to be involved

in the play. That was hardly the way to get the distance from him she needed.

But when her gaze encountered the hunger in his, distance was the last thing on her mind. Adam could say whatever he wished. She could protest, pretend and preach all she wanted about her past relationship and her lack of desire for a future one.

But something rare bloomed between her and Adam.

It was lust.

And it was more than that, too.

Which put Adam and her between a rock and a hard place.

There could be no funny stuff between them.

"What has changed between us?" she asked, then answered. "Nothing."

He didn't say anything.

"We are still two people, attracted to one another, who won't do anything about it for good reason. You're not my daddy, you're not my friend and you're damn sure not my lover. You're exactly what you said you are—my probation officer."

"You're wrong," he said. "I am your friend."

"Maybe. But it doesn't feel quite that way. I don't think about my friends this way. This feels different."

He stared at her and she couldn't read his expression.

"I want to get this over with so I can move on with my life. I'm sure you want the same." She entered the center and shut the door behind her, wishing it was as easy to shut out her thoughts.

Obviously fate cared nothing for her wishes.

CHAPTER FOURTEEN

ADAM FLIPPED ON THE RADIO as he started down the driveway of Phoenix House. Bob Seger's haunting melody about life on the road filled the car, complementing the stickiness of the night. Dusk had given way to full night and a velvet sky full of stars winked above. As he turned onto the road, the beams of the headlights caught a dark shape hidden behind a screen of pampas grass.

What the hell?

Adam slowed the cruiser and inched past the grass. He stopped, put the cruiser in Park and eased from the car.

The shape moved.

Fast.

It was a man. A man who loped toward a car parked in the entrance to the pasture across from Phoenix.

"Hey," Adam called. "Stop!"

The figure kept going, scrambling toward the dark sedan.

"Ah, hell." Adam ran after the man. Nothing pissed him off more. He hated to chase suspects down on foot. Especially over uneven ground on a dark night.

The man had just reached the car when Adam slammed into him like a linebacker.

"Oomph!" The air went out of the man. Adam immediately shoved him, facedown, near a rainwater-filled ditch, pressing his head into the mud.

"Okay, okay!" the man yelled as Adam reached for the cuffs he didn't have in his back pocket. He'd nearly forgotten he wasn't in uniform.

He flipped the man over and cocked his fist.

"I give up," the man cried when he saw Adam poised to deck him.

"Who the hell are you and what are you doing lurking in the bushes?"

"I'm Chris Miller." The guy winced and turned his face away from Adam.

"What are you doing here?"

"Just trying to get a picture, dude."

"A picture?"

The man pointed toward his car. "My camera's over there. Somewhere. Hell, I hope it's not broken."

The man was a reporter. Adam stood and pulled him up by the collar of his shirt. "You're a reporter?"

"Nah. I'm a photographer. Paparazzi, you know?"

"Paparazzi?"

"What are you? Stupid? I get paid for taking pictures of celebrities. Get it?" The little man tugged at his collar and dusted at his jeans. His upper lip held a slight sneer.

"Don't be a smart-ass. I know what paparazzi are. I also know you're trespassing."

The man adjusted the glasses that had slid down his nose during his takedown. "I wasn't hurting nobody. Just tryin' to feed my family, you know? I have to do what I have to do."

"What you have to do is get in your car and get your ass out of here."

"I will as soon as I get a picture of Scarlet Rose with her gang members. The editor of *Star International* wants one for his articles on celebs and community service. I drew the straw."

"The hell you will," Adam snarled. "Get in your car and leave."

Chris's eyes narrowed. "I noticed you were all chummy with the starlet. You got something going on with her? Something you're trying to hide?"

"Of course not."

"Hmm. I wonder. You look guilty. She's a fine piece of ass. I don't blame you, brother."

"Look, you piece of filth, Scarlet Rose is serving a sentence and I'm the chief of police. Nothing is going on between us. Now, pack your raggedy ass up and get out of my town."

"This—" Miller extended one finger in the air and made a circle "—ain't your town. And I don't have to go anywhere. It's a free country."

Adam bit down on the impulse to say "Not really," the way he had to Scarlet over a week ago. Instead, he gave the squirrelly photographer a sneer. "I feel certain I speak for Sheriff Lee and Rick Mendez when I tell you to pack up and get the hell out of here. Or I can make a call and they can do it for you. Leave Scarlet and this facility alone. She is serving her sentence and nothing inappropriate has occurred between her and me or any other member of the community. You're barking up the wrong tree, *brother*."

Miller shrugged. "I see smoke. And where there's smoke there's usually a fire. Bet a fire with her would burn a man up."

Deep anger seared Adam's gut. His fist flexed. He wanted to beat the ever-loving hell out of the man but couldn't allow himself the pleasure. Plus, the piece of garbage had sniffed out what he knew to be true.

Adam did want Scarlet to strike him like a match struck against sandpaper. To burn out of control with her.

"Think it over, Chief. I can get you big bucks if you give me a story on her. On what she's like between the sheets."

"You little sack of shit."

"Go ahead. Punch me. We can add a lawsuit to the story of you bopping the vampire queen."

"You're not worth the time. Get out of here before I teach you a lesson in manners."

Miller picked up the camera that had fallen near the tire, then opened the car door. "You know, you may want to be more worried about that creepy dude who's been following Scarlet around."

"What creepy dude?"

"That old dude who got the book tossed out."

"Harvey Primm?" Adam had seen Harvey hold fast to a grudge, something that usually resulted in the offending person ending up in his sham of a paper. But stalking seemed extreme, even for him. Of course, Scarlet had injured his pride, had embarrassed him in the national news.

Miller climbed into the car and cranked the engine. "Yeah, that's the dude. I saw him earlier. He's freaky. Me? You got nothing to worry about. I take a pic and then I'm gone."

"So go," Adam said.

Miller drove away, leaving Adam to mull over what he'd learned. Harvey's visit to the station to complain about Scarlet following him hadn't set right with Adam, but he hadn't given it any more thought. So why was Harvey spying on Scarlet? Had he become obsessed with her? Or was it something more dangerous? Some kind of revenge because she had embarrassed him?

Adam walked to the cruiser, taking a moment to look hard at the landscape around him. Phoenix sat miles outside Oak Stand. The nearest house was Cottonwood, an estate owned by Rick's father-in-law. In fact, the land the rehab center sat upon had been part of Justus Mitchell's vast property before Justus deeded it to the foundation for which Rick and Kate served as directors. They lived in a smaller rustic cottage that sat adjacent to the center, but no one else lived within miles of the place. The only consolation Adam could find in the situation was that Scarlet's class contained six street-savvy, tough gang members who wouldn't hesitate to protect their acting coach.

Suddenly he was very glad he'd decided to be a part of their production. Acting had never interested him, but that insinuation that he didn't need to participate had him throwing his hat into the ring. Adam hated being told he couldn't do something.

Which was how he had ended up a police officer in the first place.

Years ago over breakfast with his parents, he'd mentioned law enforcement as a possible career. He'd been fresh out of college and without any direction career-wise.

"Absolutely not," his mother had said, spearing a grape with her fruit fork. "I won't have a son who is a police officer. Can you imagine, Hal?" She'd said *police officer* as if being an enforcer of the law was cousin to the crap she scraped from her mare's hoof when she came in from riding.

His father had smiled. "Not a bad way to earn a living, son, but you really don't need to earn a living, now do you? I thought we'd agreed upon law school."

Adam shoved his empty plate away. Marta immediately cleared it and refilled his coffee cup before his father waved her away from the terrace where they often had breakfast on Sunday mornings. "That will be all, Marta. Have Thomas bring the car around in forty minutes. We'll be attending church this morning."

The maid nodded, then melted away inside the house.

"I don't want to go to law school," Adam said.

"Hinton men always go to law school, darling," his mother said. "Then you could get your MBA as your father has done. Very useful for when you take over the companies. Your father can't very well work forever."

"Who said I was taking over?" Adam asked, raising his voice. Having finished his undergrad at Texas A&M University, he had no intention of applying for law school. He wanted to go to the police academy. Get a regular job. Be a regular guy. He wanted to take scissors to his custom-made suits, slice the polo guy off all his golf shirts, toss the keys to his Benz in the ornamental fountain filled with Japanese carp.

His father frowned. "You want to sow some oats? Fine. Go to Europe for the summer. Backpack and do whatever it is your friends do. When you come back, you'll be ready to start. I've already sent your application in to Tulane, Stanford and Harvard. I even sent one to Rice for the MBA program."

Adam shoved his chair back and stood. "I don't want to go to Europe, I don't want to go to law school and I don't want to live here any longer."

"Darling," his mother said in the same syrupy voice she'd used on his father for years. The voice that accepted the way her life was, the voice that forgave the incessantly philandering husband as easily as it forgave the maid who'd burned a hole in her favorite designer suit. Placating, accepting…whiny. "You can't be serious. A police officer? Really, what—"

"Would the ladies at the club say?" Adam finished for her. "Maybe they would say I got a clue. That I broke away from this farce of a life. That I did something that *I* wanted to do for once in my pitiful existence."

His father's eyes grew cold. "If you go to that academy, you will be cut off without a dime. Think hard about it, son."

Adam threw down his fifty-dollar linen napkin. "I have. I'm leaving for the academy on Monday. And I don't need your money. I have a trust fund Grandfather was smart enough to give me control over when I turned twenty-two last year. I can live comfortably off the interest."

He'd stalked away—nearly knocking poor Marta down on the way—to his room to pack. No one told him what to do. No one.

Ten years later, and that outlook still held true. Pride had always been his downfall.

He climbed back into the idling cruiser, thinking about not having what he wanted. He wanted Scarlet. The way he'd once wanted Angi. He'd met his ex-wife four years ago at a bar in Tomball when he'd gone out to celebrate his partner's birthday. She'd been half-drunk and smoking-hot. All the guys had made a play for her, but she had eyes for Adam. They'd dated for two blissful months. Then she'd gotten pregnant.

Maybe not getting what he wanted was a good thing. Angi, the miscarriage, his father's meddling in his affair—all had led him to the breaking point.

So what would Scarlet lead to?

If he could have her. Which he couldn't.

But how in the hell would he resist her? When she was so deliciously forbidden to him?

Maybe the answer lay with Sophie Waters. Maybe his date with the very appropriate mayor's daughter would straighten him out. Maybe hanging around the right kind of woman, the type of woman who could be his future, would purge him of these crazy urges. Maybe he needed exposure to good women to cure him of wanting inappropriate women. And there was nothing inappropriate about Sophie. She was exactly the kind of girl he needed to date.

And exactly the kind of girl he didn't want.

He watched one of the best examples of the exact kind he craved walk down the steps of Phoenix and climb into her convertible She hadn't bothered to even check the area around her. A deranged madman could have jumped her and made off with her as easily as a knife slid through hot butter.

He needed to have a talk with Scarlet. In a strictly official capacity. He'd tell her to exercise caution, pay attention to what was happening around her. And, yeah, there would be a little warning for himself.

SCARLET CLOSED THE DOOR to her room at Serendipity Inn and fell across her bed with a deep sigh.

Teaching the gang members at Phoenix sucked.

It wasn't as if they didn't have potential.

On the contrary, their lives on the street had given them plenty of varied, if not a little scary, experiences to pull from their acting closets. It was the emotional toll that had her topsy-turvy. Throw the sexy police chief in the mix, and she was like a swimmer tossed in the middle of a stormy sea. Very tired. Very waterlogged. And very uncertain about her fate.

The door to her room flung open, scaring her.

"Aunt Scarlet!" Henry cried. "Check out my progress report!" He landed beside her on the bed and waggled a yellow piece of paper in front of her eyes.

She squinted in the dimness of the room, trying to distinguish the writing. "Get the light, will you?"

Henry switched on the bedside lamp and sat beside her like a puppy awaiting a treat.

"Five A's and two B's. Most excellent!" Scarlet gave him a high five.

"So what are you going to give me for them?" Henry asked, picking at a scab on his forearm.

"Stop," Scarlet said, knocking his fingers away from the sore. "Why do I have to give you something?"

Henry looked shocked. "Because you're supposed to. Those are *good* grades."

Scarlet rolled her eyes. "This isn't a report card. It's a progress report. Shouldn't you be satisfied with getting a good grade?"

"Well, yeah, but I thought it was at least worth something. Like an ice cream." Henry dropped his head then snuck a peek under his lashes at her. His cuteness was a pistol to her temple.

"Okay, okay. Maybe a hot-fudge sundae from the Dairy Barn."

"Yay!" Henry bounced up and down on her bed.

"Stop, before I get seasick." Scarlet laughed, tugging her nephew into a headlock and giving him a noogie. "We'll go tomorrow after I film my audition."

"What are you auditioning for?"

"Nothing you need to worry about." Wasn't as if she could teach him about bisexual hookers. Yeah, that would be a little hard to explain to the sister who had pulled strings to get her an appointment with a production company in Shreveport. She would head over tomorrow to film her audition and be back before lunch. "Hey, kick your shoes off."

Henry's sneakers were caked with dirt and had already marred the perfection of the white chenille spread.

"'Kay," Henry said, toeing them off. An unholy smell filled the room.

"Good heavens, Henry. Put them back on," she cried, holding her nose.

Henry laughed like a deranged clown. And then he farted.

"Out!" Scarlet commanded, launching herself from the bed and pointing her nephew out the door. He complied, but not before farting again. "Henry!"

Brent appeared at the door. "What smells so bad in here?"

"Me!" Henry yelled before disappearing around the corner.

"Phew," Brent said, wrinkling his nose. "Rayne shouldn't have let him eat those black beans with the quesadillas tonight."

"Here, give him back his nasty shoes." She pinched the back of the tennis shoes and handed them to Brent.

He took them but didn't look happy doing it. "Hey, some guy called today. I told him to try your cell phone, but he said you never check your messages."

Only one person had teased her about that. "Who was it?"

Brent shrugged. "He didn't leave a name, but caller ID said Hammerstein. No first name."

John.

Scarlet's heart skipped a beat. How had he tracked her down to Serendipity? Duh. She'd been all over the news and John knew who her sister was. Wouldn't take a rocket scientist to figure out she was holed up at Serendipity Inn. "Oh, yeah. He's an old friend."

"Wouldn't be John Hammerstein, would it? The actor?"

"Um, yeah." Scarlet averted her eyes. She didn't want Brent to see the truth. He was intuitive—a trait she'd missed in him many years ago, mostly because her first impression of him was that he was a pure man-whore.

"What do you think he wanted?"

"What does any man want?"

Brent lifted his eyebrows. "Wow. You and Hammerstein, huh? He's like, what? Twenty or thirty years older than you?"

Scarlet bristled. "We're not together. Just old friends."

Brent grinned. "Stress on the *old* part, right?"

Aggravation flashed inside Scarlet. Yeah, John was older. Salt-and-pepper hair, white at the temples, craggy good looks, lean, only slightly paunchy in the middle. He had been more than capable in bed. *Old* was not a word she'd ever ascribed to John.

"That's none of your business. Did he leave a number?"

Brent stopped smiling. "Wait. This man, did he hurt you?"

Scarlet swallowed and tried not to look guilty. "We had a relationship of sorts. A mentorship, so to speak. We had a disagreement, and I haven't heard from him in well over a year. Just surprised me."

Her new brother-in-law didn't look convinced, but neither did he probe further. "Check your cell phone. Maybe he called you on it. By the way, Rayne left dinner for you in the fridge. Some kind of cold soup she cooked on her first segment."

"I don't get quesadillas like Henry?"

"She makes her quesadillas with goat cheese."

"Soup it is. Then I'll call it a night."

Brent tromped off to do lord only knew what. Probably watch a ball game or read on the toilet or other guylike activities, and Scarlet was left to wonder why her ex-lover had called. Was it because he'd seen the news? Was it something more?

Maybe she didn't want to know.

Maybe she did.

She pulled her cell phone from the drawer she'd dumped it in. Most actors clung to them like holy grails, but Scarlet considered them to be rather crippling. She didn't have to play Angry Birds while she waited in a grocery line and she didn't have to check her email every hour. She hated seeing everyone walking around looking at a stupid device. What was wrong with talking to an actual person?

Of course, it had come in handy with Destiny.

So, they had their uses.

She pressed the button that lit the screen. John had called but had not bothered with a message. She allowed her finger to hover over the little telephone icon. Should she call him back and see what he wanted?

No. If he wanted her to return the call, he would have left a message. So why hadn't he?

She flopped back on the bed, deciding against food, and wondering why she hadn't thought about John in days. For the past year, she'd allowed him to trickle into her thoughts the moments before she closed her eyes at night and those sleep-soaked moments when she awoke. For the past week, she'd had Adam on the brain. Not John.

Strange.

It was as if losing her necklace had allowed her to empty out the hurt and open herself to something more…something like the serious police chief who hid a dazzling smile and totally hot body beneath his starched shirts.

She yawned and tucked her head against her folded forearms.

Too bad she had to keep her hands off him. She really wanted to find out how he felt beneath her touch. Longed to see those clear eyes cloud with passion, those straight white teeth nip—

She yawned again.

Did this mean she was officially over John?

She was pretty sure she was, but was she falling for Adam? Maybe. Falling in love would be a huge mistake. Texas-size mistake. But could she stop herself?

Maybe she'd think about all these things later.

Like her namesake, she'd think about it tomorrow.

CHAPTER FIFTEEN

"SCARLET!"

The voice penetrated the fogginess of her consciousness. She was at Disney World, watching Cinderella dance with the big character who wore the tiny green hat. She had been pointing out where her Japanese tour group could buy cotton candy before they boarded the tour bus. Her plane would leave in thirty minutes, but she still had to ride the water ride that took her through Norway. And she wanted cotton candy.

"Scarlet!" The sound of knocking succeeded in waking her.

Scarlet sat up and rubbed a hand over her face. Where was she? Oh. Yeah. Her aunt's inn. Oak Stand. "What?"

"Open the door," Rayne called with another insistent knock.

She slipped off the bed, twisted the lock and threw the door open. The harsh light of the hallway had her blinking. "What?"

"Oh, you were asleep."

"Crown you Queen of Obvious," Scarlet grumbled.

"Sorry to wake you. Adam is downstairs. He wants to talk to you."

Scarlet's stomach tripped. Adam. Hadn't she just dreamed about him? No. It was Disney World. "What does he want?"

"I don't know. He seemed kind of pushy about it. Want me to tell him you'll call tomorrow morning?"

She shook her head. Her ponytail felt lopsided and her mouth thick with sleep. She may have even drooled on the Battenberg lace throw pillows. "Give me a minute and I'll be down."

After she brushed her hair, scrubbed her teeth and smoothed out the ugly navy top, she headed down the stairs. No one was in the foyer, but she heard voices from the family den.

"Okay, I'm up. What's the emergency, Chief?"

Adam looked up from the leather sectional where he sat beside Henry, who had fallen asleep reading a sports magazine. Brent munched on popcorn and watched soccer on TV.

"No emergency, but I would like to have a word with you, if that's okay?" As usual, Adam's question wasn't really a question. It was a command.

Brent didn't look away from the television.

"You mean, privately?" Scarlet asked, wondering if it were a good idea spending any time alone with Adam. She didn't trust herself around him, because he crushed her good intentions under the boot of his colossal sexiness.

He glanced at Henry. "That would be best."

"Let's go out back."

They wound through the kitchen, where Rayne stood at the stove, focused on whatever was in the saucepan. She merely grunted when Scarlet told her they were going outside. Scarlet pushed through the screen door her aunt had insisted on keeping when her sister had overhauled the inn that past spring.

The moon hung low, barely a sliver in the deepening darkness. Bright stars laced the inky night like fireflies woven in a tapestry. Crickets chirruped and a thick humidity settled around them like a cloak. It was intimate, sticky and seductive. Not what she needed.

"So?" She settled on the second step from the bottom.

"Nice night," he said, avoiding her question. He crossed the flagstone pavers, crushing the herbs planted in between with his cowboy boots and releasing their scent. Beneath a recently planted weeping willow was a cedar swing, polished and framed by iron scrollwork. He sat on it.

She cocked her head. "Did you come to pontificate upon the weather or was there another reason?"

"You're grumpy when you wake up."

"Most people are. Who jumps out of bed crapping sunshine?" she snapped. The man showed up at 9:45 p.m. and wanted to trade civilities?

She had every reason to be ill-tempered. His life hadn't turned sideways and bassackward. He wasn't serving a probation sentence under someone he wanted to knock boots with. He hadn't received a phone call from a former lover…one he hadn't heard from in over a year. And he wasn't teaching ex-gang members how to find truth in their characterization of a damn blackbird. Scarlet felt as if she'd been tugged into an alternate universe. And it made a girl cranky.

"So nicely stated," he muttered, setting the swing into motion.

"So sue me. I'm not a happy camper when someone wakes me up and doesn't tell me why he bothered to pull me out of bed."

She closed her mouth because the look Adam gave her could cook bacon. It was that damned sizzling. Must have been her mentioning getting out of bed. She frowned the prickle of awareness away and concentrated on the fact she'd rather be in bed. Alone. At least that's what she told herself.

He cleared his throat. "Right. I came by to discuss the weather. How astute of you."

"Okay. Sorry."

"First, I want to apologize for making things difficult for you. I've tried hard to ignore whatever this is between us. I know it's made—"

"You didn't have to come by to say that again. Haven't we had this conversation a bazillion times? We know the score. So—"

"Yeah, we do." He took a deep breath. "Actually, I came by because you have a few crazy fans."

"I have more than a few. Last time I checked my Twitter account had close to half a million followers." She wasn't arrogant. People followed her on Twitter and Facebook. She didn't know why. She rarely posted anything remotely interesting. She couldn't figure out people's fascination with knowing things like what other people had for dinner or how many times their dog had chewed a shoe.

"Yes, but these are more up close and personal."

"What do you mean?" She hadn't told him about Harvey Primm lurking in the bushes. She'd nearly forgotten about the loony bird of a deacon.

"I caught a photographer waiting to snap a pic of you with the gang members at Phoenix. Oh, sorry, I mean *paparazzo*. He seemed particular about the designation." Adam leaned forward and propped his arms on his knees. The movement made his shoulders seem broader, more virile. She noticed and wished she hadn't.

"Oh, well, that's par for the course. Tabloids are always looking for scoop. Americans love catching celebrities misbehaving. They even take pictures of them squeezing oranges at Whole Foods."

"Maybe so, but this paparazzo said he'd seen Harvey Primm watching you. That doesn't sit well with me."

She felt uneasy. The man had actually followed her around? Mark her as officially creeped out. "What do you mean? He's been stalking me?"

"I don't know, but you need to be careful. Check your surroundings and keep a cell phone with you."

Guilt tapped her on the shoulder. Okay. That was another good reason to take her phone. She had to stop being stubborn. "Why's he doing that?"

Adam stood. "Not sure. He's obsessive when he has something on his mind. I've been here almost a year and there always seems to be some issue he's tackling. Usually he uses his newspaper to attack a person, but he seems to have taken this censorship thing personally."

"I don't get it. Having a difference of opinion is what makes us American. It shouldn't lead to forcing his beliefs down a person's throat. He's confronted me before and I—"

"When?" He took a few steps toward her until his shadow fell across her.

"About a week ago. He showed up while Henry and I were tossing the ball around. He waved a newspaper around and said I was trying to make him look crazy. Honestly, he does that all by himself."

"Why didn't you tell me?"

"It didn't seem like a big deal. I told him to leave. He did."

Adam clasped her shoulders. "You have to tell me things like this, Scarlet. A guy showing up like that, pissed and confrontational, could be bad news."

She shrugged out of his grasp. "I really didn't think it was a big deal. If I had, I would have told you. I'm not stupid. Or stubborn."

He quirked one eyebrow. The gesture felt so familiar. In fact, he felt so familiar. As though she'd known him much longer than she had. "Adam, I'm *not* brainless. If I felt it was something more than an old man peeved because he thought I'd done something to ding his rep, then I would have come to you and reported it."

A few seconds ticked by. Something passed between them. The same thing that had passed between them many times before. Raw hunger. Yet something more. His features softened. "I like when you say my name."

Seduction. She could feel it vibrating off him. "Adam?"

He laughed a soft, dangerous sound. The kind that invited trouble. "Yeah, that's it. You tend to call me *chief* a lot."

"I thought you liked being called chief. Seems important to you."

He tilted his head, looked pensive. But the tension didn't melt away. Only intensified. "It's my role."

"But doesn't define you." He'd boxed himself so firmly into the role, he'd forgotten that he was also Adam. A man. Who had desires. Needs.

"Hard to separate. The town doesn't. To them, I'm the law. Not a man."

"That doesn't seem fair," she murmured, wanting to touch him, but holding herself back. She'd wanted to respect his wishes. Wanted to remember all the good reasons not to indulge in anything other than business with Adam. But it didn't stop her from wanting to toss that reason away. To touch him. Kiss him. Feel his body against hers.

"Life's not fair," he said quietly. So quietly his words sounded like a caress. "If it were, you'd be a lot closer than you are now."

She stood and the action put her closer to him, close enough to smell him. Woodsy, expensive aftershave. The scent wasn't overpowering, just enough to intrigue. She met his gaze. The sleepy green eyes made her want to step closer still. So she did.

He closed those eyes and groaned. "Damn, woman."

"What? You don't want me close? Don't want me to tempt you?"

He opened his eyes. "You know what I want. I want to taste you. Touch you. Play you like a melody."

She released her breath and moved forward so only inches separated them. She felt the heat of his body. Perhaps she could even time the beats of his heart. "Somehow I knew poetry lurked beneath that badge."

He smiled. Slow. Sexy. Sweet. "That's not all I got under here."

She slid her tongue along the curve of her bottom lip. "Oh, yeah? Since I can't take a peek, you want to tell me?"

His expression promised something naughty. He'd gotten caught by the pull of the moon, by the whisper of desire that brushed over them.

"No, baby, you go first. What do you have under that grandma shirt?"

"I knew it. It's ugly, isn't it?"

The corner of Adam's mouth kicked up and she felt it low in her belly in a place that hadn't felt anything in quite a while. It felt delicious, like a new leaf unfurling inside her.

"So?"

"What's underneath?" he whispered in her ear. But he didn't touch her. It was kinky torture indeed.

Scarlet moved her lips so they almost touched the shell of his ear. Almost, but not quite.

"Lacy black bra. Do you like lace, Adam?"

His breath brushed her ear. "No, I like what's underneath lace."

"Oh," she breathed. "Your turn."

"I don't wear lace," he said, blowing against her neck.

Oh, he was a bad boy. What she'd always suspected. The heat from his body competed against the sultry night and won out. Impish desire took hold of her, urging her to tantalize until she got what she wanted. "So we're really gonna do this phone-sex thing…without a phone?"

He pulled back, his delicious lips twitched in amusement. "I wouldn't know. Never had phone sex before. I prefer the real thing."

She moved closer, near enough that her hair brushed against the front of his shirt. She was immensely glad she'd washed her hair with the specialty shampoo Stefan had insisted she buy when they'd been poking around Greenwich Village. It reeked of sensuality. "Oh, baby, you've been missing out."

"Obviously. What's next?"

She rose on tiptoe. "You have to tell me what you want to do to me."

"I'm not sure there are words."

"I'll show you how."

She slid behind him, almost touching her back to his. Almost, but not quite. She emerged on the other side of him, leaned in close and whispered, "Follow me."

She walked across the lawn toward the shadows thrown by the neighbor's maple tree and leaned against the fence. A clump of azaleas hid her from the house. Adam propped a hand on either side of her head. He ate her up with his eyes.

She touched the tip of her tongue to her upper lip and slipped one button open on her blouse. "Maybe you should have a peek."

He rubbed a hand over his face. "Maybe I should."

She slid another button open, tugging the shirt so he could catch a glimpse of the black lace covering the plumpness of her breast. Her nipples ached for his touch. It was nearly unbearable.

She slid another button loose, so the tops of her breasts were visible. She leaned against the rough wood of the fence, arching her back slightly. "Now you know I'm not a liar."

He groaned.

She gave her most Veronica-like smile, but the vampire queen was nowhere to be found. Scarlet's emotions were all her own. "Now, let me show you how it's done. First, I'd have to get that shirt off you. It's a nice shade of green, complements your eyes. But it's got to go. So, I'd unbutton it slowly, maybe stopping to lick your collarbone or give you sweet little bites on what has to be a magnificent chest."

He exhaled. "This is going to kill me."

"If you're lucky."

She met his hungry gaze, loving every minute of the sweet torture. She wanted to drive him crazy, wanted to see him lose control. "So, then I'd pull your shirt from those jeans, Maybe slide my hand beneath your waistband so I could make sure your ass is as hard as it looks."

"I am a hard-ass."

"And you have a nice one," she said. "I would push

your shirt from your arms, making sure I brushed my nipples against your chest. So you'd feel how turned-on I am."

He closed his eyes. Again.

"Your turn," she said, pushing herself from the fence so she stood in the circle of his arms. Not one part of her actually connected with him, but she'd never been so aware, so utterly turned-on in her entire life. Her body was tight as a guitar string, and her lacy panties likely drenched. And it felt so damn good.

His eyes were dilated, lids heavy. If she were a betting woman—and she was—she would say the slightest touch could drive him over the edge. But she wouldn't touch him. Couldn't.

They were playing a game, one in which only their words crossed the line. Okay, and maybe her shirt being opened to his gaze was a bit risky.

But if anyone peered over the fence or glanced across the yard, they would see two people talking.

Even if they were using words that had her near climax.

ADAM INHALED, TAKING in all that was Scarlet. She smelled like a woman turned-on and it drove him insane. He'd never seen anything as beautiful as Scarlet standing barefoot in the dying grass, wearing that ugly blue shirt. The freshly painted fence created an appropriate backdrop for her vivid beauty. Moonlight poured over her, bathing her in luminescence. She was a wicked temptress and an innocent Madonna rolled into one. She would be his undoing.

"My turn, huh?"

"Mmm-hmm." She tilted her head and her dark red hair fell to the side. A diamond winked in the delicate ear revealed. Then he made the mistake of looking at her lips. Lush, beckoning. He felt a shudder rip through him. Hell, he could spend all night on those lips alone.

"I don't think I'd waste time. No teasing. No unbuttoning. I think I'd shuck those shorts of yours, lift you up and worry about picking splinters out of your back later."

She laughed. "Oh, you're one of those guys, huh? Wham, bam, thank—"

"Oh, no. You'd be thanking *me.*" He laughed against the softness of her throat. It was so tempting. He could lower his lips half an inch and they would brush against her satin skin. But if he did that, he wouldn't stop until she was naked beneath him. So he pulled back. "I'm not sure I can continue this, not without touching you. And if I touch you-—"

"We'd both spin out of control."

He sighed and stepped away. "I don't think you know how much I want you, Scarlet."

Her gaze slid to his crotch. He swore it felt like a caress. He nearly gave in. Nearly grabbed her, took his pleasure, be damned the consequences. Her eyes met his. "I think I do."

He grimaced. "You know, this is hell. This whole integrity, moral-compass stuff."

"Yeah, but it's who you are. I like that about you."

He started toward the porch and the light of reality burning steadfast in the night. "Come on. Before we're tempted to say to hell with it and strip down naked."

She sighed and buttoned her blouse. "A girl can dream, can't she?"

They crossed the yard shoulder to shoulder and, like moments before, they were so close, yet so far away from what they both wanted. Rayne appeared at the screened door. “Hey, where did you two get off to?”

Her voice was teasing and it bothered him Rayne would assume they were up to no good. Of course, they had been up to no good. Kind of.

“We were walking the perimeter. I stopped by to let Scarlet know Harvey Primm has been following her around. I want her to be doubly careful over the next few weeks.”

Rayne pushed the door open and stepped out. Worry creased her face. “He was here the other day. Did you tell him, Scar?”

Scarlet nodded. “Yeah. He’s probably looking for some dirt on me or you. Maybe some sort of leverage to shut me up, but he’s a little weird. Who knows with people nowadays?”

“Exactly. So what are you going to do, Adam?”

“Not much I can do other than keep a closer eye on him. As long as he doesn’t trespass on your property, he’s not crossing a line.”

“Well, thanks for coming by and checking on me,” Scarlet said, climbing the porch steps to stand beside her sister. “Your concern was…touching.”

He didn’t miss the play on words. Neither did Rayne. “What does that mean?”

Scarlet chuckled. “Nothing. I nearly lost my way out there and the chief kindly redirected me.”

“Y’all are talking in circles,” Rayne said, her gaze swinging from her sister to him.

He cleared his throat. “Nothing to worry about, Rayne. Scarlet likes to tease.”

That was the understatement of the decade. He hoped like hell his erection wasn’t too visible. He was still halfway hard from the *teasing* she'd given him earlier. Naughty girl.

"Survey your surroundings before you get into your car or check the mail. If you see anything funny, call me at the station."

Rayne nodded. Scarlet merely watched him, her gaze hard to read. Would he ever understand her? She was a puzzle—saucy, bold but also surprisingly levelheaded and sincere. A man could go years and years and never solve her.

"I'll head around the side. Night, ladies."

He saluted, then crunched through the crushed gravel toward the front of the house, allowing his eyes to swing left and right, combing the shadows.

The most logical explanation for Harvey's illogical behavior was that he hoped to catch Scarlet acting inappropriately in order to paint her in a bad light in his tattler newspaper.

All the more reason to keep his vow when it came to Scarlet. Even if it were the hardest thing he'd ever had to do.

Adam reversed the cruiser out of the drive, and headed toward the station. He needed to add a notation to the file he kept on Harvey and it would be best to stick one in Scarlet's, too. He'd learned early on that documentation was the best protection for a policeman. That and a bulletproof vest, of course.

When he got to the station, it was stifling hot. One of the former chief's rules—turn the thermostat way up after hours as to not waste taxpayers' money. Adam didn't want to waste money, but neither did he want to sweat his balls off while he tried to work. He tapped the thermostat down and grabbed the files from Roz's cabinet.

His office was painfully clean—the way he liked it. But the order made the fact the desk drawer was open well over an inch stand out as though it was under a spotlight.

He jerked the drawer open and plunged his hand toward the back.

Shit.

The tape was gone.

He yanked the drawer open as far as it would go, exposing the well-ordered contents. Stapler. Sticky notes. Pencils. Pens. Blank sheet of paper folded over…nothing.

Son of a bitch.

Adam closed the drawer and looked around.

Who?

Wasn't Roz. She wouldn't even inch a toe inside his office. And Jared seemed too damn lazy. Roy Killough was nosy enough, but also respectful of Adam's rank. The other officer, Ian Fox, was new and eager to please. No way he'd be caught shuffling through his chief's desk. So who?

Harvey's image appeared.

The old man had balls enough to pull it off, but Adam's desk had been locked. And while Primm had been accused of getting information in unorthodox ways, Adam couldn't quite see him resorting to jimmying locks. Of course, Adam had once caught him going through Emile Prothro's trash the morning after the man had complained about the article on the pesticides sold to the local farmers' co-op. A man who resorted to that behavior would be the type to carry picks. And really, it wasn't hard to pick a desk lock. Harvey could have stopped by this afternoon while Adam was at lunch. Probably told Roz he'd wait in the chief's office. Broke in, took the tape, then said he'd come back later. Roz wouldn't have suspected a thing.

Adam sat. He'd be willing to bet the old geezer had the equipment needed to view the 8-mm tape. Adam rubbed a hand over his face. How had he screwed this up so badly?

One little kiss.

It had been good. Very good. But had it been worth risking his career? One whiff of his misconduct and the press would have a field day. With balloons, hot dogs and a dunk-the-police-chief booth. He was screwed.

Of course, Harvey might not have swiped the tape. But Adam couldn't think of a better suspect. Hell. How had everything gotten so complicated? Of course, he knew the answer to that question. It had been the day Scarlet had blown through the Welcome to Oak Stand sign and plowed straight through his certainty of who his woman should be.

Now his one indiscretion as police chief was out there, floating around in someone's hands.

CHAPTER SIXTEEN

SCARLET WAVED HER ARMS. "Cut!"

Juan frowned. "What? I said it right that time."

"But this is a tender moment. You've learned your grandmother, the dear woman who tucked you in your bed and told you lovely fairy tales, is the Magpie. Her spirit inhabits the bird and is guiding you in the quest for the jewel. We need more emotion. How do you feel? Imagine it is *your* grandmother," Scarlet said, stomping up the steps and stepping across the masking-tape-lines stage of the Oak Stand auditorium.

"Yo, my *abuela* smoked unfiltered Camel cigarettes and ran a gas station. She was too damned tired to tuck me in," Juan muttered.

Tito snickered. "My *abuela* was a hooker."

Scarlet snapped her fingers. "Focus. This is acting. Feel free to pretend your grandmother is a freaking fairy godmother. Summon tenderness."

Miguel II raised his eyebrows. "Tenderness is for pussies. I'm hard. Wanna come check me out?"

Scarlet whirled around and stabbed a finger at Miguel I and II. "Okay, busters, I'm tired of all the sexual innuendos. You're not clever. You're not sexy. And I don't want to have sex with either of you."

"Damn, dude. She smoked your ass," one of the guys said.

Scarlet blinked. "I'm not trying to hurt your feelings, but what you're doing is considered harassment. This center is preparing you for the world, a different world than the one you've been living in. Women are people. They are colleagues. They are bosses. You cannot make those types of comments and not expect to be reprimanded or sacked for it. Mind your tongue and put the brakes on your sexist comments."

Silence fell. Miguel I looked, dare she say it, ashamed.

"Now, get your asses up here and let's get this scene right."

"I hope I get a boss like her," Marco said, trudging across the stage.

Scarlet closed her eyes and counted to ten.

"What, *gringita?* I hope I get a hard-ass like you. You want it right. Perfect. I used to work at Subway for this dude who spent all day in the john, looking at porn. He blamed me and the other girl every time something went wrong. I hated working there."

She smiled. "Okay. Just so you mean it in that way."

Marco shrugged. "Whatever. Let's do this scene."

"Places." She pointed out marks as Aunt Frances appeared stage right. "Okay, let's run it. Action!"

The guys started going through the motions of the scene without any real enthusiasm, so she stepped over to her aunt. "Thanks for asking the principal to allow us to use the auditorium. It really makes a difference."

Aunt Frances patted the curve of her hair and delivered a secretive smile. "I know how to get what I want from a man."

Scarlet arched an eyebrow. "I bet you do."

"He owed me a favor. Besides, he thinks it will be a good thing for the community. He was opposed to the book at first...until he read it. Now he doesn't want others to do what he did—make a snap judgment."

"Funny how people make assumptions without really knowing what lies beneath. Facades. We're surrounded by them."

"We all wear them, don't we? Me. You. Especially you."

"Because I'm an actress?"

"Mmm." Aunt Frances watched the guys on the stage pull on the curtains. "You boys stop messing with those curtains. Do you have any idea how much those things cost?"

The former gang members straightened as if a drill sergeant had stepped on deck. It made Scarlet smile. Something she hadn't done since Adam had left her several nights ago. Thoughts of John, Adam and her career swirled around and around in her head. It all felt so heavy. The play. The probation. The fact Stefan hadn't answered her phone calls.

"Yo, can we go now?" Marco called. "We've done it eight times today. How many more run-throughs do we need? If Miguel don't get his shit together and learn his lines, we're gonna look like a bunch of—"

"Watch your language," Aunt Frances said.

"Yes, ma'am." Marco said. Miguel II's response was to flip his fellow actor the bird. Marco reciprocated.

"Okay, enough," Scarlet called, moving onto the stage. "We need to adjust some lighting. Stand in your places for scene two."

The guys dragged their feet and stood at their marks so Scarlet could make notes on the clipboard she carried with her. This time the clipboard served a purpose. She scratched a few instructions for the high-school kid who ran the light-and-sound booth. "Okay. Practice tomorrow at nine o'clock. Now, get out of here."

Her actors dispersed, their goodbyes moderately more polite than in the past. Aunt Frances drew the curtains into place, turned off backstage lights, then disappeared into the dressing room. Darkness descended, broken by the exit signs. Scarlet sank onto one of the auditorium seats and allowed her sigh to fill the space.

Hmm. Good acoustics.

Scarlet pulled the cell phone Adam had insisted she carry from her pocket and stared at the message icon. She had one message.

John.

She pressed the button, opening the screen where his voice mail sat awaiting one little tap of her finger. Before she could think too much about it, she pressed Delete. She didn't want to talk to him anymore, not after what had occurred between her and Adam in the backyard. Something had changed her as she stood not quite in Adam's embrace. It was as if the very meaning of the bed-and-breakfast had taken hold of her. *Finding things where least expected.*

Adam had wiped her clean and she was a blank slate, awaiting a new story.

So why would she want to hear what John had to say? There had been days upon days for him to say something about why he'd chosen to end their relationship. But he hadn't bothered. He'd refused her calls and turned away from her when she'd seen him at a premiere, giving no other explanation than "It's over."

Scarlet shook her head, as frustrated now as she'd been over a year ago. He didn't deserve her acknowledgment.

She shoved the phone into her pocket as someone

sat down beside her. "You've got your work cut out for you, chickadee."

"Ugh, stop scaring me like that, Aunt Frances."

"CIA, remember?"

"But do you really have to sneak up on people? Wear a charm bracelet or something."

"I recognize that little wrinkle in your forehead. You were deep in thought, staring at that phone of yours. What's got you upset? The play?"

"Nah, I don't expect perfection. Just something passable."

Aunt Frances smiled. At least what seemed to be a smile. Could have been a grimace. It *was* dim. "That doesn't sound like you. Passable? Ho-hum? Not my Sum—Scarlet."

"I can't make them care. It's not important to these guys."

"So make it important. Give them a stake in it. Do they know how the town feels about the book? It's pretty much the way the town felt about the center and Rick when Phoenix was being built."

"What do you mean?"

"Many folks around here didn't want the rehabilitation center near our town. Terms like *thieves* and *lowlifes* were tossed around. They sure changed their tune when those fellows showed up to help rebuild the community after the tornado. Rick and his ex-gang members were a godsend. So compare *The Magpie's Jewel* to the center. Let them create a platform about judging a book by its cover."

Scarlet studied her aunt's hands as they tapped a tune on the wooden arm of the chair. "You're pretty damn smart."

Her aunt smiled. "Yes, darling, you get it from me."

"Well, not my smarts. My sass maybe. When it comes to some things, I'm as dumb as a…as a…"

"Post? Brick? Sick camel?" Aunt Fran said.

"Sick camels are dumb?"

"Got carried away."

For a moment, they sat in silence.

"Can I ask you something, Aunt Fran?"

"Shoot."

"What do you think of Adam Hinton?"

"The chief?"

"Yeah."

Her aunt gave her a piercing look. "Why do you ask?"

"I don't really know much about him. Like how he ended up in Oak Stand."

Aunt Frances seemed to be digging around in Scarlet's psyche with that gaze. Scarlet hated when she did that. Hated more the thought of what she might uncover. "You're not trying to get dirt on him or something, are you? He's a good man."

"You know me better than that," Scarlet said. "I don't have a grudge. I like him."

"As in *like him* like him?"

She didn't want to answer. So she didn't.

"The council hired him out of a pool of applicants. They were smart for once and brought in someone from the outside. Let's face it, Dan Drummond was a good ol' boy and some changes needed to be made."

Scarlet had deduced as much. But she wanted to know about Adam. Who was he? Where had he come from? And why had he chosen Oak Stand?

"He's divorced. I got that tidbit from Roz. She says his ex-wife calls every now and again, which makes Adam grumpy."

Scarlet almost blinked. Now, that was something she'd not known. His words about making something work, building a relationship on sand, came back to her.

"Roz also said his family is loaded to the gills with old money. His mother came to town a few months back, wearing fancy clothes and driving a Jaguar, but Adam certainly doesn't act as if he's wealthy. He lives in a small house and the only expensive thing I've seen is his classic Corvette."

"Old money, huh? I'm surprised girls aren't lining up."

"Oh, they have. Don't think for a minute there aren't some mamas around town pushing their daughters toward the good chief. In fact, the mayor's daughter has a date with him for the picnic Monday."

Pain struck her hard and low. Adam had a date? Monday? She hoped her aunt couldn't see her shock. Her hurt. She swallowed. "Oh."

But Aunt Frances was like a hound dog on a scent. *"Oh?"*

"Don't say it like that. I have a little crush. No big deal." So what if Aunt Frances knew she had a thing for the chief?

"That's not like you, either. Accepting defeat?"

"I'm not accepting defeat." Scarlet felt the sting of irritation. She wasn't giving up. She didn't have a chance to begin with, no matter what they'd done, or not done, in the shadows of Mr. Hines's maple tree. "I can't mix it up with him anyhow. It would be misconduct."

"Why?"

"Because. I'm under his jurisdiction for my community service. He can't risk his career for a little horizontal mambo with the trashy actress."

"That's how you see yourself? And is that all you want from him?"

Scarlet deflated. "I don't know what I want. Everything feels so backward. My professional life is going gangbusters but my personal life is sucking…is sucking…"

"I'm not going to touch that one."

At that Scarlet smiled. "Yeah, I'd let it go, too."

Aunt Frances pushed a strand of hair behind Scarlet's ear. "Listen, baby, life ain't no fairy tale, no matter what you read in a book. It knocks you around sometimes and just plain hurts. Sometimes a girl can't wait on a guy to rescue her."

"That's the last thing I need, Aunt Fran. I don't want a guy who thinks he has to save me…even if it's from myself." Her thoughts flitted to John. Was that what had happened? Had she relied on John to save her? To guide her career? To give her direction at a time when she lacked her own game plan? Maybe he'd seen the writing on the wall and abandoned ship. "I'm not looking for a knight on a white horse, or in a police cruiser."

"That's not what I meant, child. I meant, sometimes a girl has to go after what she wants. Some men are worth that. Your uncle Travis was, and the good Lord knows I had to make him sit up and take notice. I actually had to ask the man out myself."

Scarlet smiled at the thought of her aunt giving chase to the quiet, humble man who'd planted blueberry bushes on the property line of the elementary school so the kids could eat the berries at recess. It had pissed the teachers off…and a couple of mothers who couldn't get the stains out of their kids' clothes. Uncle Trav hadn't thought of anything other than pleasing the kids of Oak Stand Elementary. It was Scarlet's favorite

Uncle Travis tale. *Oblivious.* That was what her aunt had always called him. "That man didn't stand a chance."

"You are more like me than you know. I'm thinking you need to go to that picnic."

Scarlet didn't answer. She hadn't planned to attend the town's annual event, but the thought of Adam with another girl messed with her intent. She could see Sophie. Probably blond hair, cut in a shoulder-length bob. Blue eyes. Rounded cheeks. She probably smiled a lot and knew how to tell homemade cookies from store-bought ones. She would wear a floaty skirt and a demure top, spread out a patchwork quilt her grandmother made and set the chicken she'd fried that morning on a platter in the center. Sophie would laugh at all of Adam's dorky jokes.

Scarlet hated her already.

"Sophie's a sweetheart. Teaches at Oak Stand Elementary and has such a way with kids. She's perfect for Adam. Already half in love with him."

She knew what her aunt was doing, but couldn't stop herself from falling in the trap. "Really? Half in love with him?"

"Uh-huh. If it were me, I'd do whatever it took to step over Sophie's broken body to get to that man."

Scarlet didn't respond. The spring of hurt gushing from her heart had joined forces with jealousy and was mixing it up with anger. She and Adam had had phone sex, or whatever the hell it was. The man had virtually screwed her with his eyes, and now he was going out with some paragon of virtue? What the hell?

"If you're merely interested in the horizontal mambo, you might as well leave him to the girl. He'd probably be perfectly happy with milquetoast. He seems to look for that in everything he does. Like he's afraid to color his life too much."

Hmm. That seemed to be true. Everything about the man was discreet, neat and orderly. No bright colors. No coloring outside the lines. No mess. Yet, she sensed he'd so enjoy the wind in his hair, blasting Metallica on the radio and sex on the hood of his Corvette.

"You know what color would look good on that man?"

She turned to her aunt and lifted an eyebrow, à la Bette Davis. "What?"

"Scarlet."

ADAM FIDDLED WITH THE CORD of the telephone on the wall of his kitchen. It had been a while since he'd had a phone with a cord. The retro style suited him fine, even if it did mean staying in the one room while talking on it. "No, Mom. I appreciate your wanting to come to Oak Stand for the picnic, but it's not necessary. I actually have a date with a nice, acceptable girl."

"Acceptable? In Oak Stand?" his mother said.

He closed his eyes and counted to only three. "Yeah, they have some of those around here. Go figure."

"Don't get smart. You may be nearing thirty, but—"

"I just turned thirty-two, Mother."

"Let's keep that between you and me."

He felt his lips twitch. His mother sometimes made him want to stab his eyes out with a pin, but he'd forgo the whole Oedipus thing. She was a giant snobby pain in the ass, but she was still his mother…and he loved her.

"I'll leave you to your acceptable girl and come another weekend. I have swatches of fabric I'd like to test against the walls in the living room. You did call the painter, didn't you? And that handsome contractor? I've already paid him to refinish those floors."

"Um, no. I like white walls and the floors are fine."

Her huff of breath was all too familiar. Why did she have to meddle? And try to decorate his life with curtains, paint and women?

"It's bad enough you're living in a veritable shack, but to refuse to spruce it up… I don't understand you, Adam. You settle for the ordinary when you could have the extraordinary."

"I like ordinary, Mother. It suits me."

"Does it really? Or have you convinced yourself playing Average Joe will solve all your problems? You're not average. You're something pretty damn special, and I'm not talking money here, son. I'm talking about who you are. Why in the world would you desire to fade into the background?"

He studied the refrigerator hunkered against the stove that rattled when he boiled water. Rust formed on the bottom of the appliance, marring the white surface with a spot of undesirable color. "I'm not settling. I like this town and who I am in it. I know you don't understand, but I've always been a Hinton and that's not easy. Here, I'm the chief. I go to church. I fish. I mow my own grass. I—"

"I understand. But I feel as though you're searching for something you won't ever find. Your life as a Hinton wasn't perfect, but your life as Adam, the chief of police, won't be, either. You can't line up your life and expect it to fall into place as pretty as you please. Doesn't work that way."

He chewed on her words for a moment. Guilty as charged. Maybe that's why the idea of taking Sophie to the picnic had never sat right with him. Not only because he'd tumbled into something he didn't want to put a name to with Scarlet, but because Sophie seemed made to order. Cookie-cutter perfect for him. But not what he wanted to taste. "You're right, Mom."

"Lord have mercy! Let's mark this day on the calendar."

He chuckled. "I'll get my pen out."

"Adam, I love you. And I want the best for you, even if I'm snooty, somewhat oblivious and too concerned with the color of your walls. I'm still planning to visit. With my swatches."

His mother's voice had grown soft, sweeter than he'd ever remembered. Was there something wrong with her? A thread of fear squeezed his throat. "Mom? Are you okay?"

"I'm fine. I simply don't say that enough to you, and I should."

Adam twisted a knot into the cord. "I love you, too. And I might even unlock the door if you leave those curtain samples in Houston. I don't want anyone girling up my bachelor pad."

"Deal."

They said their goodbyes, he hung up the receiver and stared at the rust spot. He needed to get some paint to cover the stain or it would spread. Or he could get a new fridge. And maybe he should cancel his date with Sophie. Wasn't fair to lead her on. Yet to bow out at such a late date would be ungentlemanly. Besides, Sophie was a nice girl. Maybe she'd grow on him.

Because Scarlet couldn't be the right woman for him. After next week, she'd be gone. Back to New York. Maybe even back with the man she swore she still loved.

Jealousy flooded him, hot and vicious. He had no right to feel envious of a phantom lover. Yet he did.

He hated whoever had broken Scarlet's heart. The man should have his damn head examined to toss her over. She was extraordinary.

His mother's words floated back to him.

You settle for ordinary.

Maybe he should go for extraordinary. Allow life to fall outside the lines he'd drawn for himself. He could end up hurt. Or fired. But could he be happy sitting between his plain white walls with the knowledge that he settled for ordinary when he might have had a chance with a woman who made his heart pound between his ribs? A woman who made his hands sweat. Made him laugh. Made him want to take a walk in a thunderstorm. Make love beneath the night sky. And paint his front door a vivid crimson to match her hair.

Maybe, for once in his life, his mother made sense.

CHAPTER SEVENTEEN

SCARLET SHIFTED THE picnic basket into the crook of her elbow and looked for her sister and Henry among the sea of blankets, lawn chairs and tailgate tents.

"Scarlet!" She heard her sister's voice but could not locate her. She craned her head and felt very un-Scarlet like. Damn. No New Yorker showed up to a tiny park and acted lost. Hell to the no. But she didn't feel very New York at the moment. She felt pretty much lost.

"Over here. By the zinnias," Rayne called.

What were zinnias? Scarlet swiveled her head and finally saw her sister waving her arms as if she were guiding in a jumbo jet. Scarlet picked her way through the crowd, very well aware everyone stared at her. In fact, conversations died as she passed by.

Maybe the whole country-girl-with-a-twist look had been a bad idea. The denim shorts were Katy Perry short as was the gingham shirt knotted between her breasts, baring her midriff. She'd parted her hair and braided it, finishing off with grosgrain ribbon. She'd purposely left her shoes at home.

Brent gave her a once-over as she stepped onto her aunt Frances's quilt. "Did you escape from a country-music video?"

Scarlet scowled. "It's a festive look."

Rayne snorted. "If that's what you want to call looking like a prostitute on *Hee Haw*."

Scarlet rolled her eyes and dumped the picnic basket at her sister's feet. "Aunt Frances said I looked perfect. She sent chicken-salad sandwiches and extra lemonade."

Rayne glanced at the small table laden with food. "Set it on the table, I guess. And you look…cute?"

Scarlet had been going for hot. Drop-that-sweatered-bitch-because-I-can-rock-your-world hot. But she guessed cute would work. She rifled through the contents of the basket, withdrawing the plastic-wrapped plate of sandwiches from the depths, along with the jug of lemonade. She used the busyness to secretly comb the area for a glimpse of Adam with his little friend.

She didn't see them.

"So," she said, pretending to casually survey the gathering, "looks like everyone in town showed up."

She didn't see Adam on the right side of the gazebo, either. Maybe he was behind the structure. Next to the bridge. It looked like a romantic spot. A little hideaway, perfect for some privacy.

"Yeah, everyone usually comes. Mostly to see their kids sing or clog. Jasper Boyett will be doing his ventriloquist act in ten minutes. After that, the Dance Factory will perform a tribute to the Beach Boys." Brent didn't look overly excited. Henry stuck his finger down his throat and pretended to gag.

"Has Roz's granddaughter sung yet?"

"I don't think so," Rayne muttered, fussing with the lid on a plastic storage dish.

"I think I'll go look for her. You know, to say hello to little Mary Ellen."

"Mary Claire," Rayne corrected her.

Scarlet pulled out cherry lip gloss and swiped it across her lips. "Yeah, whatever."

She stepped over Henry's feet, walked around a tent of older ladies playing gin rummy, then skirted the gazebo. A few people waved and one moron gave a wolf whistle. But she focused on finding Roz, which was totally her cover for finding her sexy lawman.

Scarlet spotted Roz near the temporary stage, dabbing rouge on a pudgy girl who looked to be about ten years old. But she didn't see Adam. Where in the world was he? Aunt Fran had said he had a date. Maybe he'd backed out. Maybe after their little adventure in the backyard, he'd realized no other woman compared to her. Maybe he'd canceled.

But then she saw the car.

She stopped right in the middle of Kate and Rick Mendez's quilt. And stared.

It was bright yellow and gleamed against the green shrubs sitting behind it. A classic muscle car with shiny rims and a fresh coat of wax. And sitting right on the hood was a thin blonde in a strapless sundress and thong sandals. In her hand was a plate holding a piece of pie… and she was feeding it to Adam.

Scarlet felt her heart drop to her toes.

That little bitch. She was feeding pie to her—

To her what? Her man? Not hardly. But it felt that way, as though Sophie had her elegant—and no doubt sanitized—hands all over Scarlet's man.

That pissed her off and hurt her like nothing else she could recall. Not even when John had tenderly, and almost gentlemanly, revealed he no longer loved her. Unfathomable to think she felt this way about Adam, but it was true.

The waves of pain were followed very swiftly by rage. She clenched her hands and shot darts of poison at Adam, who chewed slowly, then gave a sweet smile to the laughing blonde.

"Scarlet?" Kate said. "Are you okay?"

Scarlet ripped her gaze from Adam and looked at the pregnant woman sitting at her feet. "Hmm?"

Kate wrinkled her nose, probably because Scarlet's bare foot had pinned down a paper plate holding several cookies. She then turned her head in the direction Scarlet had been staring. "Oh."

Scarlet didn't bother answering. She was too busy with the tsunami of emotions washing over her.

That bastard had never looked at her that way. Sweet. Tender. Like a suitor.

She stepped off Kate's blanket and charged toward the couple. She may have stepped on a few quilts and she was fairly certain she'd knocked a kid's Nintendo DS from his grasp, but nothing would stop her from giving Adam Hinton a piece of her mind. *Nothing.* A freight train. Wild horses. And any other stupid euphemism that didn't make sense in the twenty-first century.

No one.

Except John.

Her former lover stepped right in front of her.

"Scarlet."

She stopped. Took one step backward. Then another. John. Here in Oak Stand. Adam holding Sophie's hand. People staring.

Her heart thudded so loud in her ears that she lifted her hands to them.

"Scarlet." John reached out a hand as if in slow motion. She looked at him. At his hand. Then she saw a swoosh of color. Green. Blue.

Then black.

ADAM HAD NOTICED SCARLET heading his way just after he'd taken a bite of the lemon pie Sophie had made. He caught sight of her out of the corner of his eye and his mind shouted a warning. Because the fireball actress looked incensed. Like pissed off, pissed on and ready to knock his teeth out.

Part of him had been secretly pleased she was jealous. And part of him had him reaching down to protect his balls.

But then a man had stepped in front of her, and her expression had Adam pushing the plate Sophie held aside and sliding off the car. Scarlet looked scared. Stunned. Lost.

"Scarlet!" he called, his exclamation mixing with that of the older gentleman who had also said her name.

She stepped away from the man. Then her eyes rolled back in her head and she went down like a lightweight riding a knockout punch.

Someone screamed amid several shrieks of dismay. Adam ran, but the older man reached for her first.

"Move back," Adam said, pushing against the man's shoulder. But the man didn't budge. Adam shifted to her other side and crouched. She had landed in the middle of Kitty Lou Monk's floral quilt, and her face had collided with a plate of potato salad.

He rolled her over. "Scarlet?"

She didn't move.

"Let's get her feet up," he said, relieved to see her chest rising steadily. He turned to the older gentleman who clutched Scarlet's hand. "Take her feet and lift them up."

"Huh?"

"Her feet. We need to elevate them."

"Do you want me to call 911?" Kate said, pushing

people back from where they'd started gathering around Scarlet's inert form.

"I am 911," Adam said, turning Scarlet's face toward him. He wiped a glob of potato salad from her cheek. Damn, she was pretty. Didn't matter what she was covered in. A warm, protective feeling stole over him. He tenderly tapped her cheek. "Scarlet?"

"I *know* you're the police chief," Kate said. Adam almost smiled because he had the feeling she had almost tacked on *dumbass,* but smiling was hard because Scarlet had him terrified. "I meant, an ambulance."

"Find Phillip Patterson," he said, "I saw him with his wife near the stage a few minutes ago." Though he had basic life-saving certification, having a doctor around would be best. He looked at the older man, who had propped Scarlet's long, smooth legs on his shoulder. Something about that made Adam want to pop the man right in his patrician nose. He looked at the woman who had made him so crazy he needed a straitjacket. He slapped her cheeks a bit harder. "Scarlet? Wake up."

She didn't respond. He placed his hand where he'd so longed to place it for the past two weeks. Right between her breasts. She had a strong, steady heartbeat. He looked up at the circle of people who'd formed around the quilt.

Then he slapped Scarlet hard.

Her eyes flew open.

A few people gasped. Kitty Lou said, "Well, good lord, Chief."

Scarlet blinked once. Twice. "Adam?"

"Yeah, I'm here. You okay?" He smoothed a few stray hairs from her eyes. He knew it looked more tender than it should, but he didn't care what everyone thought at the moment. All he cared about was Scarlet.

"What…what happened?" she asked, trying to lift her head.

"No, no. Lie back." He gently pressed her shoulder. "You fainted."

"What?" She looked confused. "I don't faint. I've never—"

Then she stopped talking, and her beautiful hazel eyes widened. "John."

"I'm here, Scarlet," the older man said, patting her calf. Adam glared at the man. Was this the man she'd been in love with? This old dude? He looked vaguely familiar. Perhaps Adam had seen him in a movie or two. A commercial maybe?

Scarlet struggled against his hand. "Let me up."

"Kate went to get a doctor. Lie still," he said, pushing her back. But she wouldn't comply. Why was he not surprised? Had she ever complied with anything he'd asked her to do over the time he'd known her?

She sat up and stared at the man patting her leg. She pulled her feet from his shoulders and tucked them beneath her bottom, moving closer to Adam.

John gave her a crooked smile. "Wasn't quite the greeting I'd hoped for."

"Oh, really?" Scarlet asked, narrowing her eyes.

"My Scarlet. Always making a—"

But he didn't finish his sentence because Scarlet's fist collided with his cheek. The older man wobbled, grasping the air as he fell back. He sat down hard and looked absolutely stunned. He didn't say a word. Just cradled his cheek with one hand.

Scarlet looked taken aback that she'd decked the man. She stared at her fist, then at Adam.

"And you." The piercing glare she gave him made

him wish he'd received the right hook she'd given to Daddy Warbucks instead. "You, you—"

Her gaze locked on Sophie standing on the perimeter, still holding the plate. Scarlet's eyes filled with tears and Adam felt knocked down and out of the fight.

He'd hurt her.

"You men need to stop staring at that girl and get her out of this heat." Kitty Lou's bright blue eyes gave him that snap-to-it-quick look moms had perfected around the dawn of time. Of course. He needed to get Scarlet out of the heat to await the doctor.

"We're going to take you to Tucker House. It will be cool there. You need to see a doctor."

"No, I—"

"Yes, you do," John said, struggling to his feet.

Adam didn't wait for any further protest or agreement. He scooped Scarlet into his arms and pushed through the gathering crowd, toward the senior center housed in the antebellum mansion across the street.

Scarlet didn't say anything. For once. It was as if all her fire had been extinguished, which bothered the hell out of him. He ignored John, who tagged along, and said to Kitty Lou, "Send the doc over."

The sun was hot and Adam tried to avoid Sophie's eyes. She gave him a halfhearted smile as he strode past. Well, hell, if she wanted to be in the running for his wife, she would have to learn to step aside when his job called.

Not that she had even indicated she wanted to run for the position of the chief's wife.

He climbed the steps to Tucker House and knocked once before entering the cool parlor. He set Scarlet on the sofa that seemed more decorative than comfortable.

"Okay?" he asked, settling her against the flowered pillow.

"Fine."

John lowered himself onto an armchair. A bright red spot marred his left cheekbone. Scarlet's punch wouldn't even leave a mark.

"How could you?" she muttered, staring at the white ceiling above her.

Was she talking to Adam? Or the older guy? Or the ceiling?

"What?" Adam said.

"How could you look at her that way? Like you could fall in love with her."

He took a step back. "Fall in love?"

Her eyes shimmered, and he saw it within the depths. Something elusive and precious. It both warmed and terrified him.

For most of the time he'd known Scarlet, he'd assumed she'd been playing with him. The way Angi had. A little fun. No harm. No foul. But this didn't feel that way. Scarlet looked heartbroken. "Scar—"

"No." She waved her hands frantically. "No, don't say anything. Don't." She eased back and closed her eyes. Tears leaked from the corners and dripped into her braids. A soft sob heaved in her chest.

Adam felt his stomach sour.

He hadn't known. Or he hadn't wanted to know. Hadn't wanted to know she'd been doing more than biding her time with a small-town police chief. What had grown between them was about more than sex. More than friendship. More than admiration. And Scarlet had embraced it. Felt it.

Just like he did.

Adam looked at John. He gave a slight shake of his

head—clearly not willing to touch this situation. Adam couldn't blame him. Scarlet had heartbreak written all over her and, this time, it wasn't John's fault. It was Adam's.

Scarlet looked so beautiful, almost like a princess, as she tried not to break down. Sleeping Beauty…with a broken heart.

He did the only thing he could think of.

He became her prince.

And he kissed her.

SCARLET HAD BEEN THINKING about the least painful way to die when she felt someone move above her.

Adam.

His hands slid up her cheeks, smudging the stupid tears that had escaped, mixing them with something she must have fallen in, something with pickles in it. They threaded a bit painfully through her braided hair, tugging a bit at her temple. She opened her eyes as he lowered his head.

His lips met hers.

"Oh," she said against his lips, but she didn't stop him. It felt too good. He tasted like lemon pie and his lips were soft and sweet. He kissed her the way he'd looked at that stupid Sophie. Tender. Romantic.

Scarlet felt his kiss all the way to her toes. She was certain little chill bumps had broken out on her body.

She lifted herself on her elbows and kissed him back.

In the back of her mind, she knew they shouldn't be lying in the parlor of a seniors' center, kissing as though they were starved for love. But the knowledge wasn't enough to stop her from drinking Adam in, reveling in his mouth on hers. She wasn't turned-on, though it could easily shift that way if she opened her mouth a bit.

No, this was something…wonderful.

Then it ended.

"Are you giving her mouth to mouth?" a voice asked, breaking into Scarlet's subconscious and ripping her from the world she and Adam had created.

Adam jerked his head up. "No."

Scarlet felt heat suffuse her cheeks. Was she blushing? She never blushed. She looked at the man who had interrupted their intimate moment. At least somewhat intimate since John had been witness to the whole melodrama.

The man looking at them wore khaki trousers and a golf shirt, but had a commanding sort of presence. Totally a doctor.

"She fainted," Adam said, rising and offering his hand to the man. "I think she's okay, but you might want to check her out."

The man took Adam's spot on the edge of the settee. "Hi, Ms. Rose, I'm Dr. Patterson. Let's check you out."

Scarlet shook her head. "I'm fine."

The door to Tucker House flew open and Rayne skidded in, followed by her assistant, Meg, and Meg's boyfriend, Bubba Malone. "What the hell is going on?"

No one said anything.

Finally, John leaned forward. "Scarlet fainted and this guy gave her mouth to mouth."

"What?" Rayne looked at Scarlet then Adam. Then she looked at John, whose hands dangled off his knees. The sight of the red mark on his cheek should have made Scarlet feel bad, but it didn't. He'd deserved it. Thirteen months of pain had driven her fist. Not in the least ladylike, but Scarlet had never been one for decorum.

Rayne turned on John. "Who *are* you? And why would Adam give mouth to mouth? Did she stop breathing?"

Dr. Patterson stopped his whispered counting. "Not the medical kind of mouth to mouth. The fun kind. Your sister passed out."

"I'm John Hammerstein." John stood and offered his hand. Rayne took it, but didn't look interested. She was more focused on Adam, who had the appearance of a kid caught raiding her cookie jar.

Everyone exchanged looks, before finally landing on the doctor, who was busy trying to get the timer on his diver's watch to work. Meg and Bubba shifted their feet and inched toward the door. Discomfort was the name of the game. Scarlet felt she'd fallen into a sitcom. All they needed was a hipster doofus to skid into the room and crash into the piano in order the break the tension.

Scarlet took in a deep breath.

"Relax," Dr. Patterson said, pressing an insistent hand on her shoulder, but she didn't want to lie back. It felt too vulnerable, and after all that had occurred, she didn't want to be lying down when the shit hit the fan.

Because it would.

She'd fainted into something squishy and picklely.

She'd slugged her ex in front of the whole town.

And Adam had kissed her in front John and Dr. Patterson...who felt obliged to share the 411 with her sister. Not to mention Bubba and Meg.

Dr. Patterson grabbed her wrist and started taking her pulse again.

"Scarlet had a little episode, but she seems fine now." Adam looked less guilty and more determined to control the situation.

Scarlet was glad he felt better about things because

she certainly did not. She'd allowed her emotions to boil over and ruin the agreement she and Adam had…the one where they kept their feelings for each other under lock and key.

"So why did you kiss her?" Rayne kneeled beside the sofa and pushed Scarlet's hair back to study her eyes. "Are you okay? Do you feel lightheaded?"

Scarlet shrugged off her sister's ministrations. "I'm fine. Totally fine."

"Is she okay?" Rayne asked the doctor.

"I can't be absolutely certain without running tests, but her color is good and her pulse is normal."

Scarlet pushed her sister away and stood. Her legs felt a bit shaky, but she could stand just fine. She waited for Adam to say something, but his expression was shuttered. He was in take-charge mode. Or clean-up-in-aisle-Scarlet mode.

"Adam?" she whispered, very aware everyone wanted the answer to Rayne's earlier question. She could feel their curiosity. What had the good-as-gold police chief and the bad-girl actress been up to? How long had they been getting it on? Why would he risk his career for a woman who would be gone before the first cold front came through East Texas?

He smiled, then shrugged. "I'm no saint."

Rayne shook her head, making her corkscrew curls fly around her shoulders. "What's going on here?"

"Come on, Rayne," Scarlet said. "You know I love a challenge. Do you know how long I've been trying to seduce this man? If I had known fainting would do the trick, I'd have hit the pavement a week ago."

"Well, hell, Summer Rose," Bubba Malone said in a deadpan tone. "If you needed a kiss that badly, I'da done you a solid."

Meg elbowed him in the gut, causing him to grunt, but Adam didn't move. His unflinching gaze held Scarlet's. She was the first to cut eye contact.

"This one was hard to break. Thought I'd have to pull the ol' catsuit out of the closet and play Veronica to get him to notice me." She rubbed her sweating hands against her denim short shorts, unwilling to risk glancing at Adam in case the truth—that she'd screwed up the moment she put her bare foot on the town square—was plain on her face.

Bubba chortled. "Well, if you ain't using that catsuit, can Meg borrow it? I've got this fantasy where—"

Meg reached up and twisted her boyfriend's ear.

"Ow!" Bubba hollered, swatting at her hand.

"Pardon this hick for a moment. I need to remind him of the manners his mother taught him, and I think you guys need some privacy. Come on, Brandon." Meg tugged on Bubba's arm and they escaped to the front porch, where Scarlet could see Adam's date sitting on the steps.

Guilt crept around the corner of Scarlet's conscience.

Sophie was probably a nice girl, but Scarlet wasn't as nice. She didn't want someone so pretty, thin and, well, so good to have Adam. If any man needed a little kinky in his life, it was him. He wore pristine running shoes, a tucked-in T-shirt and not one strand of hair was out of place. Here was a man who needed a little mussing up in his life. He needed…

Her.

She pretended to crack her knuckles. "Well, I guess my mission here is accomplished. Now, who else can I go out there and seduce? Who is the man least likely to want me?"

"Harvey Primm," Rayne drawled, tilting her head.

Scarlet knew her sister was in the process of making connections, drawing conclusions and creating a game plan for dealing with Scarlet, her ex-lover and her not-yet-but-she'd-really-like-him-to-be-next lover.

"Good idea. I'll work on Harvey next."

"Well, you might have some success," Dr. Patterson said. "I heard from Rita Frasier over at the library that the old man asked for a copy of the book *and* she saw him reading it in his car."

Scarlet faked a brittle smile. Inside she felt a little sick and a lot scared because she and Adam had blown it. Her little charade had fooled no one. "Then maybe I can loan Meg my catsuit after all."

Rayne put her hands on her hips. "You can stop with the whole acting thing. Everyone can see what's going on here."

"Well, if you've got a handle on it, I wish you would share it with me because I don't know my up from my down anymore," Scarlet said, feeling better, stronger and not willing to deal with her sister's admonishments. "And did I hear right? Did Meg just call Bubba *Brandon?*"

CHAPTER EIGHTEEN

JOHN HAD REMAINED virtually silent throughout the melodrama. Scarlet didn't blame him. After the way she'd hit him, she was surprised he'd stuck around. But he had to have good reason to be there. No man left New York City and traveled over a thousand miles merely to say hello to an old lover.

"John?" Scarlet said, ignoring the others. The place smelled like roses and baking bread, which should have relaxed everyone, but no one seemed to be soothed by the smells nor the comfortable, old-fashioned parlor. "We need to talk."

She glanced at Adam, who spoke quietly with an elderly lady wearing an American-flag shirt and a sun visor. He caught her gaze and gave an imperceptible nod, and it felt as if a guiding hand pushed her John's way. She had to deal with the past that had cropped up before she could move on to Adam and her future.

If there was one.

John stood close by, watching her with wariness in his eyes. He seemed so out of place in his Gucci loafers and stylish linen pants. He'd lost a good deal of weight, but it didn't look bad on him. He appeared older, but it had been over a year since she set eyes on him.

"Do you mind going outside?"

He took in all the people covertly studying him under the guise of chitchat. "That would probably be best."

"Y'all can go out back, sugar," the older woman said. "Plenty of places to talk away from prying eyes."

Everyone watched as she and John left, moving through the dining area, into the kitchen and finally out the back door. The backyard of Tucker House, peppered with bird feeders, large potted plants and benches, was fairly secluded. Scarlet waved John toward a stone bench near a wooden garage.

"I'm sorry I hit you," she said quietly, glad the grass was lush and thistle free. "You didn't deserve that. Well, maybe you did, but I still shouldn't have done it."

"I deserved it."

She pressed her lips together, smearing the leftover lip gloss. "What are you doing in Oak Stand?"

"I came for the picnic," he said with a wry smile.

She didn't answer. Simply lowered herself onto the bench, still a bit unsteady. He took her elbow.

"Thank you," she said. John had always been solicitous, taking her under his wing long before he'd taken her into his bed. He'd been a mentor, a sort of father figure, and she'd wondered many times over the past year if that had been her fascination with him. He'd given her something she'd never had.

Oh, she loved her father. Both her parents loved her, had given her gifts many parents could not give their children. They'd given her room to grow and flourish in any spot she so chose. But they hadn't given her much stability.

John had been her stability, grounding her, advising her and protecting her.

"I'm sorry I surprised you like I did," he said, settling beside her and plucking a blade of grass from the planter next to the bench. He twirled it between his fingers. "I tried to call your phone. I even called your aunt's inn."

"Not so good with my phone. And I'll be honest. I erased your message without listening to it."

"I'm not surprised. I handled things badly."

She sighed. "No, you didn't handle them at all."

"Touché," he muttered, moving to take her hand, but she shifted away. She didn't want him to touch her so intimately. Those days were long over. She didn't know when it had happened, but she knew she no longer loved John. If she did, she would have been overjoyed to see him, despite her anger with him. She'd felt nothing. Nothing but shock that he'd turned up in the middle of a world he had no business in.

"So do you hate me now?" he asked, splitting the blade of grass and tossing pieces of it onto the ground at his feet.

"No, of course not."

He smiled. "You wouldn't. You're a good person though you sometimes allow people to think the worst of you. Like that little sham with the police chief."

She flinched. "What do you mean?"

"Come now, Scarlet. It was evident to everyone in that room he is head over heels for you. To pretend you'd been trying to seduce him was akin to saying the sky is falling. Total falsehood."

She looked up at the cerulean sky. "But the truth is, he hasn't touched me. We've shared one kiss, now two. But that is all. So there was truth in what I said. He's a man of character."

"That may be, but he still wants you."

"Why are you here?"

"Ah, you want to avoid talk of the chief?"

She met his gaze with a hard one of her own. "Not

any of your business, John. Instead, why don't you tell me how it is you're sitting here after a year of silence."

"I've been seeing a good therapist, and she helped me realize I've been grossly unfair to you. I never told you the truth about why I ended our relationship."

"It took a therapist for you to see what a shit you were? Why come all the way to Texas to tell me that?"

His face held no expression, but tenderness crept into his eyes. "Scarlet, your anger is not unexpected. I hurt you, but I want you to know I did it out of love."

"What a bunch of crap. This is a different version of 'It's not you, it's me.'"

"No, I loved you. That's no lie. But, eventually I realized I held you back."

Her mouth dropped open. "Seriously? That's your excuse for dumping me after screwing my brains out the night before? You wanted to set me free?"

"Jesus, Scarlet."

"The truth isn't glossy and pretty."

"That's not accurate." He paused a moment. "Or maybe it's only half-accurate."

The silence pressed down on them.

"I was sick, and I was scared."

"Sick? What do you mean?"

He sighed and clasped his hands between his open knees. "You remember that night in Central Park? We danced under the trees and talked about going to Italy."

"It was a beautiful night."

"It was," he said. "The next day I went to the doctor. I'd been having some pain in my ribs—a nagging that wouldn't go away. They did some tests and found a mass. I had bone cancer."

"Oh, my God, John," she said, touching his arm. "I'm so sorry. Why didn't you tell me? I don't—"

"I intended to." He gave her a sad smile. "You met me at that coffeehouse, remember?"

How could she forget? She'd been wearing a new sundress, one she'd bought for their trip. Later, she'd stripped it off and thrown it in the trash. "I remember."

"You were brimming with plans. Hiking in Trentino. Dancing in Rome. You talked nonstop about everything we'd do. And I listened to you, watched you. So young. You deserved those things, those experiences. You didn't deserve to have to watch me get ill from chemo or traipse around Manhattan with a shrunken, bald man."

Scarlet felt anger creep alongside the pity. "You didn't give me a choice in the matter, did you? You broke things off and—"

"No, I didn't give you that choice. That was wrong of me."

"You made me think I was unlovable. That's what you gave me. Not a choice. A death sentence to a woman who thought she was in love for the first time in her life."

"I thought I was saving you from pain. From hurt. I thought I was freeing you."

She plucked a blade of grass and tore it until little remained, much as John had done earlier. The bits scattered around her bare feet, a symbol of their relationship. Torn, scattered, not destined to be whole again. "But you weren't."

"That's why I came here. I needed to tell you. I thought I was being selfless, but Monica helped me see I wasn't being fair. You deserved the truth. You deserved to make your own decision about your life. I needed to fix things with you before I could move on in my life. So I came to Texas."

She nodded, her heart conflicted, a regular occurrence these days. She wanted to be angry, hold fast to the bitterness that had been her constant companion for many months. Somehow it didn't seem to matter as much as it had weeks ago. Somehow the gash in her heart had been healed. "You protected me."

He slid his hand along her arm. At one time it would have warmed her, but now she felt nothing. "I always wanted the best for you."

She studied his tanned hand against the fairness of her arm. She'd loved him once. But no longer. Her heart had moved on before she even realized it, and filled itself with tender new feelings for Adam. "I can forgive you, John, because I no longer carry that burden of heartache. I won't lie. It hurt, but I'm in a new place in my life. I can't go back."

He dropped his hand and stared out at the dying vines clinging to the wooden fence a few feet from them. "I had hoped we might have a chance. But if I go away with your forgiveness, I can live with that."

She didn't say anything more.

"So that guy. Is he the one who's helped you move on?" he asked eventually.

"Maybe."

"He doesn't have your passion."

"No, but he needs it."

John threw his head back and laughed, startling her.

"What? He needs me to unleash his inner passion. The man is a walking time bomb."

"Don't ever change, love," he said, tenderness etched on his face.

She shook her head because she wouldn't. She was who she was, and nothing, not even love, could alter her.

They shared a peaceful moment. Finally, John rose and held out a hand. “Shall we?”

She accepted his hand. “Your cancer? Are you better? Or…” She didn’t want to think about John being worse.

He smiled. “It’s in remission for now.”

“I’m glad to hear that. Life wouldn’t be good without John Hammerstein in it.”

He curled an arm around her, and she allowed him to hug her. “You are so special, my dear. They broke the mold when they made you.”

She gave him a squeeze. “Thank you for finally telling me the truth.”

“I will always be sorry I hurt you. Do know that I loved every minute of life when I was with you? And if this new fellow doesn’t treat you like the queen you are, I will personally take him to task. Tan his hide.”

Scarlet’s lips twitched. “He already knows I’m a drama queen. I just hope he thinks I’m a risk worth taking.”

“Well, if he doesn’t, he’s an idiot.”

“I’m definitely not an idiot.”

Scarlet and John turned toward the sound of Adam’s voice. He stood next to a pecan tree.

John didn’t acknowledge Adam. Instead he dropped a light kiss on her cheek. “If you ever need me, you know where to find me.”

John walked toward the house, stopping to study Adam. For a moment, they looked like dogs squaring off against one another, hackles up, tails straight. But when John extended a hand toward Adam, he took it. “You’ve been handed a treasure. Don’t squander it.”

Adam nodded but didn’t respond. He released John’s hand and approached Scarlet. A moment later they were alone, or as alone as two could be across the street from a town picnic. She could hear the shouts of children and the twang of a banjo in the background.

"You okay?"

"As okay as a girl can be after taking a header into what I think was potato salad."

He didn't smile. Instead he studied her. She didn't wiggle under the duress of his regard, though she wanted to. It seemed every brush of his gaze weighed, measured and dissected all that she was. And maybe spotted the mayonnaise coagulated near her temple.

"Your cover-up speech about trying to get me to kiss you didn't work. A blind man could have seen the truth."

"Do you?"

His smooth forehead furrowed.

"Care for me?" she asked.

"All I know is we've spent the past few weeks avoiding everything we've felt for each other. I can't do that anymore."

"But you have to." She had twenty more hours of community service to fulfill. Nothing had changed. Yet everything had changed. He'd tossed his convictions aside in front of eye witnesses. Everyone in Oak Stand would be talking about it by the time the sun went down.

"We can't pretend this away," he said.

"We have to." What other choice did they have?

"You think we can? You freaked out in the middle of a picnic because I was with another woman."

"Correction. Another woman was feeding you pie and you looked like you enjoyed it." Scarlet felt anger rise again. Anger at him, Sophie and the whole situation. "I didn't mean to get so—"

"Emotional? But that's what this is between us. Emotional stuff. It's not about sex, though I can't say I haven't been fantasizing about you beneath me, on top of me, all over me during a good part of every day since we met."

"Just a good part? Not every waking moment?"

"And some sleeping ones."

"So what do we do about it?"

He rubbed a hand through his hair. It stretched the fabric of his polo shirt against his flat stomach. "Honestly, I don't know. I'm into you. You're into me. But—"

"There's always that, isn't there?"

There was a resigned look in his green eyes. "What I said about you not being what I'm looking for in a woman was wrong. I form these ideas in my head about what life should be, about who I should be, and I can't let them go. It's not very open-minded of me. I judged you because you're sexy, because you seemed like a self-absorbed actress. I was wrong."

She turned away from him. She'd figured that out long ago, but his words still hurt.

Why did both he and John see her as less than what she was? John thought she was too immature to stick with him through his illness, so he gave up on her. And Adam had thought her too shallow to be worth loving. Sure, he'd corrected himself. But that didn't change the fact he'd tossed her into some category he'd created. This man thought he could label everything and everyone, and, though she hadn't yet reached the age of thirty, she'd learned long ago not to make assumptions. It was one rule her parents had hammered home. No lines. No judging.

"You still make assumptions about me. You think you know me, and you don't. Not really. You can't create a perfect world or a perfect girl. Nor can you hide who you are beneath a badge. At some point, you have to accept life and people for who they are, including me."

"You aren't good on paper."

"What?"

"Sophie's good on paper. You aren't. But I realize being good on paper doesn't mean being the right person for the job. It's a gut-feeling thing, and my gut tells me the *right* girl is standing before me."

She sighed. "This isn't a job, Adam."

"That's not what I meant."

She couldn't handle much more. The drama had been epic, but even a vampire queen had her limits. She looked down at the red leather watch on her wrist. "It's nearly two o'clock, and I promised Roz I would watch her granddaughter Mary Ellen sing."

"Mary Claire," he corrected.

"Whatever."

"But we're not finished." He reached out to stop her.

"We are for now." She sidestepped him. "You better get back to your date."

CHAPTER NINETEEN

SCARLET LAID LOW for the next several days. She tweaked a few scenes for the play, creating a final script that she dropped off at the high-school drama teacher's house for an edit. She spent hours driving along county roads less traveled, with the top of the convertible down, her hair whipping in the wind and the sun hot on her shoulders. It was freeing and gave her tangled thoughts and emotions time to unknot.

By Thursday night, when she'd pulled up to the parking area of Phoenix, ready to start full run-throughs of their patched-together play, she'd reached a decision about her and Adam. She would do nothing.

She'd fought so long and hard against what she felt for him that to not do so felt more exhausting than before. She didn't know where they were headed. Or if there could even be any sort of future between them. But she wasn't going to overthink it anymore.

Overthinking had gotten her nowhere except lost in the Texas countryside.

Without her damn cell phone.

So she was done with thinking and aimless driving.

"Hello, magic woman," Georges said, opening the door. Cool air-conditioning and her actors met her as she stepped inside.

"*Hola,* Georges." She dropped her canvas bag holding a few props Rayne and Aunt Fran had whipped together, including the magpie's jewel. "*Hola,* guys. I wanted to talk to you about why this production is so important before we start our run-throughs tonight."

She delivered the speech Aunt Frances had inspired that day in the auditorium and had helped her perfect last night. For once, the guys paid attention.

"So you're saying this play is like us?" Miguel II asked. "The community thinks this book is bad? And they thought the center was bad? Man, that's—"

"Don't say it," Scarlet warned. "I'm pretty sure it's a rule violation."

"Then we gotta do this right, *gringita.*" Tito nodded his head emphatically.

"Right." She handed out the final script, which consisted of five scenes adapted from the book. Brent had pulled some strings, gotten in touch with the author and received her permission for an adaptation. Scarlet wasn't a screenwriter, but she had been pleasantly surprised at how much she'd enjoyed translating the author's words and ideas into a script. "I've taken the liberty of highlighting each of your parts."

Tito frowned. "What about the cop?"

"Chief Hinton?"

"Yeah, he's doing this, too. He's Valken's servant, right? He eats the poison leaves from the fenberry tree and turns into another raven. That's the best part. When Marco kills him."

"You bloodthirsty pirates," Scarlet said, setting Adam's script on a chair with her bag.

The door to Phoenix opened and the man who'd haunted her thoughts stepped inside. Scarlet's heart sped up, beating like a thundering herd of Thoroughbreds around a racetrack. She wondered what he had been doing since they last spoke. Had he been trying to rationalize his feelings for her? Had he been wrestling over the dilemma of falling in love with the totally wrong person?

Wait. Love? *L-O-V-E?*

She blinked, then rifled through the tote, looking for the faceted jewel. Anything to look busy. To distract herself from the revolutionary thought that had invaded her mind.

"Hey," Adam said, weaving around scattered chairs as he approached. He didn't look at her. "Only a few days until we perform this. You guys ready?"

"I was born ready," Miguel II said.

She looked up and Adam glanced at her. "Are you ready?"

He seemed to be talking about more than the play.

She studied him as he stood beside men who had once mistrusted him. It had taken them several rehearsals, but finally they had come to an understanding. They weren't friends, but they weren't enemies. Adam was light to their darkness. Erect carriage, golden skin and hair. His green eyes were steadfast, his jaw strong. So damned handsome. Was there any other man in Texas as good-looking as this one?

Not to her.

"Yeah," she said, with a smile. "I think I am."

He smiled. "Good."

The undercurrent was broken, and the former gang members began to rehearse. When it came time for Adam's character, he read the part with exactly the right emotion and emphasis. Scarlet had no role beyond providing the mysterious voice of the magpie. She read her lines with an upper-crust British accent, which amused the guys greatly.

They went through the scenes three times, then Scarlet called an end to practice.

As she stepped onto the porch with Adam, she paused to appreciate the evening. It was that magical time of day, with the deepness of night chasing the sun away. Fingers of orange and pink reached out from the horizon as if to cling to the earth as stars overtook the light.

"Beautiful night," Adam said.

"Mmm-hmm." Scarlet shouldered her canvas bag. "You like to talk about the weather a lot."

He gave a soft laugh. "A habit from my mother."

"She likes the weather?"

"No, she likes to avoid problems."

"And I'm a problem."

His smile was warm. "Haven't you been since I first laid eyes on you? From the very beginning, you pecked at my defenses. I had no recourse but to surrender."

"I don't want to be the woman who tears you apart, destroying all you are. You make me sound like a plague, and I'm not. I'm a woman. I'm not defined by anything other than that."

"Nope, you're not."

"And I'm not a job. You can't pick who you'll fall in love with from an applicant pool."

"No, you can't."

She narrowed her eyes. "You're being awfully agreeable."

"Because I'm done with fighting what I feel for you. And I no longer want to hold on to my crazy idea of what life should be." He nudged her with his elbow. "Come on. I'm trying to go with the flow here."

Who could resist smiling at that?

He reached into his back pocket and withdrew a paper. "I got this today." He held it out to her.

She took it. It was a court letter. She quickly scanned the missive. "I'm done?"

"Yep. I signed off on the paperwork today. The judge got a call from the Texas State Trooper's office about your visit to the hospital, and it seems your unsolicited community service warmed her heart enough to shorten your sentence. You've already completed twenty hours and the rest of the time was suspended."

The enormity of that hit her. "I can leave Oak Stand?"

"If that's what you want." Something flashed in his eyes. He didn't want her to go.

She should go. It might be best.

But there was the matter of the play next week. When she'd first arrived, Rayne had accused her of not finishing what she started. If Scarlet left Oak Stand now, the six guys inside would be left with no direction. And what of the play itself? She'd wanted to bring healing to the community still split over the censorship of the book.

And beyond those reasons, the most important one, was Adam. How could she leave him?

"I can't leave," she said, passing the paper to him.

"You can't?"

"No. The play is next week. We have to show Oak Stand the phenomenal acting skills these guys have."

He shifted his gaze from her, staring at Banjo as he ran along the fence on the scent of something. "The play. Of course."

She resisted the urge to physically reach out to him. "Did you think there was some other reason to stay?"

His gaze clashed with hers. "Actually I did."

"What reason is that?"

"This." He stepped toward her, wrapped his arms about her and covered her mouth with his.

Sheer elation flooded her body as she opened her mouth to him, slid her hands up his shoulders to his short hair. Sweet desire awakened as it had the first time he kissed her, except this time there were no bars in the way.

Liquid heat pooled in her stomach and she felt every hard inch of his body against hers. His fingers wove through her hair, angling her head so he could deepen the kiss, as his tongue traced her bottom lip before plunging inside her mouth, then withdrawing again.

She groaned against his lips, tugging him closer, holding him tighter.

"Yo. Get a room," Marco called through the door they'd neglected to shut all the way.

Scarlet laughed against Adam's mouth, but he didn't stop kissing her.

Finally, he pulled back and gazed at her. "Was that enough?"

His kiss had drugged her. "Enough what?"

"Enough for you to stay awhile?"

"You're pretty persuasive, Chief Hinton."

"I've got more tricks up my sleeve if you need more persuasion."

She gave him a smile. "I might take you up on that, but where would that leave us?"

"I'll show you," Adam said, taking her hand and tugging her toward the drive. Banjo looked up and wagged his tail, but he didn't leave whatever he chased. Adam's hand felt so right in hers. They'd spent so long not touching, not giving in to what they both wanted, she delighted in the simple contact.

When Adam reached the bright yellow Corvette, he dropped her hand and reached into the backseat, withdrawing a quilt and picnic basket. "Mind if we take your car? The guys are detailing the 'Vette tomorrow."

"Go where?"

"I want to show you something."

"Oh, really?" she drawled.

His laughter echoed around them. She loved the way he laughed. Reckless abandon. Just as she'd always suspected. "I love that your mind is halfway in the gutter."

"I could easily toss it all the way in." She looped her arm through his. He tossed his keys to Georges, who, true to form, had appeared out of nowhere. "I think Georges must work with Aunt Frances."

"I won't even ask," Adam said. "Keys?"

She handed him her keys, tossed her bag in the back then slid into the passenger seat. Adam cranked the engine and they roared down the driveway.

As they sped down the highway, Scarlet didn't speak, feeling the moment was too sacred, too tender and poignant to ruin with nervous chatter. Adam handled the car as if it were an old friend, taking the curves smoothly, winding over the empty Texas back roads with ease. They came to a cattle gap, rattled over it, then proceeded down a bumpy dirt road around a thick stand of trees. The view opened up to reveal a small pond glittering in the soft moonlight.

"Oh," she breathed, "how pretty."

"I bought it when I first moved to Oak Stand, thinking one day I'd build a house out here. It's only ten acres, but perfect since I can't even pretend to be a farmer." He pulled onto a stretch of grass and killed the engine.

"I've never brought anyone here. It's my secret place,

a place where I get away to think. I've been out here for the past few days." He faced her.

"I probably drove right past you. I spent most of my thinking time riding around in this car."

His face remained expressionless. "So what did you conclude?"

"Nothing. Other than this is not about just sex."

"No, it's not about sex." He kissed her gently. "It's about way more than sex. I didn't bring you here to ravish you. I'm tired of all the prying eyes around town. I love Oak Stand, but there isn't much privacy to be had."

She touched her tongue to her lips, savoring his taste. "This would be easier if it was only a physical thing. And so you know, I'm not opposed to being ravished."

He folded her into his arms, brushing his lips against the hair at her temple. His lips were soft and the moment tender. She tilted her face to his and he met her lips with his. The caress said more than "I want you," and the pleasure of knowing that wrapped around her like a cashmere blanket, soft and priceless. She brushed her fingers through the short hair at his nape and opened herself up to him, physically and emotionally.

He broke their kiss. "I have wine."

"You don't have to get me drunk to score."

He closed his eyes and shook his head. "I didn't bring you here to score."

"You don't want to score?"

He opened his eyes. "I'm not stupid. I'd never turn down the vampire queen."

"Smart man. Let's have some wine."

Adam climbed from the car, grabbing the blanket and basket, pulling her with him. Crickets and the occasional sound of a barn owl were their only companions. The grove of trees hid them from the road, and, for once, Scarlet thought she could dig being a country girl. Moonlight, summer grass and a hot, willing man. What more could a woman want?

Adam chose a dry spot and spread out the quilt. Scarlet slipped off her flip-flops, then sank onto the cover as he busied himself with uncorking the wine and setting out strawberries, grapes and chocolates. Feast laid out, he pulled her into his lap.

She took the plastic glass of wine from his hand. "You're pretty good at seduction."

He sobered. "It doesn't have to be seduction. Honestly, I was going for romance."

"Mission accomplished. I can't imagine anything more romantic than this." She took a sip, savoring the rich taste on her tongue. The surface of the pond sparkled in places as the katydids started a serenade. He kissed her. He tasted like spicy cabernet when she opened her mouth to him, and it caused an intense wave of desire to crash over her. He tasted divine.

"Adam," she groaned as his hands moved over her, sliding from her hip to her shoulder, tipping her onto the quilt. He took her glass and tossed it onto the grass, following with his own glass.

Adam covered her, still cradling her head. His mouth was soft, yet demanding. She met his passion with that of her own, running her hands over his shoulders, down his back and back up to the scruffiness of his jaw. She allowed her fingers to move along his lean cheek, memorizing every detail.

"I like romantic, Adam, but would seduction be okay, too?"

He worked his way from her mouth toward her ear. "I thought that's what I was doing," he whispered.

She smiled at the branches above her and pulled him

even harder to her, shifting the mood from sweet to searing. Adam tugged her T-shirt up, cupping her breast through the lacy bra. His thumb found her nipple as his mouth began a journey down her neck.

He struggled with her shirt, so she lifted herself and yanked it over her head. But she didn't stop there. She wiggled out of the shorts and kicked them aside, too. Then she lay before him in the black lace bra and matching panties she'd tempted him with the night they'd played games in the inn's backyard.

"Damn," he groaned, tracing one of her ribs with a single finger.

She inhaled the night air and watched as his gaze devoured her flesh. He stroked her as if she were a great treasure and he the fortunate man who'd discovered her.

"You're beautiful." He lowered his head to kiss her shoulder before working his way toward the edge of lace that held her breasts. "You smell like summer, like heat and flowers."

"That's my name," she breathed, reaching for him, drawing his mouth to hers. "My real name is Summer."

He smiled against her lips before tasting her again. "But you are much more a Scarlet. Hot, vivid and—" he tugged her hair "—red."

She tugged the T-shirt from his waistband. "I'm ready to see what you tempted me with that night at Serendipity."

He pulled his shirt over his head and tossed it on top of her abandoned one. She ran her fingers over his chest. He was magnificent. Tight, lean and tough. "Very nice." She licked his collarbone.

"Ah, hell, don't do that." He grabbed her wrists and pinned them above her head. "Do you want me to come like a schoolboy in my shorts?"

"You're not wearing shorts."

But he wasn't paying attention to her words. His focus was on her body. His mouth blazed a trail over her skin, leaving fire in its wake. He licked, suckled her through her bra and nipped sensitive spots along the way. Finally, he released her arms and unhooked the front clasp of her bra and her breasts popped free.

"Oh, yes." He cupped her with an almost reverent touch. "You are lovelier than anything I've seen."

And Scarlet believed him.

He worshipped her breasts for what seemed like hours, driving her mad, all the while stroking her body, dipping and testing the boundaries of her restraint.

"Please," she groaned as he teased her through the lace panties. "Adam, please."

He glanced up and gave her a most wicked smile. Then he unbuttoned his jeans, slid them, along with his boxers, off his body. She raised her head to watch.

Her uptight, by-the-book lawman looked like a naughty Greek god. No other way to describe how delicious he was lit by the moon. Hard and unyielding, a marbled statue in the softness of a summer night. Then he peeled her panties from her hips, down her legs. But before he allowed them to join the other clothing strewn on the grass, he feathered a kiss through the hair at the juncture of her thighs, and his tongue tasted her, light and quick.

She wanted more.

She tugged his hair.

"Ah, not yet, my love. Not yet."

She tugged harder and he laughed against her belly.

"Adam," she pleaded, stroking his shoulders. How dare he be so bad?

He pulled her to him, allowing their naked bodies to

touch completely for the first time. The heat between them intensified as her breasts pressed to his chest, his erection pulsed hard against the softness of her belly. Even their feet intertwined. He insinuated one of his legs between hers, applying delicious pressure where she needed it most. She whimpered.

He grinned.

Damn, he knew exactly what he was doing. He was on a mission to drive her insane. "Are you punishing me?"

He bent his head and sucked one of her nipples into his mouth. She moaned.

"Someone shouldn't have crumpled her speeding ticket and thrown it into a fast-food bag," he murmured against her belly button.

She laughed. "Oh, you're a wolf in sheep's clothing, huh? Pretend to be righteous, but exact revenge at the right moment."

He did something spectacular with his tongue and she lost the ability to communicate for a few minutes.

He lifted his head. "Are you complaining about my method of punishment?"

"Please, continue. It's the best punishment I've had."

He laughed and went back to teaching her why crime sometimes paid.

AFTER BRINGING SCARLET to a splendid climax, Adam took a moment to treasure the taste of her on his lips, the feel of her soft body beneath his hands, the sound of her panting in his ear.

He'd never experienced a woman who was so sexy. He'd been with many, but none he'd loved. This one he was fairly certain had caught his heart well and good.

Her breasts were large and perfect, rose-tipped like

her name. They jiggled as he pulled her against him, causing his erection to throb and his balls to tighten.

No more playing around. He needed to sink inside her, bind her to him in that way men had been claiming mates throughout time. For there was one certainty he knew. Scarlet Rose had been made for him.

He rolled her to her side and kissed the crook of her neck. He could taste the salty sweetness of her release in the thick night air, and he felt out-of-control lust for this woman.

He reached for the picnic basket and withdrew a condom from the side pocket. Quickly, he sheathed himself and pushed Scarlet onto her back. Her eyes were still closed and they flew open.

"That was—"

"Good?"

She shook her head and lifted herself onto an elbow. "No, it was beautiful."

She slid a hand down his stomach and clasped his erection. The pressure of her hand nearly drove him over the line. "Easy, I'm close."

She smiled, and pulled him down for a kiss. Then she shoved him onto his back and rolled on top of him.

"You've been naughty," she said, capturing his mouth in a kiss. He kissed her back. Hard.

"I wasn't always a good boy," he said, capturing one of her satin breasts and bestowing a kiss upon it.

Scarlet lifted herself, then lowered onto him, sheathing him in the hot wetness of her body.

"Oh, good—" He couldn't finish because she'd begun to move.

"Yes, *good* would be the word." She nipped his ear.

And then his sweet redhead became the vixen he loved. She sat back, tossing her red tresses over her, shoulder and rode him. Her breasts bounced in the moonlight as she taught him a lesson about playing games with a temptress.

And he loved every millisecond of that lesson.

Within minutes, his cries mingled with hers as they both catapulted into mindless bliss, riding wave upon wave of sheer pleasure until Scarlet crashed onto his chest.

Then nothing more was heard, except them gasping for breath with the accompaniment of the sounds of the countryside.

CHAPTER TWENTY

SCARLET ENDED UP with poison ivy, which was one mark against the whole country-living idea. However, it was a small price to pay for the wonderful night she'd spent in Adam's arms on the bank of his secret pond. It had truly been one of the best nights of her life. Not because their lovemaking had been explosive, but because they'd lain wrapped in the quilt, sharing favorite memories of their childhood, sipping cabernet and devouring decadent dark chocolate.

A few fireflies had shown up to celebrate with them and the stars had steadfastly observed Scarlet fall head over heels for the man she'd once thought of as humorless and tight-assed.

And that head-over-heels thing had been both spiritual and literal.

The man was good at everything he did.

"What are you smiling about?" Rayne asked, passing the morning newspaper to Brent. "You're almost cheerful. Are you that happy to be leaving Oak Stand?"

Scarlet set the lid on the butter dish. "Who said I'm leaving?"

Brent lowered the sports section to peer at her.

Rayne shrugged. "Well, you said your community service was over. I figured—"

"I have the play coming up. I can't leave."

Brent smiled. "That's unexpected."

"Why?" Scarlet asked, taking a bite of toast. She was ravenous. Strawberries and chocolate had only gone so far in supplying her with the calories she'd lost last night. She scratched her ankle.

He shrugged. "Because don't you have an audition or something?"

"I sent a tape. And why wouldn't I follow through on my obligation to direct the play?

"Oh, I forgot. You think I can't finish stuff." Scarlet grabbed the last piece of bacon. Henry had left for school over an hour ago so there was no one there to protest her pigging out. "See? I finished the bacon."

The phone interrupted the rebuke she had intended on delivering to her sister and her henchman.

Rayne answered it. "It's for you. Some assistant who wants you to hold for a David Sparrow?"

Scarlet's fork clattered to the plate. She almost knocked over her juice glass in her scramble to grab the receiver.

Rayne held it out of reach and mouthed, "Who is he?"

Scarlet ignored her sister, gesturing impatiently until Rayne gave up the cordless. Scarlet left the toast behind as she pushed through the swinging door into the kitchen.

"This is Scarlet Rose," she said into the receiver.

"Hello, Scarlet. This is Etta. Mr. Sparrow would like to speak with you. Can you hold?"

She paced while she waited for David to come on the line.

"Hi, Scarlet. This is David Sparrow."

They exchanged niceties, then the director got down to business. "I received your audition tape. Casting really liked it and I'm also intrigued."

"Thank you," Scarlet murmured, feeling nauseous. Her hands shook because she knew what this call meant. Knew she was on the verge of something big.

"I'd like to have you do a private read for us. Perhaps let you do it with Hugh and see how you two play off each other."

She screwed her eyes closed and tried to keep her cool. Hugh flippin' Jackman. Or was it Hugh Grant? Oh, snap! Either one would be huge. "I'd love to do that. When would you like to meet with me?"

"I know it's short notice, but I'd like to meet with you Saturday afternoon with the read the following morning. Is that doable for you?"

Oh, crap. *Scenes from The Magpie Thief* would be performed on Sunday afternoon at 2:00 p.m. There would be no way to audition for Sparrow in L.A. then make it back to Texas in time to direct the play. Dress rehearsal and dinner at the center had already been set for Saturday evening. Half the guys in rehab had family coming in and the tickets had sold out.

"Sorry, I've got a commitment then. I could try to move things around. I want to—"

"I wish I could offer you another time," he interrupted, "but we're already behind schedule. The production will be tight on this one, so if you can't make it by Saturday, we'll have to move forward and look at other possibilities."

"I understand," Scarlet murmured. "I don't want to pass up the chance to work with you, so I'll move my commitments here. I'll be in L.A. tomorrow morning."

She wrote down the meeting place and time, then hung up.

She sank onto a stool, overwhelmed with guilt. What else could she have done? This was her big break, her chance to step away from the small screen and onto the big screen. The part wasn't huge, but it was cleverly written and deeply emotional and would stretch her acting ability beyond any other role she'd ever taken.

Adam.

Her heart skipped a beat. What about him…and her? And the magic they'd shared last night? A mere six hours ago, she'd left him with a tender kiss, a sweet promise for a beginning.

Not an end.

But she had to go to L.A. Acting was her life. The guys at the center would be disappointed, but they would understand. Tipsy Nolan, the drama teacher at the high school, could step into Scarlet's shoes without blinking. The show would go on, the town would see the message hidden in the children's book and Scarlet would get her biggest break since she'd donned her vampy catsuit.

But nothing would be solved with Adam.

She didn't know how she could leave him after last night. When she'd gotten so attached to the idea of being with him. Everything felt so confusing, like being stuck in a mirrored fun house, not knowing which was the right direction to head. Nothing familiar and everything disjointed.

Rayne stuck her head in the door. "I've got to head over to our office for a preproduction meeting. We're filming here in a few hours, so you'll need to clear out. Is everything okay?"

"I'll be clearing out to L.A.," Scarlet muttered, running her finger around the uneven tile of the bar.

"L.A.?"

"I've got a callback on Saturday."

"I thought the dress rehearsal was on Saturday."

"It is."

Rayne lifted her eyebrows. "Oh, I see."

No, she didn't see. This wasn't about the play. Well, it was. But it was more about Adam. She didn't want to leave in the middle of their beginning. Even though it wasn't really their beginning—they'd been circling each other for weeks. It *was* the beginning of something really good for both of them.

And she knew what Rayne thought. Another thing Scarlet has left unfinished. Unfortunately, it was true.

This time she left more than one thing unfinished.

She might be leaving her chance at love behind.

IF A DESIGNER WERE TO DESCRIBE Adam's small home on Hickory Street, she would use words like *blank slate* or *austere and simplistic* to basically mean undecorated. Everything was colorless and plain.

White siding. Black shutters. Black door. Beige carpet. Blue couch. No art, save what Scarlet thought might be an original Picasso, or a really good knockoff.

But there was nothing simple about the man pacing the carpet. "I don't understand why he can't wait. I thought movies took forever to get made."

From her perch on the couch, Scarlet spread her hands apart. "They do, but there are schedules and they are behind. They can't proceed without a complete cast. It's a huge production, juggling actors' other commitments, locations. I could go on and on, but really, what it boils down to is I have to go."

He stopped, his green eyes flashing. "You couldn't if you were still serving your sentence."

"But I'm not."

He grimaced and resumed pacing. Several seconds ticked off on the clock hanging over the one armchair.

"Adam, I don't want to leave, but I have to."

He stopped again. "Why? Why do you *have* to go to this audition? It's not a commitment you already have. It's one you want."

"Because it's my career. My future."

He sank into the armchair. "But you have a career. You're on a new show, one that's generating tons of interest. Why do you need this other role?"

She sighed. "Look, I didn't pursue the feelings we had between us because of your career, because of your reputation. How can you ask me to toss aside the opportunity of a lifetime, when you weren't willing to do the same for me? That's a double standard."

He looked at her flatly. "That was misconduct. Not a selfish need to maintain my career."

"Are you calling me selfish?"

He didn't say anything.

She rose and took her turn at pacing. "Look, I know things will be tough if we pursue a relationship—"

"*If?* I thought we'd already embarked upon a relationship. Not just sex. Remember? You're willing to toss that away?"

"I'm not tossing it. I simply have to leave."

"For how long?"

"Not sure."

He leaned back. "I see. Well, that will be small comfort on cold, sleepless nights."

She wanted to feel his skin beneath her hand, but didn't touch him. Had it been only last night she'd dozed in his arms, content as she'd ever been? She'd lay there, listening to the owl hoot and slapping at the occasional mosquito, fantasizing about a life she'd never known. A life with a man she could love, and who would love her back.

One phone call had changed everything.

"I will come back to Oak Stand at some point. I have to get my car," she said, knowing her voice sounded unconvincing. Life could get crazy for an actor juggling filming schedules on two different coasts. Not to mention Bert had left her a message about a possible advertising campaign with a cosmetic company. They wanted her lips on their ads.

"Sounds like you believe that." He sighed. "I'm such a stupid ass. I knew this would happen. Knew the moment I saw you that I would fall for you and it wouldn't work."

"Don't say that. Two people can be different and still have a relationship. Neither one of us has to sacrifice who we are to be together."

He shook his head. Regret leaked from him, permeating the room. She felt it to her core. "It won't work, Scarlet. You're on a path that will always lead you away from me, and I'm not going to follow you around New York or L.A. like some damn lapdog. I need to have purpose. And you need to shine. We're too different."

She rubbed her eyes. Was he right? Maybe they were merely two ships passing in the night, two stubborn ships unable to change course. She wiped her eyes. "You want this to be goodbye?"

"It is what it is."

His attempt to comfort her made her angry. "There you go again, scratching lines in the sand, making up rules for the way life should be. Who says I have to stay and be the little woman? You are giving up. Not even caring enough to fight."

"I can't give up on something that never got out of the starting gate."

"We got out of the gate. We had sex three times last night. That's out of the gate, mister!"

"Calm down, Scarlet," he said, patting the chair arm next to him. "Sit down. Please."

"No. You sit down," she yelled, even though he was already sitting. "You don't want to make it work because it's easier for you that way. You get to say, 'I screwed Scarlet Rose and then I dumped her.'"

"Please sit. We'll talk about this like rational adults."

"No. No, I won't. Everything is screwed up. I shouldn't have gone with you last night. I shouldn't have opened my heart to you." Scarlet felt her emotions gallop out of control. Her heart squeezed so hard in her chest she thought she might die. It had happened again. She'd fallen for a man and he didn't think her worthy enough to take a risk on. How had she been so stupid?

He watched her with a mixture of resignation and wariness, but he didn't try to calm her.

She dropped to the couch and put her head in her hands. She didn't want to cry, she wanted to pretend everything away. Adam was right. Their relationship was impossible. She jumped to her feet. "I've got to get out of here. I can't deal with this right now. I can't go through this another time."

Adam rose and grabbed her arm. "Scarlet, don't leave this way. You're being overly dramatic once again."

She twisted her arm from his grasp. "I'm not being dramatic. I'm being honest. We were a mistake from the beginning, and nothing, not even last night, can change the fact we're not meant to be. You said so yourself weeks ago. I'm not the right kind of girl, yet I let myself believe in a fairy tale. This isn't some movie or romance book. There isn't always a happily-ever-after. Sometimes things end and no one is happy."

He flinched and stepped back. He didn't seem to know what to say, and she damn sure had no words to make anything better.

She picked up her purse and headed for the door.

He didn't follow her. When she took one last look over her shoulder, she felt something in her chest break loose and flood her with grief. He watched her heart break from the center of his living room. She couldn't believe this was happening. That they were over.

"I'm sorry, Scarlet," he said. "I want you to stay. Direct the play. Plan a future. But I can see it was never in the cards. We want different things from life and maybe there is no way to overcome that. Sometimes the timing is wrong."

She had no words left in her. So she turned and walked out of his life.

CHAPTER TWENTY-ONE

ADAM STARED UP AT THE myriad of lights above him. He almost lolled his tongue out but was afraid it would be overacting.

"Cut!" Tipsy Nolan yelled.

He pushed himself to an elbow and studied a grinning Marco, clad in a flowing cloak. "Watch that damn sword. You almost emasculated me."

"If *emasculate* means cut your *cajones* off, then I nearly accomplished my mission."

Adam gave the former gang member a scowl and rose from the dusty wooden floor of the high-school stage. The dress rehearsal had gone smoothly and Tipsy had pitched only two fits in the past hour. He figured the show would go on.

He'd intended to not show for the play, but his sense of duty won out over his utter despair. She'd left yesterday. Jared had seen her roar out of town and hadn't bothered with a ticket because he'd been in the middle of eating a banana split at the Diary Barn.

Adam wanted a do-over on their last moment together. Maybe then he wouldn't feel so damned empty. Maybe then he could have fixed what had broken so easily between them.

Perhaps Scarlet had been right. Perhaps he should have fought for their future together. But what difference would it have made? She'd still be gone. He'd still feel broken.

The only bright spot had come when he found the stolen videotape in his desk drawer. The thief could have made a copy, but Adam would never know unless the person came forward. Still, something about the gesture spoke of forgiveness. He liked to think that threat had been neutralized, and if it hadn't, he would deal with whatever repercussions came his way.

"Okay, that's a wrap, folks," Tipsy said, her bright pink fuzzy shoes clacking up the steps to the stage. The shoes looked like something out of a black-and-white movie. Except the color, of course. "Everyone be here at one o'clock for hair and makeup. No exceptions."

The guys looked at each other with horrified expressions.

"I ain't wearing no makeup," Juan said. "My old lady's coming and she ain't seeing me looking like no—"

Tipsy clapped her hands. "This is theater, gentleman. Not a beauty salon. On this stage, your job is to become someone else. Don't forget to tell your old lady that."

With that, Tipsy sashayed away.

Adam's radio crackled to life. "Chief, give us a twenty-one."

He dialed dispatch. "Hinton," he said into his phone.

"Some lady called in about a body part on Leonard. At least that's what it sounded like. She was hysterical," Jared said.

A body part?

Adam rushed out the double doors of the auditorium into the late-afternoon sun. "What sort of body part? Are you sure this isn't a prank?"

"Sounded real. Want me to check it out?"

"No, I'll go, but send backup."

"Ten-four."

Adam slid into his cruiser, fully alert but suspicious about the nature of the call. He'd never in his ten years as a police officer had someone find a body part. A body? Yeah. A part? No. Very strange.

He headed southeast toward Leonard Road. The sun had dropped in the sky, but still caused heat to radiate in waves off the asphalt. It took him four minutes to reach the turn to Leonard Road, and two more to pull in behind a black convertible BMW.

What the hell?

He glanced at the license plate. It was Scarlet's car, but she wasn't in sight.

Terror filled him as he automatically checked the gun on his belt. Could Scarlet be in trouble? Harvey's hard smile invaded his thoughts. Surely he hadn't done anything to Scarlet.

Adam flipped open the snap on his holster and opened the door, stepping onto the gravel on the side of the road. It did not escape him that he stood almost exactly in the spot where he'd pulled Scarlet over for speeding. The day he'd first laid eyes on the woman who would flip him upside down, yank him sideways and hang him out to dry.

He hoped like hell she was okay.

He drew his gun from his holder and cleared the car, surveying the perimeter. He could see no one at all. He needed backup quickly so he reached for his radio, and then he heard it.

Crying.

The sound caused his hackles to rise. What the devil was going on? He holstered his gun and walked around to the front of the car.

Scarlet sat on the pavement, knees drawn up to her chin, crying as if there were no tomorrow.

She looked at him with the most fragile look he'd ever seen, and if he hadn't been so damn relieved to see her unharmed, he might have chewed her ass out.

"What in the hell are you doing, woman?"

She shook her head and continued to sob.

He looked left than right again, wondering if he were on some kind of prank show. Like maybe Ashton Kutcher might jump out and shout, "You've been punked!"

But no one was there.

"Scarlet, I got a call about a body part."

She threw something at him. It pinged against his boot.

"You are stupid!" she shouted, unfurling from her position against the bumper of the car. She wore a pair of high heels and a very short skirt. His mind registered the fact she was off her rocker, but it also sent a message to nether regions about long, bare legs and a spectacular ass.

He took a step back. "Have you lost your mind?"

She jabbed a finger in his chest. Right beneath his badge. "You didn't even bother to come to the airport. You were supposed to come get me."

"Jared said there was a body—"

"It's my heart, you jackass. That's the body part, the one you stole and threw away."

He blinked. "You called in a false report?"

She wiped the tears from her cheeks. "So arrest me."

He didn't know what to do. The crazy broad had called in a false report. But then again the crazy broad stood in front of him. In Texas. On Friday night.

She hadn't gone to Los Angeles.

She'd stayed.

"I—" He snapped his mouth closed.

She pushed her hair back. "You are the biggest idiot in Howard County. Don't you know the hero always comes for the girl?"

Huh?

He begged his brain to click, whir and figure out what in the hell she meant. Maybe he was an idiot. Maybe he'd always failed at relationships because he didn't understand women. Especially not the rather complex one glaring at him.

"You wanted me to stop you from achieving your dream?"

She crossed her arms. "No, I wanted you to *want* to stop me."

"I don't understand. I thought—"

She pressed a finger over his mouth. "Stop. Aunt Fran was right. I'll have to do everything in this relationship."

She pulled her hand away.

He stared, not sure what to do. She no longer cried. Instead she looked aggravated, yet pleased with herself.

"Let me ask you something." She tossed her hair over her shoulder. "Do you love me?"

He swallowed. Did he love her? Was that what this was? This constant pressing in his chest, sort of like indigestion. And the ever-present yearning for her smile, her laugh, her cranky frown when she didn't approve of something he said. He thought about her night and day, wondered where she was, who she was with. Was that love? "Uh, yes?"

"You don't sound sure."

"No, I'm sure. I love you."

"Good," she said. Then she slapped him.

"What the hell?" he said, grabbing his cheek. Damn, she'd put her weight behind that.

Scarlet strolled toward his police car. He watched as she placed her hands on the trunk and spread her legs. "I intentionally assaulted you. Are you going to arrest me now?"

"Are you out of your goddamn mind?"

"Yes. You not only stole my heart, but you also wrecked me mentally. So, come here and frisk me."

He stalked toward where she stood. "Scarlet Rose, stop playing games and tell me what is going on in that beautiful, but also scary, head of yours. Why are you doing this?"

She rolled her eyes. "If you arrest me, I can't be at an audition, can I? I'd probably have to do more community service."

Then the reason for Scarlet's whole fabricated call and ensuing slap hit him. She wanted him to arrest her.

From somewhere deep inside him, laughter welled. "Oh, my God. You are the craziest women I've ever had the pleasure of—"

"Pat me down. I could be packing heat."

"Oh, you're packing heat, all right," he said, trying not to smile, but failing. He hadn't felt too much true happiness in his life. Life mostly felt like business, with no time for gut-wrenching laughs and silly daydreaming beneath the glow of fireflies. Scarlet Rose had changed that the minute she'd asked him to kiss her. And she'd cemented it into his heart by coming back to Oak Stand, choosing him over a role as a bisexual hooker.

He pulled the handcuffs from his belt.

"You're going to cuff me?"

"You're dangerous," he said, clipping one cuff around

her left wrist. "Besides, I thought you liked being cuffed."

"Only if they are lined with fur," she said, as he snapped the other over her right wrist. Now her hands were immobile. Exactly what he wanted. Scarlet at his mercy. His mind tripped to his thoughts after the first time he'd ticketed her, the way she'd arched over the car, tempting him, and the way he'd guiltily desired to have her under his control.

"Now I'm going to pat you down," he murmured in her ear. She shivered. He smiled.

He slid his hands down her shoulders, reaching beneath her arms to brush the undersides of her breasts, pausing to flick the rigid nipples he encountered a little higher. She sucked in her breath.

"Why, Officer, I think this is inappropriate."

"Do you give up your rights?" he asked, sliding his hands over her ribs before cupping the curve of her hips and pulling her spectacular ass against the hardness of his erection.

"Ooh, Officer, is that a nightstick or are you glad to see me?" She giggled, grinding her bottom against him.

He leaned forward and brushed his lips against her ear and whispered, "You'll never know how glad I am to see you."

She rested her head on his shoulder. "I think I do."

He kissed her neck and spun her so she faced him. Her eyes shimmered in the Texas sunset. He lifted her and placed her on the trunk of the car, settling himself between her knees. She looped her cuffed hands around his neck and kissed him.

It was sweet as summer melon, and for the first time ever, Adam's blood didn't sing at a kiss. His heart did.

She pulled back and looked deep into his eyes. "I love you, Adam."

"But what about the audition? About Hollywood and that director?" he asked, thrilled with the declaration she'd made, but afraid too much still stood between them and a happy-ever-after.

"I drove away, thinking you and I were through. That Hollywood and this role were my new beginning, my key to happiness. But I couldn't get a flight until morning, so as I lay in the hotel room in Dallas, bawling my eyes out, it occurred to me I'd stepped out on the chance to be truly happy. To be truly loved. Not for a month or two, but forever."

"You think this is a forever kind of thing?"

"That's why I'm here. Everything happens for a reason. You leaving Houston. Me canceling my villa on the Riviera. Oak Stand. A speeding ticket. Community service. Fate."

He slid his hands up to cup her face and kissed her tenderly. "It won't be easy."

"Nothing worthwhile ever is, but I want you."

He smiled. "I'm going to have to take you in."

She laughed. "I was counting on that. Rick smoked a brisket and all this drama has me starved."

"You really didn't call in a body part, did you?" he asked, pulling her close so he could nibble on the sweetness of her neck.

"No, Roz helped me. I waited at the airport, missing three flights, hoping you'd show up to bring me back. But sometimes a gal's got to do things herself." She licked his ear, heating his blood and making him forget they were in plain sight on the side of the highway.

The blast of a horn ripped him from the perusal of

the sexiest earlobe he'd ever had the pleasure of sucking into his mouth.

"Now, that's what I call *po-lice* harassment," Bubba yelled, pulling up parallel with them.

Normally, Adam would have been appalled at being caught necking on a county highway while in uniform. But today he felt too good holding the woman he loved in his arms to worry about it. Misconduct be damned. Scarlet tipped her head and smiled at the man in a Dallas-size diesel truck. "And he's good at it."

"When you going to sign me up for the squad, Chief? I'm seeing more benefits than dental in wearin' that uniform." Bubba grinned as he readjusted his Texas Longhorns ball cap. "'Course, I already got a broad."

"Better not let Meg hear you call her that," Scarlet said, removing her hands from around Adam's neck. "We might have another code…what was it, Adam? An appendage discovered?"

"And I know which one that'd be." Bubba nodded toward town. "I'm headin' to Phoenix. Rick's got the smoker goin' and I don't miss them kinda meals. Y'all goin', too?"

Adam helped Scarlet from the back of the car, steadying her on the uneven gravel. "We'll be there shortly. Scarlet has broken the law and will have to be punished."

She turned as red as her hair. It was the first time he'd seen her embarrassed, and something about her blush pleased him.

"Then I'll be gittin' gone." Bubba grinned. "See you later, Chief."

The truck roared away.

Scarlet held up her hands. "Are you going to let me go?"

He shook his head. "Not a chance."

"Well, in that case, can I get another pat down?"

He wrapped her in his arms, trapping her handcuffed hands between them. "I may never let you go again."

She sighed. "We've got a play to put on. But later… I never got to test out your mattress and I've got mosquito bites you can scratch, not to mention a patch of poison ivy."

"So you're staying?"

She nodded, nipping his neck. "When I'm not biting people in Collinstown."

"And maybe you can think about taking the other job?"

"What job?"

"The police chief's wife?"

"Hmm. Not sure. Phone calls at night about dog poop on the square? Stolen goats? Might be too exciting for a city girl like me."

He took out his key and unlocked the cuffs binding her hands. "Then you've never seen the Saturday-night poker game at Tucker House. Sometimes we have to raid and confiscate Efferdent and Alka-Seltzer. It gets wild."

They linked hands and walked to her car. "I think there is no place I'd rather be than in Oak Stand, Texas," she said. "With you."

* * * * *

COMING NEXT MONTH

Available November 8, 2011

#1740 CHRISTMAS IN MONTANA
North Star, Montana
Kay Stockham

#1741 TEMPORARY RANCHER
Home on the Ranch
Ann Evans

#1742 ALL THEY NEED
Sarah Mayberry

#1743 THESE TIES THAT BIND
Hometown U.S.A.
Mary Sullivan

#1744 THE SON HE NEVER KNEW
Delta Secrets
Kristi Gold

#1745 THE CHRISTMAS GIFT
Going Back
Darlene Gardner

Harlequin® Special Edition® is thrilled to present a new installment in USA TODAY *bestselling author RaeAnne Thayne's reader-favorite miniseries,* THE COWBOYS OF COLD CREEK.

Join the excitement as we meet the Bowmans—four siblings who lost their parents but keep family ties alive in Pine Gulch. First up is Trace. Only two things get under this rugged lawman's skin: beautiful women and secrets. And in Rebecca Parsons, he finds both!

Read on for a sneak peek of CHRISTMAS IN COLD CREEK.
Available November 2011 from Harlequin® Special Edition®.

On impulse, he unfolded himself from the bar stool. "Need a hand?"

"Thank you! I…" She lifted her gaze from the floor to his jeans and then raised her eyes. When she identified him her hazel eyes turned from grateful to unfriendly and cold, as if he'd somehow thrown the broken glasses at her head.

He also thought he saw a glimmer of panic in those interesting depths, which instantly stirred his curiosity like cream swirling through coffee.

"I've got it, Officer. Thank you." Her voice was several degrees colder than the whirl of sleet outside the windows.

Despite her protests, he knelt down beside her and began to pick up shards of broken glass. "No problem. Those trays can be slippery."

This close, he picked up the scent of her, something fresh and flowery that made him think of a mountain meadow on a July afternoon. She had a soft, lush mouth and for one brief, insane moment, he wanted to push aside that stray lock of hair slipping from her ponytail and taste her. Apparently he needed to spend a lot less time working and a great deal *more* time recreating with the opposite sex if he could have sudden random fantasies about a woman he wasn't even inclined to like, pretty or not.

"I'm Trace Bowman. You must be new in town."

She didn't answer immediately and he could almost see the wheels turning in her head. Why the hesitancy? And why that little hint of unease he could see clouding the edge of her gaze? His presence was obviously making her uncomfortable and Trace couldn't help wondering why.

"Yes. We've been here a few weeks."

"Well, I'm just up the road about four lots, in the white house with the cedar shake roof, if you or your daughter need anything." He smiled at her as he picked up the last shard of glass and set it on her tray.

Definitely a story there, he thought as she hurried away. He just might need to dig a little into her background to find out why someone with fine clothes and nice jewelry, and who so obviously didn't have experience as a waitress, would be here slinging hash at The Gulch. Was she running away from someone? A bad marriage?

So...Rebecca Parsons. Not Becky. An intriguing woman. It had been a long time since one of those had crossed his path here in Pine Gulch.

Trace won't rest until he finds out Rebecca's secret, but will he still have that same attraction to her once he does?
Find out in CHRISTMAS IN COLD CREEK.
Available November 2011 from Harlequin® Special Edition®.

HSEEXP1111

SPECIAL EDITION

Life, Love and Family

This December

NEW YORK TIMES BESTSELLING AUTHOR

DIANA PALMER

brings you a brand-new Long, Tall Texans story!

Detective Rick Marquez has never met a case he couldn't solve or a woman he couldn't charm. But this smooth-talking Texan is about to meet the one woman who'll lasso him—body and soul!

Look for TRUE BLUE

November 22 wherever books are sold.

www.Harlequin.com

SE65637DP